NOT YOUR AVERAGE JO

NOT YOUR AVERAGE JO

GRACE K. SHIM

Kokila

KOKILA
An imprint of Penguin Random House LLC, New York

First published in the United States of America by Kokila,
an imprint of Penguin Random House LLC, 2024

Copyright © 2024 by Grace K. Shim

Visit us online at PenguinRandomHouse.com.

Library of Congress Cataloging-in-Publication Data is available.

Printed in the United States of America
ISBN 9780593462768
1st Printing
LSCH

This book was edited by Zareen Jaffery, copyedited by Kaitlyn San Miguel, proofread by
Jacqueline Hornberger, and designed by Jasmin Rubero. The production was supervised
by Tabitha Dulla, Nicole Kiser, Ariela Rudy Zaltzman, and Hansini Weedagama.

Text set in Sabon Next LT Pro

This book is a work of fiction. Any references to historical events, real people,
or real places are used fictitiously. Other names, characters, places, and events are
products of the author's imagination, and any resemblance to actual events or
places or persons, living or dead, is entirely coincidental.

The publisher does not have any control over and does not assume responsibility
for author or third-party websites or their content.

To anyone who's ever had to settle for average.

And for Tyler, Troy & Kate.
May your voices be heard.

ONE

When you're an Asian American in an area where there aren't many Asian Americans, there's a cultural expectation people have of you that is clear from day one. You become the resident expert on all things Asian, whether you like it or not—whether you're *qualified* or not.

Can you tell me what this says? (Points to random Chinese word.) Bro, not every Asian is Chinese.

Oh, you're Korean? I love K-pop/K-drama/K-beauty. Um, you're welcome?

Riley Jo? Are you sure "Jo" is a Korean last name? Because I've never heard of it before. Well, then, it must be a mistake. I'll tell my parents, and the Korean Ministry of Last Names, that you, random white lady from Arkansas, are right and they are wrong.

Where are you fr— Nope!

Bentonville, Arkansas, is the only home I've ever known. And yet "at home" is not quite how I feel here. The way I have to convince people I'm from this city/state/country is like a form of verbal MMA I don't have the stamina for. I gave up trying to explain myself after the first few—I don't know—hundred times, when I began to sound like a broken record.

I mean, if you think about it, it's kind of like a pickle. (Just hear me out.) Pickles are made by submerging a cucumber in a container filled with saltwater brine or vinegar. The process doesn't happen in an instant. It takes time for the briny water to infuse the cucumber, changing its texture, flavor, and even appearance. And then, when it's finally ready for consumption and it's sliced up for hamburgers or speared for sandwiches, does anyone consider it a cucumber anymore? Of course not. Because it's had a completely different environment—a completely different *life*—that changed the cucumber into something else entirely.

Anyway, my point is, no matter how many times I tell people I'm a pickle, all they see is a cucumber.

For the record, the pickle doesn't count as a vegetable serving because it's too salty—also relatable.

To be fair, no one I've encountered in Bentonville, Arkansas, is mean-spirited or belittling. It's not like anyone here is telling me to "go back to my country" or calling me any variation of the C-word (*chink, ching-chong*, and, more recently, *China virus*). It's the kind of microaggressions derived from a type of lazy curiosity that should be their issue to deal with. And yet somehow the problem inevitably becomes mine.

If I don't meet people's cultural expectations of who they think I am, they start backing away like I'm someone to be wary of. Because if they can't place me, then I—all five feet, two inches of me—must be evil. I'm seriously lol-ing at that because aside from my mildly lethal form of snark expressed in the most subtle way (a contradiction if there ever was one), I am a classic eldest child, and as such, I am biologically incapable of doing anything that goes against the grain. As far as I know, I'm the farthest thing from evil. I'm the polysynthetic fluff inside a Squishmallow. I'm a friggin' PEEPS Marshmallow.

If people here don't understand me by now, they never will. So, instead, I choose passive-aggressivism. I'll show you, random cashier-dude at the deli who assumed English wasn't my first language. I'll speak the most unaccented English in my very outdoor voice inside this teeny tiny convenience store just to prove my point. If people think I'm supposed to like K-pop, I'll go out of my way to show them there are other genres of music I like/play/listen to. If they think I'm supposed to be friends with the other Asian kids at school, I'll steer so clear of them it's like I don't even know they exist.

But that's where my plan sort of backfired. Without interest in football or pep rallies, I didn't have many options for friends. Because that's Bentonville High School in a nutshell: one big sports arena with way too many chants about winning/dominating/defeating.

I started playing the guitar to avoid having to join a sports team. But it didn't take much to realize I had a natural knack for it. One chord, and I was sold. I discovered I could play back tunes I'd heard only once or twice. Somehow, chord progressions made more sense to me than conversations with my classmates.

My instructor (aka the internet) showed me a list of songs every guitarist should know—the Red Hot Chili Peppers' "Under the Bridge," one of the most performed songs ever; Green Day's "Good Riddance (Time of Your Life)," one of the best beginner songs for guitarists; Metallica's "Enter Sandman," another great starter piece to learn easy riffs and basic song structure; and so on. In a matter of months, I could play anything from James Taylor to Taylor Swift.

Then, by the middle of my freshman year, just when I was finding my rhythm with my music, something happened that changed everyone's lives: The Pandemic.

I tried the virtual hangout thing for a hot second, played a few rounds of *Among Us* or, as my sister, Elise, likes to call it, *Amongous like Humongous.* Probably the most entertaining thing about the game to be honest. Because sussing people out felt even more uncomfortable online than it did in person. I felt like the imposter every time without even being the imposter. Anytime I'd get down on myself, mourning what few acquaintances I'd had (RIP social life), I'd turn on the TV and be reminded that people all around the world were losing their actual lives, which shut me up pretty quickly. I should consider myself lucky. And besides my health, I still had my guitar. With it, I never felt lonely. In fact, while we were on lockdown, when music was all I had, I was the most myself I'd been in my life. Which is something I don't admit out loud, since I don't want to be insensitive to others who suffered mentally/physically/emotionally during the pandemic.

By the time people started reemerging from their homes to go back to work/school/stores, music had become my everything—my friend, my safe space, my family even. It's now the only way I know how to express myself, the only place I don't have to explain myself. And as long as I have it, to quote Metallica, "nothing else matters."

The plan was to get out of Bentonville right after graduation. I had my eye on a few small liberal arts colleges—Wesleyan, St. Olaf, Luther. Not only do they have established and reputable music programs, but they are out of state. It was during my college search that I discovered Carlmont Academy, a boarding high school for the arts. I was looking for a way out of Bentonville after high school. The possibility of leaving even sooner had never entered my mind. It was the perfect plan.

"Boarding school?" Mom wrinkled her nose. "Why would you leave for high school when you already go to a perfectly good one here?"

Okay, maybe not *the perfect plan*, depending on who you asked.

My mom is a second-generation Korean American who grew up in Little Rock and is a professor of pharmacology at Bentonville U. Her whole life, she never lived outside of Arkansas. And, as far as I could tell, it's what she expected of me.

"Besides," she went on, "you have so much to look forward to here." Without saying it, I knew exactly what she was referring to. Children of faculty members at Bentonville U are given a free ride at the four-year college, pending admission, of course. It's a privilege I have a hard time seeing as one. Four more years of *this*? I may not know what I want to do in the future, but I know what I *don't* want to do: stay in Bentonville.

My dad moved here from Korea to attend college, and I thought I'd have a better chance convincing him to let me go to Carlmont, since he's a bit of a dreamer himself and knows firsthand what it's like to want something so badly you'd move halfway across the world for it. But then again, my dad came to the US on a mathematics scholarship. And as much of a dreamer as he is, he wasn't about to send me on a whim to a school without some kind of guaranteed investment in my future.

"Tuition is a lot at Carlmont, even if it's only one year," Dad said, noticing the due date to apply for scholarships had already passed. "With college right around the corner, we don't have that kind of money to spend, even if it's a good opportunity."

I could see where this was going. Mom had already been dropping hints that liberal arts colleges came with a premium price tag. That didn't include the costs of flights to Connecticut or Minnesota or Iowa.

"It says on the website that there aren't many openings for juniors and seniors." Dad frowned at his computer screen.

"What if you don't get in? Are you sure you want to put yourself through that kind of disappointment?" Mom raised an eyebrow.

But that was just it—if I didn't get into Carlmont, I'd be no worse off than I was already. I had nothing to lose by applying. So I offered something without thinking it entirely through.

"I'll agree to go to Bentonville University after graduation if you let me go to Carlmont for my senior year of high school," I said.

I'm not sure if it was the four years of free college tuition or my sheer determination that did it, but they agreed to the deal. Now all I had to do was apply.

APPLICATION TO CARLMONT ACADEMY:
1. Tell us about yourself.

The first question on the application, and I was already stumped. If I answered truthfully, I'd ruin my chances of getting into Carlmont. Because if I'm being honest, I'm a Nobody.

The thing is, I'm actually good at writing. Something I get from my dad. He writes poetry, or he used to. And like with songwriting, there's a certain freedom there that I understand. It's permission to color outside the lines, to write in incomplete sentences, a string of thoughts and emotions like a constant stream of consciousness.

After staring at the blank screen for way too long, my vision blurred. I drifted to a familiar coping mechanism: writing in verse.

Some people talk
Some people write
I need to play
That's how I convey
The feelings inside, the emptiness subsides

When I started to get on a roll, I completed the thoughts into sentences:

When people ask me about myself, it's not always easy to come up with an answer. Mostly because I can tell they don't want to hear the actual answer, but rather a confirmation of what they suspect of me. That I am the type of Asian they're familiar with from TV or movies, or the ones who sing the songs they sing along with on the radio or their playlists. The truth is, I'm more like everyone else here than they think: an average American teenager, born and raised in Bentonville, Arkansas, with hopes and dreams similar to theirs—to be liked, to be understood, to feel seen. But no matter how much I explain or try to, the words are lost. Instead, I write my thoughts down, hearing them as a melody. Some people like to talk their feelings out with a friend or write them down in a journal. What I discovered about myself during the pandemic is that I need to play them. Today I write songs that convey who I am.

For the audition piece, I'd had to submit two songs. One had to be a straightforward performance of a known song. I chose to play "Blackbird" by the Beatles. Not only is it a super-recognizable song that plays beautifully on acoustic, but it's got a melody that is impossible not to smile at when played well, which I knew I could do. The other audition piece I could take more creative liberties on. By the time I'd finished the written portion of the application, I already had a song in my head, which helped me get it started. So I played that as my second piece. It might seem reckless to submit something like this on the fly, but sometimes a song hits you and you know it's worth taking a chance on. So I clicked submit as soon as the file uploaded.

It wasn't until I got my acceptance letter a month later that it hit me what I'd agreed to. In exchange for one year at Carlmont, I'd agreed to four more years at Bentonville.

I must really be a pickle, because somehow I'd gotten myself into the biggest one ever. At least I'd have a whole year to find a way to get out of it.

TWO

It's my last night before going to LA, and we're eating my favorite: spaghetti marinara. Just kidding—it's my younger sister Elise's favorite.

My favorite is mac-and-cheese grilled cheese, if anyone cares. Which is exactly what it sounds like—a mound of creamy mac and cheese smooshed between two buttery slices of bread with an extra layer of cheese for good measure. If you haven't tried it, you haven't lived. And before anyone can food-shame me, I'm aware of its high fat/calorie/cholesterol content. Just let me carb in peace.

As soon as dinner's ready, Elise and I join Mom at the table. Dad joins us a second later, setting down a bowl of pickles. We pile pasta on our plates and a generous helping of marinara sauce, and each of us takes turns grabbing a pickle spear from the bowl. For the next few minutes, manners go out the door. It's all slurping and crunching.

"What if you don't like the food at Crapville?" Elise asks with her mouth full.

We laugh. She's got sauce all over her face, which makes it even more hilarious.

"It's Carlmont," I correct Elise. "And I'm pretty sure they'll have spaghetti."

"Yeah, well. They probably won't have it with this." Elise waves her fork-pierced pickle at me.

"That's true. I mean, spaghetti and pickles?" Honestly, if I wasn't used to it, I'd probably think it was one of those every-flavor-under-the-sun jelly beans but, like, the really bad ones. Probably not worse than Dead Fish, but definitely not better than Liver & Onions, which are actual flavors. Anyway, my point is, it's not bad . . . once you get used to it.

"What's wrong with it? It's a Jo family delicacy," Dad says, slurping up a forkful of spaghetti, then taking a bite of pickle.

"Come on, Dad. Be real. It's weird," I say.

He shrugs as if to say, *Maybe*.

"Don't yuck his yum," Elise says. Of all the Elise-isms, I like this one best.

"It's my yum too," I reassure Elise. "How'd you come up with this 'delicacy'?" I ask Dad.

"I don't think I know this story either," Mom says, leaning in. She and Dad met at the University of Arkansas when she was a freshman and he was a senior. Mom jokes that he wasn't a FOB—fresh off the boat, that is—by then anymore. When she met him, he was just an OB.

Dad clears his throat, wipes his mouth, and we all lean in like he's finally going to tell us *the great family secret*.

"When I first came here, I was homesick for kimchi."

Elise and I share a look.

"Not, like, your family or your home?" I ask.

"Or pets or stuffed animals?" Elise adds. Because of course.

Dad shakes his head. "I found on Google the closest Korean restaurant. Back then, there weren't that many Asian things around us, so I had to go to Little Rock. I brought back the smallest jar of kimchi to my dormitory and put it in the minifridge I shared with my roommate. Guess he didn't like the smell too much, so he told me to get rid of it, and I did."

My brows quirk, wondering if there's more. There isn't. "That's it?"

Dad nods. "I found a substitute." He takes a crunchy bite of his pickle. "It's not the same, but close enough."

The story's pretty underwhelming, considering Dad had to replace something that felt like home to him. He doesn't seem to mind, though. In fact, he seems happy about it. So I won't yuck his yum, and I smile along with the rest of them even though it makes me kinda sad.

After we finish eating, my parents hand both me and Elise rectangular boxes wrapped in brown paper. I rip open mine.

"A phone?! Thank you!" I'm probably the last person at my school to not have a phone. I have one of those watch thingies that call five numbers. I only need three. Guess I never cared, and my parents didn't think it was worth getting me a phone until now, which is fair.

"Just remember to call us often, okay?" Mom says.

"Of course I will," I say, hugging my parents.

Elise opens her present. It's . . . also a phone?

"Thank you thank you thank you!" Elise is jumping up and down, shrieking with delight.

I deflate. Now the brand-new phone looks less shiny in my hand.

It's sort of the deal with firstborns, isn't it? Not only do I have to be the responsible one, but I get to watch my younger, arguably less responsible sibling reap the benefits. I try but fail to pretend it doesn't irritate me that my eleven-year-old sister gets a phone at the same time I do. I'm about to say something about the unfairness of it all when my mom beats me to it.

"Now you can call each other anytime you want," she says.

Elise races over to me, hugging me so tight, the air squeezes right out of my lungs. "I'm going to call you every day so it won't feel like we're so far apart."

Resentment melts away like dirt on a rainy day. See, this is the thing about Elise. She's so completely clueless and lovable that I can't be the slightest bit resentful toward her. I hug her back.

When I look at Elise, I see myself. Smiley eyes, high cheekbones, and unruly hair that has an insane amount of what my dad calls personality. (Let's be real. It's frizz.) We could pass for twins if we were closer in age. Except our looks are where our similarities end. The second she opens her mouth, you know she and I are as different as they come. For one, she's completely random and talks nonstop. And two, she's got this rare optimism that comes from nowhere. Actually, I know where it comes from: my dad. They both see the world as half-full while my mom and I see it as half-empty. Maybe that's why we seem to butt heads when it comes to my future.

"I still can't believe you got in," my mom says, wiping her mouth with a napkin.

I would understand her disbelief if this were the first, second, or even third day after I received my acceptance letter. After about the tenth or eleventh time, though, it started to feel insulting.

"Well, believe it. Ya girl is LA-bound." I do a happy dance. Elise joins in with me, then abruptly stops.

"Wait, why am I celebrating? Tomorrow you'll be leaving us." She pouts.

"Not forever. Just for a year. It'll be over before you know it." Mom smiles at Elise, booping her on the nose.

I get the feeling that Mom thinks music is a phase. That one year is all I'll need to "get it out of my system." Naively, I thought going to Carlmont would show my mom the opposite. Guess it's part of our dynamic. We're either on the same page or we're not. There's no in-between.

The thing is, music *is* more than just a phase. I just don't know how to explain it to her. Because how can you put into words what it feels like to breathe or walk? Or to sleep or dream? Because these are things you do without thinking. Things that are natural and essential to living. Which is what music is to me.

FROM THE CARLMONT WEBSITE

VISUAL	AUDIO
Text on-screen: *A Day in the Life of a Monty* Episode One: Your First Day	
Wide shot of Dr. Warren Buckley sitting on the ledge of the water fountain on the Carlmont campus. Text on lower third: Dr. Warren Buckley, Headmaster of Carlmont Academy	Hello, I'm Dr. Warren Buckley. I've been the headmaster at Carlmont Academy for almost twenty-five years now. Carlmont Academy is a ninth- through twelfth-grade high school with a strong focus on the arts. We pride ourselves on a low student-to-teacher ratio and quality instruction with advisors who have had firsthand experience in the industry. The largest enrollment is for our incoming freshman class, with only a few acceptances for our junior and senior years, as there are limited spaces and a high volume of applicants each year. As part of our ongoing emphasis on creativity and ingenuity, we encourage students to take leadership and initiative in their pursuits. This year, it's my pleasure to introduce *A Day in the Life of a Monty*, a new web series developed by a Carlmont student in our world-class documentary program.
Drone shot of Carlmont main campus: Aerial lush hills with scattered terra-cotta roof buildings and a tall bell tower in the background.	Dr. Warren Buckley voice-over: Congratulations. You've made it to Carlmont Academy. Here's what to expect on your first day.

Tracking/gimbal shot entering the gates of Carlmont, past the security guard, and up through the campus.	Dr. Warren Buckley voice-over:
	    We have one main entrance that is gated and guarded twenty-four hours a day. The safety of our students here at Carlmont is our number-one priority.
	    Once you arrive, show the guard your student ID card that you should have received with your welcome packet. After you enter the gates, follow the long, windy road until you reach an intersection. To the right are the administration buildings and main campus, and on the left are the dormitories.

Footage of boys' dormitory: A U-shaped building with an outdoor courtyard in the middle for recreational socializing.	Dr. Warren Buckley voice-over: The boys' dorms are located on the northwest side of the campus.
Footage of girls' dormitory: A two-story building with a lawn and benches scattered in front.	Dr. Warren Buckley voice-over: And the girls' dorms are located on the northeast side of the campus.
Animated PNG of welcome letter.	Dr. Warren Buckley voice-over: You should receive your room assignment, door code, and map of the campus prior to your arrival. Roommates are assigned closer to move-in day, so you'll find that information after you arrive.
Footage of dining hall. Tall arched ceilings with chandeliers hanging over rows of wooden tables.	Dr. Warren Buckley voice-over: Meals are served throughout the day in the main dining hall.

Footage of students selling snack items behind a counter in the student union.	Dr. Warren Buckley voice-over: There's also a snack shack in the student union that stays open until study hours, then reopens for the hour of recreation time before lights out.
Animated PNG of skull flashing.	Dr. Warren Buckley voice-over: We take education here very seriously. In addition to two hours in the evening between seven and nine, the library, tech rooms, and sound booths are open throughout the day. The staff is also available around the clock and offer office hours for those who request additional help.
Wide shot of Dr. Warren Buckley.	We hope you enjoyed the first episode of *A Day in the Life of a Monty*. Stay tuned for our next one, when we talk all things arts programs.
Text on-screen: Producer: Xander McNeil	

THREE

My move-in date happens to coincide with a work conference my mom is attending in Los Angeles, so Mom says it's *convenient*. I try not to think that it means it would have been *inconvenient* if she didn't have a conference to attend while she's out here. Anyway, she's here with me now, which is all that matters. Two planes, a shuttle bus, and a long-ass line at the car rental place later, we're *finally* on our way to Carlmont.

The video on the school's website not only helped me know what to expect on the first day, it also gave me a glimpse of the type of talent on campus. The *Day in the Life* series seems pretty legit, not like some student-led project. Except the part where the flashing skull appeared on-screen, which was weird. Still, even with the glitch, it's more than we had at Bentonville High, where the extent of our creative outlet was the school paper, *The Bentonville Times* (how original). Its content was 94 percent sports-related. The other 6 percent was dedicated to school dances, something I was even less familiar with. Whatever. As of today, I'll officially be at a new school. A *better* school.

As we drive down the 405 freeway with the sun setting behind the palm-tree-lined streets, it starts to hit me. I'm in LA. I look around at the cars that are as different as the people driving them. Already everything feels bigger here. Even the freeway is six lanes wide. The stop-and-go traffic is making me antsy, like it's a song that starts and then stops just as it gains momentum. I wish we could be there already.

I turn on the radio to distract me. I'm not familiar with the stations here, so I scroll through each one, stopping just long enough to hear the song playing before going to the next one. Three back-to-back radio stations—102.7, 103.5, 104.3—are playing the same Skylar Twist song. At the same time, we pass by a billboard with a larger-than-life-sized Skylar Twist, her signature blonde curls and pink lips popping out at us. At first I'm startled by it. Guess I thought LA would have a wider song selection on its radio stations or different idols since it's so much bigger than Bentonville. Then again, it shouldn't be so surprising since Skylar's songs have been topping the charts for pretty much the past five consecutive years.

"Imagine being the biggest star in the world," I say, thinking out loud. So far, music has been the only way I can express myself fully. Being a star that big wouldn't just mean people would understand my art—they'd understand *me*.

"I can't even begin to imagine what it's like," Mom says. "I'm sure you'd hate it."

"Why would you say that?" I say reflexively.

"No freedom? No privacy?" She shakes her head. "That's no life."

Obviously we have different opinions about what having a *life* means. To me, getting called Tiffany—the other Asian girl in my class's name—half the time, being asked by our neighbors to host a Chinese New Year block party even though we're Korean, living in Bentonville my whole life and still having to explain I'm from Bentonville—*that's* no life.

For all the shade she was throwing on Skylar, my mom starts

singing along, doing the motions in her seated position. She's got some serious moves, too, but they're not like the ones in Skylar's music video.

"What's that dance thing you're doing?" I try to mimic her motions. She's going side to side, moving her arms in unison, forward, then back, when the car is in stationary position. She actually looks good.

"The CitiRokk." She glances sideways at me. "You don't know it? It's a new trend on TikTok."

Mom's on TikTok? I'm not even on TikTok.

You know what's even more weird? It's that she has this cool-mom demeanor like the moms on TV. She jokes, uses language I hear my peers use, and makes me feel like she'd understand what I'm going through. But every time I try to talk to her about me, my music, or microaggressions, she makes me feel like I'm too much for her. Sometimes I wonder, if my own mom can't understand me, then who will?

Mom exits the freeway, momentarily distracting me from my thoughts. We're here!

As we wait at the gated entrance while the security guard checks us in, Mom intermittently glances at me with a wistful look in her eyes. "I didn't think I'd have to do this for another year. I'm not sure I'm ready to say bye," she says.

"Well, consider this practice," I offer, since I'm likely feeling the exact opposite emotion of too soon. Approaching the dormitory is causing my stomach to do all sorts of flips.

"Guess you're right, since Carlmont is a onetime thing. At least next year I'll be able to see you during my lunch breaks when I'm teaching."

I don't respond. If I'm going to make the most of my year away before I go back to Bentonville, then thinking about Bentonville is the last thing I want to be doing.

The guard hands my mom a map of the campus and tells us to follow the path up to the parking lot at the top of the hill. My mom follows the directions and parks in the lot facing a two-story brick building. We each take a suitcase into the dorms. We had a layover, which got us in late. By now it's dusk, and the campus is littered with clusters of students. No one else's parents are accompanying them into the dorms, which means I'm probably one of the last to arrive.

When we reach my assigned dorm, second floor, first room on the left, I knock in case my roommate is already there. No one answers, so I punch in the assigned code to unlock my door.

"Wow, this is bigger than the dorms at Bentonville U," Mom marvels, taking inventory once we're inside the room. It's a long rectangular space with a set of identical beds, desks, and closets mirror-imaging each other.

"Looks like my roommate arrived." I spot her suitcases on the side of the room where one of the beds is made. It's, like, really nice luggage too. Matching suitcases in a happy floral print. A quick analysis tells me that a person with that kind of luggage travels a lot, which means they have the resources required to jet-set. Translation: It's not just a better luggage; it's a better life. If I quickly unpack, I can stow away my drab, uninteresting black roller boards before she returns.

Also, it's possible I could be overthinking this entirely. It's just, the longer I'm here, the more it's sinking in that this isn't just a new school. It's a completely different world. And I didn't come all the way to Carlmont to continue living the same life of obscurity I had been up until now.

My mom stays long enough to help me unpack my suitcases and make my bed. We take a quick tour of the campus before she has to leave. It's just like it is in the video I saw on their website—a lush, hilly campus that has all the charm of a fairy tale. Students are hanging out in clusters, catching up, laughing. The sun is setting, and it creates a magical glow all around; this place doesn't feel like school at all, which sets my nerves at ease when my mom says she has to go.

"I'm sorry to leave you all alone. I at least wanted to meet your roommate." Mom's supposed to meet up with a colleague in somewhere called the Valley, and it's getting late.

"Don't worry about me. I'll be fine. You should go."

She hesitates, staring at me with weepy eyes. "Before I go, I brought you something to remember us by." She rummages in her bag and pulls out a gift-wrapped box.

"Aw, Mom, you didn't have to. Just being here is a gift."

"It's nothing. Well, it's something. Just open it!" She seems excited, so I get excited.

I rip off the paper, and I can immediately tell it's a picture frame. "Oh, I love"—I stop as soon as I realize what photo it is—"it." I barely finish the sentence.

"Can you believe it's the only photo we have of us, all together on campus?"

It was Halloween. I was in the seventh grade; Elise was in first. Elise dressed up as a unicorn, and I was a thirteen-year-old pretending to care about Halloween. Just kidding—I was Elise's chaperone. We went to Bentonville U's campus to trick-or-treat. The department heads opened their offices for one another's families to stop by and get candy. My dad was hanging back with my mom in her office, helping her pass out candy, while I took Elise on her rounds. I wasn't joking when I said I came as Elise's chaperone. Anyway, we finished going around the other offices on the floor, and just as we were coming back to my mom's office, a group of older kids was coming out. I think they were eighteen or so—too old to be trick-or-treating, but that was the least of their problems. One of them was dressed as "Kung Fu Guy," wearing a kimono, and his buddy came as, I shit you not, "Asian Tourist," complete with a bad haircut, a selfie stick, and eyes taped back. Their costumes, I have to hand it to them, were creative, considering they didn't come as a set at the local Spirit Halloween costume store or on Amazon. No, they had to curate the look using years of cultural appropriation and harmful stereotyping. When we went into my mom's office, I expected my parents to be as outraged as I felt, but they weren't. In fact, they seemed . . . happy.

In the end, her colleague reported the kids, and they were sent home, but something didn't sit right with me. Later, I asked my mom why she didn't say anything to the group of students. She is, like her colleague, faculty at the university and therefore in a position of authority. She could have reminded those kids of the school's core values to be accepting of all people. Then she said something I'll never forget.

"Sorry you had to see that." She hesitated, gathering her thoughts. "But if I reprimanded those kids about their costumes, some of my colleagues would think I was being 'too sensitive' or that I 'can't take a joke.' It might even leave me out of invitations to conferences or lectures—something that would impact my future here at Bentonville U. If Professor

Wilkins, someone who can't be accused of taking it personally, speaks up, people will take her accusation more seriously. That's just how it is for people like us. So the best I can do is hope that others do the right thing." I probably didn't look convinced, so she added, "It's not always about choosing between good decisions and bad ones. Sometimes it's about making bad choices in order to avoid worse ones." She tried to smile as if to say, *It's all good*. Looking back, though, I don't know if that was more for my benefit or hers.

From that day on, I knew if I stayed in Bentonville, my whole life would be about making bad choices to avoid worse ones. My mom might be able to live like that; I can't.

"Anyway, we'll have more opportunities to take more family photos on campus. Once you come back for good," Mom says, snapping me back to the present.

Not if I can help it, I think but don't say.

FOUR

Mom leaves, and I go back to my still-empty dorm room. With the frame in my hand, I think about where to place it. Problem is, this photo doesn't just represent what I don't like about living in Bentonville. It shows how little my mom understands me. Otherwise, why would she, knowing what happened that day, leave it with me as a parting gift? After trying out different spots around the room—next to my bed, the desk, my dresser—I eventually open a drawer in my desk and put the photo in there.

With that out of the way, I'm able to focus on a more pressing matter: my roommate. It's getting dark outside, and I'm sure she'll be back any minute now. The web series mentioned that we'd be assigned roommates, which makes me somewhat nervous. I've never had much luck with school-organized pairings.

At my old school, we had an exchange student come for a semester. I was assigned to be her buddy since I was "such a good student," the administrative assistant told me. Turns out it wasn't that at all. The exchange student, Pring Srithong, came from Thailand, and the school thought it would be an easier transition for her if she was buddied up with someone who was "her own kind." *Cringe.* Both me and the other Asian, Tiffany Tran, who's Vietnamese American, had a fifty-fifty chance of being chosen. In the coin toss, I won (or lost?) and got assigned to show Pring around. What bothered me the most was that because of our outward similarities, everyone expected me and Pring to be instant BFFs, which made no sense at all to me. If a Swedish exchange student came to our school, would that person be expected to be friends with all the white kids? Anyway, explaining it to the school administration and my classmates was futile. Instead, I made my point by *not* being friends with her. Which, considering I had no friends, was pretty on-brand for me.

I always felt like the teachers were more tolerable than the kids in Bentonville High anyway. Not that they fully got me either. Like how Mr. Benson would find a way to mention his favorite K-drama in every conversation. Or how Ms. Dimitri would never fail to tell me how much she envied my complexion because "Asians have the best skin." It was uncomfortable, but at least they were pointing out things they clearly thought were compliments about my culture, albeit presumptuously. Others, not so much. Brooklyn Dennehey and her crew nicknamed me "BTS" when I dyed my hair pink for the first (and last) time. Josh Nevins accused me of eating dogs because he read somewhere that that's what Korean people do. So yeah. Hanging out with the teachers felt like the lesser of two evils.

Among other things, I hope to improve my social life (or lack thereof) at Carlmont. I have a lot riding on this year, including figuring out a way to get out of the bargain I made with my parents. Except *bargain* would imply that it's a good deal by some measure. And according to my calculations, trading one year of Carlmont for four years of Bentonville seems more aligned with a bad deal than a good one. The math isn't mathing.

When I hear the code being pushed on the keypad, I jolt upright. My roommate is here.

As soon as the door opens, déjà vu hits me with a side of disappointment.

Standing in front of me is an Asian girl who's taller than me, with long, straight jet-black hair. We don't look anything like each other, but I'm pretty sure we'll be the only ones who think so. Wonder if she feels the same dread I do. That *oh-great-they-Noah's-arked-us* feeling. Or maybe she'll ignore me like I ignored Pring.

"Oh my God, you're here. Hiii!!!" She rushes up to me, taking me by surprise. Guess that answers my questions. "I'm Aerie." She smiles wide, showing off all her teeth.

Right off the bat, Aerie seems like a person who's comfortable in her own skin. I mean, who walks into a room meeting a virtual stranger like that, all bright and cheery? I wonder if we'll have anything in common.

"Hi. I'm Riley." I do a small wave, which I instantly regret.

"When did you get here? I would have waited for you, but I got carried away catching up with people I haven't seen all summer."

"Just got here a little over an hour ago." I stand awkwardly in the middle of the room, not knowing what to do with myself.

"As soon as I unpack my bag, we can get to know each other. 'Kay?" she says cheerily.

"Um, okay," I say, finally getting my feet to move out of her way. Aerie is not what I expected. She's nicer—almost too nice. Like maybe she's too good to be true? Ugh, why is my brain such an asshole?

While I get comfortable on my bed, I can't help but notice she's got a lot of desk crap—framed photos of her family, little stuffies, mugs, key chains . . . the list goes on. When she puts up a poster of an Asian girl posing with a violin on the corkboard behind her desk, I ask, "Is that you?" Then, a second later, I regret my question. They look nothing alike. "Shit, was that racist of me?"

She laughs. "I won't hold that against you. In fact, it's a compliment if you think I'm anything like Sarah Chang." When I give her a blank stare, Aerie's eyes widen. "You don't know who Sarah Chang is?"

"Should I?"

"You're Korean, right?"

I nod, wondering how that's relevant.

"She's only the holy grail of every Korean parents' hashtag goals." Aerie goes on to explain that Sarah Chang is arguably the most famous Korean American violinist, who debuted with the New York Philharmonic at the ripe age of eight and recorded her first album at ten. I can already tell that Aerie lives a different life than I'm used to, which prompts me to launch into a series of rapid-fire questions she answers in return.

Aerie's been playing the violin practically since birth. Technically, she started at three. Since she doesn't have any memories before then, however, she stands by her original claim. Her parents live in Hancock Park, which is a historic part of LA that is central to everything: beaches, Dodger Stadium, and, most importantly, Koreatown, where they operate their textile businesses. Aerie's parents both immigrated to the US as teenagers and speak Korean with her at home. She has an older brother, Daniel, who has earned his right as the Golden Child because he attends *the Harvard*, as her parents call it.

By the tenth or so question, Aerie changes course.

"What about you? What's your story?" Aerie turns to face me, chin resting on her arms, which are folded across her pillow.

Like she's getting comfortable for the actual story of my life, not some obligatory answer.

"My story?"

"Yeah, like, where are you from? What are your interests? Do you have a boyfriend?"

Boyfriend? I swallow a laugh. I'd first have to have friends in order for that to happen. At least I think that's the way it goes. Whatever. The point is, I don't have either, and Aerie seems to be genuine in her attempt to get to know me. Like, the real me and not some expectation of who I am.

Feeling the pressure of presenting my life in the form of a one-woman show, I sit up at the edge of my bed and clear my throat.

"I'm from Bentonville, Arkansas."

"Arkansas?" She scrunches her nose.

"Have you been there before?"

"No. It's just that it sounds so . . ." She makes a face like *ew*.

I'm not sure what that's about. I mean, I don't disagree with her entirely. There are aspects of living in Bentonville that I also think are *ew*. So I don't make a thing of it.

"What type of music do you play?" she asks.

"I play the acoustic guitar. Mostly pop songs that are upbeat and dreamy with a slight edge."

"Oh my God. An Asian girl playing mainstream pop? How cool is that?" She eyes me up and down like she's just now realizing how cool I am. Wait, what am I saying? I've never been cool.

"I didn't think about it that way." I wish I could say I'm trying to break some kind of barrier. I just play what I like.

"Who is your Sarah Chang?"

A silly smile appears on my face. Less than an hour together and we already have an inside thing.

"Skylar Twist of course," I answer right away. "My lyrics and her songs have a similar confessional quality. And her guitar skills are fire. Did you know she writes her own songs too?"

Aerie stares at me an extra beat. "What about other Asian American pop stars, like . . ." She stops and thinks. Then she says, "Guess I can't think of anyone big. I wonder why that is."

"I don't know," I say when I realize she's looking to me for an explanation. It kind of throws me. I'm not sure what she's implying. Do my idols need to look like me to count? Is Aerie categorizing me the way others do? Then again, no one's ever cared enough to ask me about my music, let alone my idols. So I try not to let it bother me.

"Can I ask you something?" I say instead. There's something that's been on my mind since the moment Aerie came into the room.

"Sure." She nods.

"How do roommates get assigned here? Like, do you have a choice or . . ." I can't seem to find the right words to finish that sentence. Aerie's eyebrow shoots up, mistaking my pause for a hesitation.

"No, no, no, not like that. It's just that at my last school, I was paired up with an exchange student who happened to be Thai. The administration lady said it was because I was a 'good student,' but I think what she meant was I'm an 'Asian student.' And when I met you, I kinda got the *exchange student vibes* all over again."

She cringes. "Why do teachers do that? I've always been told to speak up and be more assertive even though I was the debate

29

team captain at my last school. I can't tell if that's a stereotype on being female or being Asian. Probably both."

"Seriously? That's messed up." I know I shouldn't say this with a smile, but I've never been able to commiserate with anyone like this, and it feels good to not be alone for once.

"Well, it's not like that here. Or at least in the dorms. Roommates are paired together alphabetically by last name. I'm Aerie Jung, and you're . . ."

"Riley Jo," I say, relieved. I can be friends with Aerie without feeling the pressure to be her friend.

"Tomorrow I'll show you around," she offers without being asked to.

Aerie is treating me the opposite of how I treated Pring when I was paired with her. Which makes me feel even worse for ghosting Pring. After a month at Bentonville High, she had two friends—Harrison Slater, a doughy white boy with a pretty obvious Asian fetish, and Tiffany Tran. Poor Pring.

Then again, that's two more friends than I had in Bentonville, so maybe . . . poor me?

VISUAL	AUDIO
Drone shot of Carlmont's arts department:	Dr. Warren Buckley voice-over: Throughout the years, this school has gone through some changes. Most recently, the pandemic has impacted our teaching methods. However, our intent has remained the same: Carlmont has a dual mission, focusing on the preparation for the conservatory arts and college preparatory academics. In short, we want to equip our students to be successful in the next stages of their lives, whether it be in the arts or anywhere else.
Aerial of scattered terra-cotta roof buildings behind the backlot of fake Hollywood.	
Text on lower third: *A Day in the Life of a Monty* **Episode Two: The Arts**	
Footage of nat sound bridge:	Dr. Warren Buckley voice-over: Carlmont has a robust orchestra program that has an international recognition of excellence from classical music organizations around the world. Our strings and percussions instructors have toured in the famed New York and LA Philharmonics, respectively.
Orchestra playing Mozart's "Violin Concerto No. 3."	
Footage of Carlmont's theater production *of West Side Story.*	Dr. Warren Buckley voice-over: The drama and musical theater department at Carlmont is headed by Tony Award–winning director James E. Brooks and works with the set and costume departments, headed by Shorty Jones and Stella Watkins, who have both worked on sets for movie productions for over thirty years. Together with the students, they create high-quality productions that are showstoppers.
The dance-off scene.	

Footage of film department filming on the set of Fake Hollywod on Calmont's campus.	Dr. Warren Buckley voice-over: Along with our state-of-the-art technology in movie and TV production, Parker Nelson brings her expert eye from her years as an award-winning documentarian. The film department is able to collaborate with the drama and musical theater departments to give our future filmmakers the tools they need to get a head start in the industry.
Footage of contemporary band (including pianist, guitarist, drummer, and bassist) playing onstage.	Dr. Warren Buckley voice-over: We pride ourselves on creativity and ingenuity, and when we were approached to open our music program to include contemporary band, we embraced it. We are excited to be partnering with Blake Collins, a pop musician and award-winning music producer who will serve as our advisor.
Wide shot of Blake Collins sitting in front of a pool in the backyard of his residential home. Text on lower third: Blake Collins, Former Lead Singer, Boyz Club	I'm pretty sure most of you know me as the lead singer of Boyz Club. Our hit single went double-platinum and stayed on the top forty for eight consecutive months. We're also the second-highest grossing record for our label.
Text on-screen: What have you been busy with after Boyz Club?	
Wide shot of Blake Collins.	After our song "Clubbin'" hit double-platinum, I decided to branch off and start a solo career. I recorded a couple of tracks, but at the time, boy bands were what people wanted. By that point, the others had moved on. Dex started working in his dad's construction company, Preston got married and started on a family right away,

	and Johnny finished college and became a lawyer, if you can believe it. [Laughs.] Anyway, by then, I had decided to move on too. My producer from "Clubbin'," Marc Rubinstein, was the one who suggested becoming a manager. He offered to hear anyone I thought was the Next Big Thing. I haven't heard anyone worthy to bring to Marc yet, but I'm hoping that'll change soon.
Text on-screen: How did you become an advisor at Carlmont Academy?	
Wide shot of Blake Collins.	A few years ago, my son, Bodhi Collins, started at Carlmont. He's talented, as are all the students there. But he's got one thing that really sets him apart—stage presence. You know, a chip off the old block. [Smirks.] Anyway, I saw his talent was being wasted in the orchestra—no offense—and I suggested to the school that they create a new program for contemporary band. Buckley said it was a staffing issue, and finding an advisor—someone with firsthand experience and knowledge in the industry—to fill that role wasn't an easy feat. Then, when the pandemic hit, I saw an opportunity. With Zoom and everything, I figured I could do it. And the rest is history.
Text on-screen: Thank you, Blake Collins. Click on the link below for more info.	
Text on-screen: Producer: Xander McNeil	

When I click on the link, it sends me to the music video of Boyz Club's "Clubbin'." I've heard the song before occasionally on a radio station that plays hits from the nineties, and sometimes it plays in the background of TV shows and movies. I've never seen the music video until now.

Blake Collins is in the front, while the three other members of Boyz Club are staggered behind him. He's singing with a mic attached to his earpiece, and all four of them are wearing the same white two-piece suit that looks two sizes too big for them. Their synchronized dance is out-of-date with their pop-and-lock moves. It's energetic and awkward but maybe impressive for its time. There's this solo dance that Blake breaks into, and the others stand in a U-shape around him. He's moving his arms and legs in a hyperactive mode like the camera speed is at 2x. I laugh out loud, wondering if this is a joke. But after I watch the entire thing play out with the credits and everything, I realize this isn't a joke. It's the real music video.

Although anyone who puts that up as Blake's bio must have a sense of humor. So maybe this is a joke?

FIVE

It's my first official day at Carlmont. Aerie follows through with her promise and takes me under her wing.

In the morning, she gives me a brief tour on the way to breakfast. The campus is an estate-turned-school that is this odd—though not unpleasant—combination of institution and resort. On the east side of the campus, the general-ed classes are taught in the original residential buildings that exude charm, with Spanish-style roofs and ivy-covered walls. Stepping into the west side of the campus, where they have the newer-built electives buildings, is kind of like stepping into a backlot on a movie set. There are theaters and music rooms and even an area that looks like a real street right out of Hollywood.

We get to the dining hall, which is in a grand building with a tall arched ceiling and wood beams hanging massive chandeliers from above. There's a buffet line of hot foods that smell savory and sweet all at once. Any other day I'd be lining up with the others. Today I have no appetite. First day at a new school is public-speaking levels of nerve-racking. Multiply that by about a thousand and that's how I'm feeling right now. It's my last first day in high school, not to mention my last first day at this school, so I've got a lot riding on today not sucking.

You know how sometimes you build something up in your mind to be bigger than it is, so when you finally get to experience it, it's inevitably one big letdown? Like skincare dupes that promise to clear up your acne forever. Or life hacks that bloggers claim are "so easy!" *(Lies.)*

Anyway, I'd read through the brochures and taken the virtual tour online, so I had an idea of what it would be like at Carlmont. Impromptu classes in the garden/atrium/patio. Teachers who aren't only industry badasses but also hashtag relatable. And laughing. Lots of laughing faces on the glossy-paged brochures. I just assumed they were staged, like the plays and performances they put on here. Today, however, proved me wrong. So far, Carlmont is living up to the dream and is everything that was advertised.

Let's start with the classes. Here, the boring subjects are actually worth staying awake for. In math, we're starting a unit where we create a model set for a TV show using proportions and dimensions. In language arts, the assignments include writing scripts, screenplays, and film reviews. And physical education, my worst "subject" and lowest grade through no fault of my own—weak upper-body muscle tone runs in the family, and seriously, half our grade accounted for how long we could hang on to a bar—is something I'm looking forward to at Carlmont. The syllabus includes stage presence, interpretive dance, and mindful meditation.

Even the clusters of kids on one of the many grassy knolls scattered across the campus seem to be laughing unironically, like they're *actually* having the best day of their lives. I can't tell if this is what it's like to be monied or if this is what it's like to go to a school you don't feel like you're on the outside of. Probably both, not that I would know firsthand. And even if it's just for a year, it feels good to be on this side of the unending Instagram reel of awesomeness for once.

After I finish the general-ed classes in the morning, it's lunch. Which kind of slows down my momentum. At my last school, lunch was A Scene. Most everyone had a thing—sports, cheer, leadership. Acoustic guitar didn't exist in Bentonville High. Didn't matter, though. People had already decided my thing was being Asian. Of course, to prove my point, I purposefully did not sit at the diversity table. (Also not my thing: being the loser who ate lunch in a bathroom stall. For the germ factor *alone*.) So I took matters into my own hands and decided helping teachers out during lunch—grading papers, distributing flyers, that kind of stuff—was my thing. Question is, what's it going to be at Carlmont?

"Riley!" someone calls out across the dining hall, and my head whips over.

I spot Aerie motioning me to join her at the table she's sitting at with her friends. A quick glance and I notice they're all Asian. Normally I wouldn't want to give others the satisfaction of fitting into their cultural expectations of me by sitting at the Asian table. But Carlmont is way more diverse than Bentonville, and there are Asian students sitting at other tables scattered around the dining hall. So I rationalize that this is not going to be the thing that defines me here.

Scruples aside, I'm just grateful to have a place to sit.

"Hey, Aerie." I sit in the empty chair next to her and set my tray of food down. Since I didn't eat breakfast, I'm famished. I've got a huge pastrami sandwich with a side of fries.

"Everyone, this is my roommate I told you about, Riley." Aerie points to me. "Riley, this is Nari Hitomi." She looks across the table to a ghostly pale girl with dark eyes and a blunt haircut. "And this is Brandon Lee." She points to the guy next to Nari. He's tall with longish hair and thick eyebrows.

"What about me?" The guy on the other side of Aerie interrupts her.

"He doesn't matter." Aerie leans in, blocking his view.

"Ooh, burn, Jason," Nari says, and they all laugh.

"Hi, I'm Jason Liao." He shoves a hand past Aerie's face and in front of me.

"Hi." I shake it hesitantly while Aerie and Jason bicker playfully. I'm not sure I fully understand what's going on.

"They're on-again, off-again boyfriend-girlfriend. And right now they're off again," Brandon leans in and says, filling me in.

"Ah. Thanks." I nod to Brandon.

I notice one of the books Nari is holding, and I point to it. "You play violin too?"

She nods. "Aerie and I are duking it out for first chair." She pretends to fight Aerie, and they laugh. "Jason plays the clarinet, and Brandon plays the flute."

"You're all in orchestra? That's cool." I hope I can be close to my bandmates the way they all seem to be.

"What instrument do you play?" Nari asks.

"Acoustic guitar," I say.

"Whoa, that's seriously cool." Brandon glances sideways at me. He's got that James Dean squinty-eye thing going for him, which I can't say isn't attractive.

"So *you're* the new kid in the contemporary band program," Nari says, eyeing me. I could be reading too much into it, but she says this with particular interest.

"That's right!" Jason snaps his finger. "A couple of the members left the school, and there was some talk about the program shutting down last year."

"I remember them. Jake Harris and Jeremy Williamson. They lived in the same dorm as me. They didn't come back this year, though. Guess boarding school wasn't for them," Brandon says.

"I worked in the admissions office over the summer, and finding the right candidate was a top priority. Anyway, there usually aren't a lot of applicants for seniors, and less for the contemporary band program, since that's not something Carlmont is known for. So I overheard the headmaster saying they might not continue with the program. Guess they found the perfect candidate," Nari says. Again, I notice her stare lingering, like she's hiding something.

"Is there something about band I should know?" The way Nari's been eyeing me makes me wonder if I'm stepping into a minefield.

"No, not at all," Nari backtracks. "I heard the headmaster handpicked you, that's all."

They all look to me, and I sit up straighter, feeling like a Someone after years of feeling like a No One.

"Do you know anyone else in the band?" I ask.

"Not really," Nari says, and the others shake their heads.

"It's a small program, and they mostly stick to themselves. Probably because it's newer," Aerie says, thinking out loud.

"We've heard them perform, you know, before Jake and Jeremy left. And they were good. Like, *really* good," Jason says in a way that's pretty intimidating.

The only band I'd played with in public was the church band. It was just a few times, but I'll never forget what it was like when

I stepped on the stage for the first time. Like performing music was my real life, and the rest of the time I'd been living someone else's. I managed to gain a small following at the youth group, and they even asked me to hang out with them a few times. Anyway, that was before the pandemic, when I was in the minor leagues for friend groups. I may have been good for Bentonville, but I have no idea how I'll measure up here. All of a sudden, I feel the pastrami and fries I just ate trying to make their way back out.

"You have nothing to be nervous about!" Aerie says, probably noticing the blood drain from my face. "Carlmont is notoriously hard to get into. Not just because of the academics. Because of the arts electives too. They wouldn't have accepted you if they didn't see something in you."

A beat later, Nari lights up with an idea. "Maybe you can use your music as a way to create Asian American awareness in a genre that Asian Americans are severely underrepresented in. This is the type of innovative stuff Carlmont prides itself on."

"You're right," Jason chimes in. "They have a real commitment to diversity. Which sounds like a joke when I hear myself. But they really are trying to platform more POCs in the arts here. The teachers would be open to it. You could even use it to help launch your career."

My mind is spinning. Asian awareness? Commitment to diversity? *Launch a career?* As much as I'm loving their enthusiasm for my music, something that's a complete one-eighty from what I'm used to, I think they might be getting ahead of themselves.

"I just want to play music," I say with a shrug. It's the only thing I'm sure of at this moment.

"Being a POC in something that not a lot of POCs do naturally puts you in the spotlight," Nari says.

"Just think about what you could do." Aerie gives my shoulder a squeeze, probably sensing my hesitation.

"Okay, I will," I say half seriously and half trying to move the conversation along. As admirable as their suggestions are, it's only my first day here. And my brain can only handle so many firsts. After I get settled with my band, *then* I'll be able to consider the other stuff they mentioned.

SIX

After lunch, we part ways for our electives. Aerie and her friends go to the orchestra room, and they point me to where the contemporary band meets.

Close to the set of Fake Hollywood is a theater with a music room attached to it. When I open the door, I see two guys on a raised platform that resembles a stage at the back of the room. There's a guy with retro-grunge vibes and blond-tipped dark hair behind a drum kit, and the guy at the piano has a surfer-snowboarder thing going on with his cargo shorts and beanie loosely covering his wavy blond hair. They look over at me questioningly, and I can tell I've interrupted their conversation.

"The orchestra is two buildings over," piano guy says to me, then turns back to the drummer to continue his conversation.

I look down at my guitar, confirming it in no way, shape, or form looks like a small cello or an oversized violin before I say, "I'm not in orchestra." I read the number above the door again to confirm I'm in the right place. Yep, 5B. The music room. "Is this contemporary band?"

The two of them abandon their conversation and crane their necks to look at me properly this time.

"Are you . . . *Riley*?" piano guy says.

"Riley *Jo*?" drummer guy says with a raised eyebrow.

Well, now that it's confirmed I'm in the right place, I allow myself to step fully into the room. The reception, however, isn't exactly welcoming.

"Yep, I'm Riley Jo." My voice is unwavering, but my fingers tremble getting my guitar out of its case.

"You're not what I— Never mind." Piano guy shakes his head, clearly annoyed.

I refrain from telling him that I'm a *who* and not a *what*. I get the feeling correcting his grammar is going to be less appreciated than pointing out his obvious show of disappointment in me.

Drummer guy deflates, pretty much confirming my suspicions: I'm not who they were expecting. Story of my life.

The outside temp is a balmy seventy-five degrees and the room is nicely air-conditioned, yet I can't seem to cool down. Even my ass is sweating.

"Hey, I'm Griff Torres," the drummer eventually says, nodding up at me. He's got gray eyes, which are striking against his tanned skin. Despite being less than thrilled about me a minute earlier, at least he's attempting human decency, which is more than I can say about piano guy.

"I'm Riley. Guess you already know that, though . . ." I say, trailing off. I pull my guitar strap over my head, probably revealing a sweat stain forming in the armpit of my shirt as we speak.

"Don't mind Bodhi. You get used to him," he says in a low voice, leaning in.

I give Griff a weak smile. Somehow I doubt that. A lifetime in Bentonville didn't make things any easier for me there. I don't have a lifetime at Carlmont, so I better make this work somehow.

"Hi. Bodhi, is it?" I force myself to say.

Bodhi turns around and eyes my guitar. "You won't be needing that today," he says instead of an introduction.

"I won't? I thought we were going to—"

"My dad— I mean, Blake wants to figure out how to strategize our talents."

His dad? I gasp. "Pop-and-lock is your dad?" Now that he mentions it, he does look familiar.

Griff lets out a snicker, which prompts Bodhi to glare daggers at me.

My face flares. I cannot believe I said that out loud.

"I mean, Blake Collins from Boyz Club, our advisor, is your dad?" I try again, but it's too late. That slipup didn't help win me any popularity points.

Bodhi exchanges a look with Griff and points to me as if to ask, *Who is this kid?* Griff nods to Bodhi, then smiles at me. Wait. Does that mean he's siding with Bodhi, or he's sympathizing with me? Unclear.

Either way, I don't have time to be offended because I just found out that Bodhi, my bandmate, is the son of a nineties pop star who also happens to be our advisor. Even though Bodhi's coming off as a grade-A asshole, I have to admit that's pretty intimidating.

"Blake is not only our advisor, he's also a manager with connections to the A&R at Ruby Records, Marc Rubinstein's label."

"Oh wow," I say, only because I can tell it's a big deal by the way Bodhi narrows his eyes and purses his lips. Like I should be impressed. Except a beat later, I realize I can't fake my way through this conversation. "What's an A&R?" I finally gather enough courage to ask.

I catch another *this kid* look from Bodhi to Griff, which he's not even trying to hide for my benefit. "A&R means Artists and Repertoire" is all Bodhi says.

Okaaaay. Guess that means I'll be googling whatever that means later. I mean, seriously. He has to know that his explanation hardly explained anything.

"Artists and Repertoire representatives work at the labels," Griff adds helpfully. "They're the ones in charge of scouting new talent and bringing them to the attention of the music producers there. Basically, they're the go-between for artists and record labels."

Okay, that helps. A little. I'm still having trouble understanding how Blake's connection with the A&R at the record label is releva— Wait a sec. "Does this mean we're going to record a song?" I ask, thinking out loud.

Bodhi laughs. "Oh my God. Are you sure you're in the right class? Maybe your acceptance letter got mixed up with another Riley Jo." When he notices Griff shoot him a look, he holds his hands out to his sides. "What? You know you were thinking it too."

Griff doesn't disagree, which stings a little. "What kind of music do you play?" he asks instead. "Aside from your name, we don't have any other information on you."

"I play anything, really. In my audition, I submitted two pieces. One was an original, and the other was—"

"He means your sound," Bodhi says, clipped. "How are we going to know if you mesh well with us?"

I thought the audition part was over and done with. I'd gotten my acceptance letter to Carlmont. What's with the third degree?

"This isn't some high school band." Bodhi waves a flippant hand at me.

"It isn't?" Last I checked, that's exactly what this is.

"Okay, fine." Bodhi rolls his eyes—I'm pretty sure—at me. In the short time I've gotten to know him, Bodhi doesn't seem like the type of guy who gets annoyed with himself. Ever.

"This isn't *just* a high school band. If we play our cards right, we'll be the next big group that Ruby Records signs. We just need The Song for the Spring Concert."

"Seriously?" My eyes ping-pong between them. "Is that what this class is all about? Becoming actual music artists?"

"Why else would we be here?" Bodhi scoffs. "Because this looks good on our college apps?"

I came to Carlmont because I wanted to get out of Bentonville. But I'm not about to say that out loud, especially to my unimpressed bandmate who I just met. So instead I say, "No, yeah. I am also here to become a famous music artist." The words come out clunky, as if I'm speaking them for the first time. Wait, what am I saying? I *am* speaking them for the first time.

What's even more surprising is the instant relief I feel. Like a weight lifted off my shoulders. As if wanting to be a music artist was a secret I'd been hiding for a long time. Not because it was something I was ashamed of. But because I thought it was too big, too out of my reach to even think about. Within the four walls of my room at home, playing my guitar, I could be whoever I wanted. The biggest star, bigger than Skylar. Outside of my room, though, where every space I occupied made me feel like an imposter, I didn't think it could be possible. And now Bodhi's telling me that it is possible? I'd hoped to figure out how I could get out of Bentonville for good, but this is almost too good to be true. I'm sure my parents wouldn't hold me to my agreement to attend Bentonville U if I were to get signed by a major record label.

A message pops up on the screen at the front of the room saying our meeting is about to begin, snapping me back to the present.

Blake Collins's face appears on the screen. His skin is weathered, with swollen bags under his eyes and a receding hairline, but he still resembles the famous pop star from the music video. Like he's an older relative or something.

"Am I on?" Blake looks at us through the screen. "There I am." He looks off camera at something and continues talking to us. "Let's get started. We have a lot to cover today since Jake and Jeremy decided not to continue with us."

I realize I've been holding in my breath since he started the class and am now feeling light-headed. So I let out my breath. It makes a *peeewww* sound, which I instantly regret.

Blake looks back at us, squinting at the screen. "Riley?"

"Yes?" For some reason I think it's a good idea to stand at attention. As soon as I'm up, I realize it's a terrible idea. So I sit back down, face throbbing.

He holds up a piece of paper and reads from it. "Riley Jo?" He looks back to the screen for clarification.

Ugh. Not this again.

Let's just get through the uncomfortable shock that I am not who you expected. The sooner we move on, the sooner we can work on getting that record deal Bodhi mentioned.

"I'm sorry, but there's been a mistake. I'm not sure if you'll fit in with The Boyz," he says, somewhat definitively.

The boys? That's a bit sexist.

"I probably should mention that my pronouns are she/her/hers. I'm not sure if that's relevant." I don't normally talk back, especially not to a scarily intimidating advisor who was once a pop icon, but I'm having a hard time following.

"The Boyz is the name of our band. You know, a nod to Boyz Club," Bodhi chimes in ever so helpfully.

"I just don't think your sound will mesh with what we've got going on," Blake continues.

"My sound? I haven't even—"

"This isn't a K-pop band."

And there it is.

Well, at least he's putting it out there. Which is more than what I can say for most people when it comes to dumping their cultural expectations on me.

"I don't play K-pop," I say defensively.

"Oh yeah?" He raises an unconvinced eyebrow. "What kind of music do you play, then?" he asks, like he's calling my bluff.

I open my mouth to say something. Nothing comes out. Like when my mom asked me why I wanted to play music, my voice shrivels up, and I can't speak the words I feel inside. I'm frustrated with myself almost as much as I'm frustrated with Blake for his blatant microaggression.

Bodhi nudges Griff and snickers like he knew this was going to happen. That someone like me being here is a mistake.

I want to shut it down. Now.

Before I know it, the familiar defense mechanism rises in my throat, and I'm prattling off examples of how I'm not the least familiar with K-pop.

"I've never played K-pop songs.

"I don't even know any K-pop bands.

"K-pop? What is that even?"

Instead of acknowledging my words, Blake's gaze is focused on something else off-screen. *He doesn't care.*

I look to Griff and Bodhi, who are both scooting their chairs farther from me as if the shame that is currently taking over me is contagious.

"I'd say my sound is more like a mix of the Jonas Brothers, OneRepublic, Imagine Dragons." Somehow, in my panic, I think it's a good idea to start listing the all-white male bands my sound resembles since he can't be convinced I don't play K-pop. "Smashing Pumpkins." Oh shoot. Guitarist James Iha is Asian. Before I can quickly think of another band, Blake shifts.

"Smashing Pumpkins?" Blake's brow quirks up, then he nods, rubbing his chin. "I could work with that."

What does that even mean?

"Look, Riley. It's nothing against you. I'm going to get right to it." Blake adjusts his seat like he's getting ready to launch into a spiel. "I wear many hats," he starts. "It's not only my job to advise you on your craft this year, but as a manager with connections to Ruby Records, I'm giving you an incredible advantage on getting ahead of what the industry is looking for. Specifically, it means that I'll be working on the marketability of the band by asking you some key questions, like: Who are you going to identify with? Who is your target audience? How do we position you in an already saturated market? These are all front matter done before the actual music part. Because if the music industry can't place you, then they won't be able to see the potential in you."

"I wish Jeremy and Jake didn't leave," Bodhi says loudly.

"It's true. We had all that figured out when Jeremy and Jake were here. Now with Riley part of the band, we won't be able to market ourselves in the same way."

I'm assuming by Blake's tone that Jeremy and Jake weren't only dudes, but that they were white dudes.

"Now, I tried looking you up on TikTok. I couldn't find you. What's your handle?" Blake asks.

"My handle? I don't have one," I answer.

"What?" Bodhi sits up like I've offended him. "You don't have TikTok? How is that possible?"

"My parents made me do a social media cleanse," I say. After the shame-stare I got from Bodhi about not having TikTok, never in a million years would I admit that I don't have enough friends to warrant a social media presence, much less that I only just got a smartphone days ago. "I've never felt healthier. My anxiety is at an all-time low. And my sleep? Like a baby." I repeat the things I've overheard my classmates say. I wouldn't know. Honestly, I don't see how social media is relevant to my ability to play the guitar.

"How are people supposed to find you if you're not online?" Griff asks with sincere confusion. "How are you going to create a fan base to get the attention of music producers and record label execs?"

The three of them wait for a response I don't have, since I only made the admission just minutes ago that being a music artist is my dream. I don't say that out loud either. Their confidence in me is low enough as it is.

After they spend time lecturing me on the importance of having a social media platform, they walk me through the steps of signing up for TikTok with the handle @TheRealRileyJo. Which feels like false advertising on so many levels.

By the end of the class, I put my guitar back in its case, unplayed.

And to think I thought it would be about the music at a music school.

SEVEN

After class ends, I'm not sure what to think. I'm used to micro-aggressive comments—okay, that's a lie. Not sure anyone gets *used to* microaggressions. Except maybe the micro*aggressors*.

Anyway, my point is, the microaggressions I'm used to are usually passing comments. An uncomfortable moment that I can walk away from or when I can change the subject to something else. I'm not used to ones that devote an entire class period to highlighting the fact that I am not who the band expected—not who they *wanted*.

Walking back to the dorms is a chore. My feet are weighed down by too many feelings. Instead of ignoring them, I lean into them. Because emotions, deep ones, are fodder for some of the best songs I've written. As someone who is allergic to confrontation, it's the outlet I need to be able to carry on. So I let myself wallow.

Except I can't fully. There's a noise that seems to be following me. Like a xylophone playing hopscotch, the noise intermittently goes on and off, distracting me. I groan. Just let me be sad in peace. I look around for the source. Where the hell is it coming fr—

Oh, it's me.

Or my phone, rather. Guess I'm not used to getting calls. Or having a phone. And after I glance at the screen, I notice something else I'm not used to. A TikTok notification. I swipe at it, and the message tells me that @EuniceJoPharmD started following me.

My first official follower on TikTok is my mom. It just keeps getting better and better. . . .

The phone is still ringing in my hand, so I click accept.

"Rileeyyy!!!" Elise scream-talks. My hand reflexively jerks the phone away from my ear. That girl has one level of volume control: loud.

"Hey, Lise. How are—"

"Ry, did you know that avocados are fruits? And that Australia is wider than the moon?"

"No, I—"

"Also, the Eiffel Tower is fifteen centimeters taller in the summer because the heat makes the metal expand. Did you know that?"

"Lise, did you get a new book on weird facts?"

"No, why?" She's totally oblivious as to why I'm even asking the question.

"Nothing, never mind." I smile. To me, it's *so Elise* the way her mind works like a pinball machine, bouncing from one idea to the next. But to her it's "normal." I have no idea how long this conversation can go for—it could be a minute or an hour. And that's not even an exaggeration. So I take a seat at the bench in front of our dorms.

"How was your first day at Carlsbad?" she asks, still scream-talking. At least it's more manageable now that I've turned down the volume on my phone.

A snort escapes me. "It's Carlmont, Lise." She can remember a million useless facts, and yet she can't seem to remember the name of my school.

"Whatever. Is it terrible? Do you want to come home? Are you homesick?"

If I'm being honest, band *was* terrible. But I hesitate to tell her the truth. With Elise, I'm always toeing the line of older sister and second mother. I don't know if I should let her live in ignorant bliss or try to prepare her for the harsh realities of the world.

Example: When I was in middle school and Elise was in first grade, I tried out for Young Cosette in the production of *Les Misérables* at a local theater group. It wasn't a school audition where everyone was guaranteed a part, and my mom and dad tried to prepare me for rejection.

"There are so many people trying out. You might not get it, and you can't take it personally because it doesn't mean you're not good," my mom said.

"In the end, you have to know that you tried your best," my dad added. At the time, I thought my parents were trying to support me, and I appreciated it.

I was all nerves in the waiting room, but as soon as I was called up on the stage, they dissipated like cotton candy when you eat it. Inexplicable confidence took over, and I was bold. I was eloquent. I was all the things I'm not in real life. When I finished, the judges stood up and clapped. I was sure it meant that I was a shoo-in.

Except I didn't get the part. I did, however, get a handwritten note saying how much they enjoyed my audition, how talented I was, and how I should try out for their next production, *The King and I*, starring Evan Fisher as the King.

When I found out the part went to Delaney Pritchard, a tiny part of me—okay, a big part of me—wondered if I hadn't gotten the part because I didn't sound like Cosette or because I didn't *look* like Cosette. And then, later, I was mad that I even had to wonder about something like that when Megan Tisdale, Kelsey Stewart, and all the other girls who auditioned and didn't get the part didn't have to think about that. Of course I knew I didn't look like Cosette. But did that mean I could only play characters I looked like, even though white people weren't held to the same standards?

Looking back, I got the feeling my parents knew that being different from the others (read: not white) would work against me in my audition. And I always thought that if my parents talked to me about it beforehand, I would have at least been prepared for the real disappointment. Now Elise is in middle school. Isn't it better to be honest with her so *she* can be prepared?

"Well? How was your first day?" Elise asks again, pulling me back to the conversation.

"It's great, so great. I'm having a blast." I chicken out. Obviously.

"Want to talk to Dad?" Elise asks.

"Um, okay." And now I realize I totally overanalyzed the question. I should have known better. I'd be annoyed by her inability to complete a conversation, or thought for that matter, except this is Elise. If I'm the polysynthetic fluff inside of a Squishmallow, Elise *is* the Squishmallow—impossible not to like.

"Daaaaad!" Of course she has to shout right into the receiver. When I recover, Dad's voice comes through on the other end.

"Ry?" he says. Except it sounds more like *lie*.

I always wondered why someone who has trouble pronouncing his *r*'s and *l*'s would name his children Riley and Elise. I'm sure he hears it perfectly in his head, though, and I sort of love that about him. He sees the world the way he wants to and not the way it is.

"Hi, Dad," I say.

"How's my number-one daughter?"

To be clear, he's referring to birth order and not ranking his daughters by favorites. That would be absurd. Elise is everyone's favorite.

"I'm doing good, Dad."

"Do you miss us yet?"

"Of course I do." There's a sting in my nose that hits me unexpectedly. "Carlmont is amazing. I'm learning so much about the music industry already," I quickly add, reassuring him (or me?) I've made the right decision in coming here.

"Wah," he says, which isn't a mispronunciation of the English word *wow*, but a Korean word that coincidentally has the same meaning. "I didn't know there were schools like this when I was your age. But hearing about it from you is like experiencing it for myself."

The backs of my eyes prickle. I know what he's referring to without needing him to further explain. If I compare my parents to shapes, my mom is a square and my dad is most definitely a star.

When Dad immigrated to America, he came to study math. Ironically, in Korea, he was just okay at math. Poetry is where he shined. I didn't know this until I found a poem he had written on the back of his and Mom's wedding photo when I had it reframed for them as an anniversary gift. The poem was written in Korean, and I asked my dad what it said. First he read it in Korean:

Meol-go keun bada eh
Salang-ui doch-eul dalgo
Oosseum eu-ro ddeo na-ri
Geu dae wah nah

I didn't understand it, so he tried to translate it for me:

Across the far and wide sea
With sails of love
We will set out with laughter
You and I

Writing in verse always came naturally to me. And after hearing my dad's poem, after learning he was a poet in Korea before he came to Arkansas, I understood where I got it from.

When I asked him why he didn't write anymore, he said it was because even though the words were a direct translation of the poem, the feeling of it didn't quite translate. I didn't understand why he couldn't just continue writing poems in Korean. So he explained it to me.

"When I came here for school, I didn't have much difficulty with math because numbers are a kind of universal language. Adapting to the culture and learning English, however, was more difficult. I had to work harder at learning a new language. I became immersed in it, only allowing myself to speak, listen to, write in English. Now, even if I wanted to continue writing poetry, the words don't come to me—in Korean or English."

Dad calls it the immigration tax. Maybe he jokes about it because that's his coping mechanism, but I get sad every time I hear a story about him giving up a piece of his past for what he thought was a better future.

"Do you miss poetry?" I blink back the tears. It's a good thing we're not on FaceTime.

"Nah," he says unconvincingly. "Besides, I came on a math scholarship."

He doesn't have to explain what that means either. That despite his tuition being paid for in full, his parents still had to spend their entire savings to send him to the US for college. He had a huge responsibility to make a career worthy of their efforts. Even I know that left little to no room for his creative pursuits.

"What's really on your mind?" Dad is pretty good at reading the room. Or maybe it's just that he's good at reading me.

"You know how first days can be," I start.

"Sure do. I dreaded when professors called on me. They always had a hard time with my name."

"I know, right?" See, my dad gets me. His Korean name, Yoo Jin, is actually pronounced in a similar way to his Americanized name, Eugene. I can see why he changed the spelling of it, since I'm sure people still found ways to butcher it.

"Somehow, 'Eugene Cho' was too foreign, so I changed it to 'Jo' when your mom and I got married." He says this without any hint of resentment.

"Wait, what?" I can't be sure I heard him right. Dad legally changed his name . . . *twice*?

"Some people spell it 'Cho' and others 'Jo.' Even though it's the same last name in Korean, one way is easier for Americans to understand."

Understand? What's there to understand? It's a person's last name. A simple one at that.

I've never heard this story before. In fact, I didn't realize *Cho* and *Jo* were different versions of the same last name. I just assumed they were completely different last names.

"Dad, you went through all that trouble just to change two letters in your last name so *other* people could pronounce it better? That sounds all kinds of backward. If others don't understand your last name, then they should change, not you."

"It wasn't that simple, Ry." He sighs quietly, but I still catch it. "My parents sacrificed a lot to send me to the US. After I graduated from college, I applied for jobs that I never got interviews for. I needed a job. My family needed me to get a job. When I changed my last name from 'Cho' to 'Jo,' I got more calls for interviews, which led to a job offer. My parents gave up everything for me to come to here. So my choices didn't have room for right or wrong, fair or unfair. My only choice was to find a way."

My gut twists around itself. My dad's never shared this part of his story with me until now. Maybe it's because we're not face-to-face, so it's easier for him. Maybe it's because I'm older. Whatever the reason, now that I know this information, it's something I can't unknow. It's a lot to sit with.

"Anyway, that was the past. I want to know about the present," he says, changing his tone. "Tell me about your band. How's *the* Blake Collins? Is the class everything you hoped it would be and more?"

Perspective is funny like that. A few minutes ago, righteous indignation over a microaggressive comment sizzled in me like raw meat hitting a hot pan. After talking with Dad, though, hearing how much he went through when he first came to the US makes me feel like I have no right to complain. Blake assumed I played K-pop. So what? No one's life is dependent on my musical achievements. So I tell him everything is fine, because in the context of this conversation, it is.

Later, Aerie comes into our room with Nari, and they seem to be debating something.

"Oh, Riley. You're back already," Aerie says, noticing me.

"Yeah. Just got here not too long ago."

"How was the rest of your day?" Nari eyes me with piqued interest.

"It was okay." After talking to Dad, I don't want to get into it again. "How was your day?" I ask instead.

"Nari was about to tell me who her crush is," Aerie singsongs.

Nari's mouth gapes open. "She lies. I had no intention of talking about my crush."

"Aha, so you do have a crush!" Aerie points to her.

"Let's talk about what's going on between you and Jason." Nari turns it around on Aerie. "Are you on-again again?" She smirks.

"Don't you dare change the subject. Riley, come help me get it out of her." Aerie motions for me to join them.

I flop myself down on Aerie's bed, wedged between her and Nari. It feels good to have a distraction—to have friends to distract me. Which, I'm fully aware of, is not nothing.

All afternoon, we talk about their crushes. I learn that Aerie and Jason are like the Ross and Rachel of their friend group—they've either been in a relationship or on a break since freshman year. From what I gather, they break up over seemingly innocent misunderstandings, like showing up thirty minutes late to a date or forgetting an anniversary—that type of thing. But I get the sense that the real reasons are deeper-rooted issues. Not that I'm an expert on the relationship front. I also learn that Nari is extremely private about her crushes, and she has a lip tighter than Fort Knox. So we spend some time trying to guess it out of her to no avail.

"What about you? Is there anyone you're interested in?" Nari turns the attention from herself to me. It's so abrupt, it takes me by surprise.

"Anyone in band?" Aerie's brows bounce up and down.

"Uh, definitely not."

"What's with that look?" Aerie asks, not fully convinced. Both of them stare at me until I eventually crack.

I tell them the whole story. About how Blake thought I played K-pop and how they assumed I didn't play the same music as them even though I never got to play a single note for them.

"Noooo." Nari cups a hand over her mouth in horror. "That's discrimination of the worst kind."

The worst kind? *Really?*

"You think so?" Not that I don't appreciate their support and understanding, but after talking to Dad, I'm not sure it's *the worst*.

"Are you kidding me? It's blatant disregard for you as an individual in his classroom, let alone as an individual human being. He's lumping you with an entire race—lumping *an entire race* with K-pop. There are so many levels of wrong with his type of behavior." Aerie shakes her head, fuming.

I'm startled by their sense of awareness. Even if I did have the courage to correct people about why they shouldn't ask me where I'm from or assume English isn't my first language, I don't always know the right words to explain *why* it's wrong. No one talks like this in Bentonville.

"Maybe it was acceptable behavior twenty years ago when he last made an album." Nari snorts. "Someone should tell Blake that we're not in the nineties anymore."

Aerie and Nari getting upset on my behalf extinguishes the fire in me. For the first time, I feel understood. This is the sort of microaggression that happens all the time in Bentonville, and no one bats an eye. Not even my parents. Maybe what I really needed all those years was someone to listen to me and validate my pain. Because Aerie and Nari are doing just that, and it seems to make me feel instantly better.

"Thanks, guys. That means a lot to me that you understand."

"Are you kidding? We're here for you. In fact, you should report it." Aerie points to me.

"Report it? To who?" I ask when I realize Aerie's serious.

"You should tell Ms. Morales," Nari says. "She's the head of the music department. Maybe she could file a formal complaint. Or maybe even get him dismissed."

I take turns glancing at the two of them. They're not serious, are they?

"Really? Over this? I'm not sure this calls for anyone getting dismissed. . . ."

"Why not?" Aerie challenges me. "I mean, aren't you tired of being overlooked because we're the 'good' kind of minority, the kind that doesn't speak up when things are unfair? Just makes me wonder that if we want things to change, we have to change them for ourselves," she says, thinking out loud.

"Aerie's right. And someone like Blake won't change unless he's made to be held accountable," Nari says.

My eyes ping-pong between Aerie and Nari, who are both getting worked up. A little too worked up.

"At the very least, they could keep a record of the account, in case this sort of thing happens again," Aerie says, probably sensing my hesitation.

"I'll think about it" is all I say. Because I'm not convinced it would help my situation. It would make things worse. And after just learning of Blake's connections with Ruby Records and his potential for signing our band, there's more at stake now than there was before. *Sometimes it's about making bad choices to avoid worse ones*, Mom's voice echoes in me. *So the best I can do is hope that others do the right thing.* I didn't understand it then, but I'm starting to now. If she's right, then maybe it's up to someone else, someone who can't be accused of taking it personally, to say something. Not me.

EIGHT

The next day, I have music theory and composition with Ms. Morales. She's got soft brown hair, a kind smile, and, best of all, she doesn't make any assumptions about me. She teaches me the basics of music theory, which sounds like another language to me—intervals, scales, and keys. But when she *shows* me by playing it on the guitar, I instantly know it.

"You have a good foundation and a keen sense of hearing, Riley. Just memorize the terms associated with the sounds, and you're golden." She's got a stack of metal bracelets on her wrist that jangle when she talks, making everything she says even more like music to my ears.

I bask in her words. Like a lizard perched on a rock to catch all the rays it can, I soak up every last bit of encouragement from her to make up for the deficit from yesterday's class.

If only my other teachers could feel the same way about me. Teacher. Advisor. Whatever.

After class ends, I'm on my way out, and I hesitate. Aerie and Nari said I should mention something to Ms. Morales, so maybe I should. But by the time I reach Ms. Morales's desk, another idea pops into my head.

"Ms. Morales. How do I . . . learn about the music industry?" Maybe instead of looking for a problem, I should be looking for a solution. Like when I talked loudly at the guy who assumed

English wasn't my first language, I'll be loud about my music knowledge so Blake will have no question about me fitting in with the band.

She tilts her head, analyzing my question. "What do you mean specifically? The music industry is vast."

"Well, mainstream pop music. How does a band become . . . a band?" I don't even know how to ask the question.

Thankfully, a knowing expression washes over her. "I think a good place to start is the trades. That is, trade publications." When I still have a deer-in-the-headlights look on my face, she adds, "If you're looking for up-to-date music deals in the commercial music industry, start with *Billboard* magazine."

During lunch, I take a tray and eat alone on a bench next to the library. Believe it or not, by choice. I waste no time and take Ms. Morales's advice to start reading *Billboard*. After lunch is band, and I'm determined to make it go better than it did yesterday.

On the website, there are a bunch of articles that I can barely make sense of. At the sidebar, however, there's a list of external links for further reading. I click on one that leads me to a resource center. There, I find an article for people pursuing careers in music that gives an overview of the American music industry. The industry is expansive, but I'm surprised to learn that it's not that complex.

While there are various ways to get the attention of record labels, the global music business constitutes a powerful oligopoly—a market condition in which a few firms dominate most of an industry's production and distribution. There are three major record labels that control about

70 percent of the global recorded-music market. Of course, there are also independent record labels that give artists more creative control; however, without the marketing dollars or reach, it's more difficult to break out as a big artist under the indie labels.

That's not to say there aren't other ways to becoming a famous music artist. Some artists have made their rise from social media and streaming platforms. Even still, those chances are very small in comparison to working with a major record label.

In short, if you want to be a household name as a musician, your best chance is to sign with a major record label.

I think back to Bodhi's questions (more like accusations), and they make more sense to me. If I am serious about my music, then what other goal should I be aiming for than to be the best in the music industry?

While I'm lost in my thoughts, something else catches my eye on the sidebar. ANTI-ASIAN HATE CRIMES UP 339 PERCENT, the headline reads. Math isn't my strong suit, but even I know those numbers aren't good. In fact, they're the opposite of good. I click on the link to the article. It redirects me to a regular news site. The latest crime happened at a Metro stop in Downtown Los Angeles. An elderly lady was pushed off the platform and onto the rails and barely survived.

Aerie and Nari said that Blake was discriminating against me in the worst way. Honestly, though, do I even have the right to complain when things like this are happening right around us?

"The world is one giant dumpster fire, and we're making music." I look to find Griff standing over my shoulder. "Oh, sorry. I didn't mean to creep on you like that. The headline caught my eye."

"No, you're good. I was just thinking the same thing. One minute I was looking up top record sales, and the next, an attack on a person's life for no reason other than they were Asian."

"I know, right? I spent an hour last night reassuring my mom that Carlmont is safe. That shit won't fly here."

I pause, my eyes taking inventory of Griff's facial features. His last name is Torres, which suggests he's Latine. Still, he has that type of ambiguous ethnic look that makes me second-guess myself. I want to ask him directly, but I hesitate. Even I know it's difficult to ask the question.

"Hey, this might be awkward, but what is your ethnic background?" The words come out clunky, and I sound like I'm reading from a script right out of *How to Speak Woke for Dummies*. At least it's better than sounding ignorant.

He laughs, shaking his head. "The age-old *What am I* question, huh?"

"You said it, not me." I put my hands up. I loathe when people ask me that. It's dehumanizing, as if I don't qualify as a real person in their eyes.

"I know this is confusing to most people." He waves a hand over his face. "Most people assume I'm Mexican."

I try to act aloof, but my face betrays me.

"Ah, you too?" He snaps his finger and points it at me.

"I— I . . ?" Yeah, I don't know what I was going to say, because nothing intelligible comes out. "It's the last name," I finally say, feeling the need to at least give him an explanation. "I wasn't a hundred percent sure, which is why I'm asking."

"Fair." He shrugs. "And I'm not offended. Kind of amused by it. My dad's a first-gen immigrant from the Philippines, and my mom is Okinawan/Hawaiian, and her family's been in Hawaii for three generations now. I feel hashtag very Asian, but apparently I'm Mexican to everyone else." He laughs. "When I went to the DMV to take the test for my driver's license, the guy asked me if I wanted to take the test in English or Spanish."

"Noooo." I cup my hands over my mouth.

"I can't make it up." He shakes his head. "People assume shit all the time."

"Everyone always thinks I'm Chinese. Like, would it kill you to look at a map once in a while?"

"I know, right? There are other countries in Asia." He holds his hands out to his sides in mock confusion.

"So many others!" I laugh. "My last name doesn't help." I chortle. "You know, even though it's two letters and spelled phonetically accurate, people feel the need to make it sound more Asian. Riley *Joo? J-oh?*" I can barely keep a straight face while finishing the sentence with Griff busting up. God, it feels good to laugh. It also feels shitty. I'm finally bonding with my bandmate, but under such terrible circumstances. "The irony of it is, my dad changed it to 'Jo' from 'Cho,' thinking it would be easier to assimilate."

"Are you for real?" Griff shakes his head. "You want to talk about messed-up last names? 'Torres' isn't even a Filipino last name. When the Spanish claimed the Philippines as their land, they forced the natives to change their last names to Spanish ones. 'Cause that's what colonizers do—they take away your culture and identity in one fell swoop. No wonder people think I'm Mexican." He laughs it off.

I gather it doesn't bother Griff that people are always questioning his ethnic background, which makes me curious.

"Where's home for you now?" I ask.

"I'm from Bakersfield. It's north of here, a couple of hours by car."

"What's Bakersfield like? Is there a lot of diversity there?"

"There aren't many Asians, if that's what you're asking. Ironically, there is a big Mexican population." He peers over at me before we both bust up laughing again. "I know, right? My parents were like, 'How can we make this more confusing for people?'"

Instead of laughing along with him this time, I say, "Ugh, I'm sorry."

He shrugs casually. Either it really doesn't bother him, or he's really good at masking his feelings.

I can relate to him to a certain degree. Until yesterday, I didn't have anyone to talk about microaggressions with, so I had no choice but to pretend they didn't bother me.

"Well, you can talk to me," I offer. "I know how frustrating it can be." In a short time, I feel weirdly comfortable with Griff. Guess that's the upside of shared grievances. For a long time, I've been pushing people like me away. I'm beginning to think I've been missing out.

"It was at first. Now, it's like . . . a callus. It might have been painful once, but the skin toughens up, and eventually you don't feel the pain anymore. I know it's wrong. I just don't know how else to deal with it except to accept it. There are so many degrees of racism." He gestures at the article on Asian hate crimes on my phone screen. "And in the grand scheme of things, confusing me for Mexican . . . is it really that bad?"

Griff is saying everything I feel, especially when I compare what I'm going through with what my dad went through. But seeing how racism endures for generations in both of our cases makes me wonder . . . when is it going to end? When are Asian Americans finally going to be *seen* as Americans?

"That's why this year is so important for me. I gotta get out of Bakersfield, and I don't have any other goal in mind than to play in a band. So this has to work."

His determination strikes another chord in me. I don't want to go back to Bentonville as much as it sounds like Griff doesn't want to go back to Bakersfield. "Do you really think this could be your ticket out of Bakersfield for good?"

"Are you kidding? My family helps me with my social media and religiously posts my stuff on TikTok. I have a good following too. But my posts keep getting taken down to be reviewed for 'suspicious activity.' I'm pretty sure it's the racist algorithm, not that I can prove it. All I'm saying is that once I had a lot of traction, my posts became more and more 'controversial' even though it's been the same content the whole time. Anyway, the connections Blake has at Ruby Records is the farthest I've gotten in the music biz."

Speaking of racist algorithms . . . "Can I ask you a serious question?" When Griff nods, I continue. "Why doesn't Blake give you shit for . . ?" I wave a hand around his face.

He presses his lips together and nods his head, understanding my question. "Yeah, I'm sorry that happened. Must've been hard for your first day. And nothing against you. We have to start over, and it's not easy to insert-replace band members and expect the same sound, let alone chemistry."

"Jake and Jeremy must have been really talented," I say. People talk about them as if they were legends.

"They were all right," Griff says, which startles me. "But they had one thing that we don't." He motions to our faces. "And don't think they didn't give me shit for that in the beginning either, calling me 'the brown kid' and whatnot. Sometimes you keep going because you have no choice. And with this year being my last at Carlmont, I'm going to do whatever it takes to make ourselves white-famous, even if it means I gotta keep my head down and earmuffs on." He motions putting on pretend earmuffs.

"*White-famous?*" Did I hear that right?

"It means you're not famous in obscure circles or play eclectic music or you're big in insert-random-Eastern-European-country-here. It's the type of famous that mostly white people achieve," he says casually.

"Oh," I say. If I didn't have the language to express why I was upset about Blake's K-pop comment to Aerie and Nari, then this is an entirely new ball game.

"You know what you have to do? You have to find your thing." He goes on to explain what he means. "I came up with a drum solo no one else has done before—it's insanely fast, rolling around the full kit three times and then doing a double bass break that leads to the final verse. I practiced until my fingers bled, and now it's an absolute masterpiece."

"Wow," I say. I'm not sure what's more impressive, his work ethic or the actual skill.

"My point is, it's my signature move. If you want to secure

your spot in the band, find your thing and make yourself indispensable."

Becoming indispensable seems impossible, since just yesterday Blake made it very clear that I was easily dispensable. Still, I thank Griff for his advice. At least he's trying to be helpful.

NINE

"Did you know that Skittles are all the same flavors?" Elise calls me during school. For *this*.

"Lise. Aren't you supposed to be at school?"

"It's a minimum day. Teacher conference week," she says. "Anyway, if you melt away the outer layer of a Skittle, you're left with this chewy, tasteless white center. You should try it."

"Ew, no. I'm seventeen, not five."

"I'm not five either," she points out. "It's still fun anyway."

"Maybe . . ."

"If you think about it, Skittles are kind of like people. On the inside, we're all the same—gummy and tasteless. Without the outer shell, we're missing some of the best parts."

I snort. Only Elise would be able to make that comparison.

"Oh, I have to go. The squirrel came back. Bye!" She abruptly ends the call without warning. By now I've learned to just roll with it.

After I check the time, I pocket my phone. There are a few more minutes before lunch is over and band practice starts, and I just happen to be by the student union, which is a large building in the middle of our campus that's kind of like Central Perk minus the funky furniture. People hang out, play board games, and grab coffee at the self-service station. It's also coincidentally where the snack shack is, so . . .

Long story short, I get the Skittles.

Even longer story shorter, I do the experiment Elise mentioned, and it's true. Once the outer shell of the Skittle dissolves, the inside is flavorless. Who knew?

I lose track of time eating candy, of all things. The old-timey bell at the top of our campus rings, signaling the end of lunch. So I head to class with Skittles in my hands.

When I get to the music room, Bodhi's already there. No *hi*, no *hello*. But when Griff comes in shortly after I do, Bodhi bypasses me and gives Griff the broey-est handshake/hug there ever was. If it wasn't clear yesterday, it definitely is today: They're homies. I get it.

While we wait for Blake to join via Zoom, I notice I'm still holding a handful of Skittles. I must be nervous, because the sweat from my hand melted the outside candy coating. *Ew*. I quickly toss them in the trash and sit back down.

Bodhi's doing that thing where he's talking loudly about his dad but only to Griff.

"Isn't this *so* something my dad—I mean Blake—would like?" Bodhi shows something on his phone to Griff, loud enough to make me think he's including me yet clearly not allowing me the privilege to see what he's referring to.

Bodhi reminds me of the pick-me girls back in Bentonville, the ones that were all, "Oh my God, don't take a pic of me. I'm hideous." Meanwhile, they're all duck lips and angled bodies with a hand on the hip and an arched back. Whatever. I don't care.

Except that I do care. Especially when Griff seems interested.

"He totally could be into that. I'm thinking something with a strong beat, heavy on the bass, and a staccato interlude." Griff's face lights up, and he and Bodhi exchange an IKR face, and suddenly, I am dying of FOMO.

"And if he likes it, Marc will like it." Bodhi fist-bumps Griff in a pre-celebratory move over some song they won't stop yammering on about.

Okay, fine. I'll bite.

"What song is it?" I can't help but ask.

As I knew he would, Bodhi clicks his phone off and pockets it. "It's the music track of an original I'm working on. You wouldn't understand it." He sniffs. "You know, textbook stuff."

I feel stupid for falling moth-to-flame for it. I knew how it was going to end, and yet I couldn't resist. I deserved that burn. Griff at least offers an apologetic look.

Blake joins the Zoom meeting, and in seconds, his face appears on the screen.

"Great, you're all here. Let's get started." He leans back in his chair, placing his arms behind his head. "I've been thinking a lot about how to brand us now with Riley part of the group."

My face flares. *Thanks for pointing out once again that I am the problem.*

I catch a glimpse of Griff, who gives me a fleeting look of sympathy. I get why he can't really say anything as the other Asian person in the room, but it sucks to be under such a negative spotlight. I rub my hands on my jeans only to realize too late that one of my hands is stained with the colors from the Skittles. I try to wipe it off with my sleeve. It only makes it worse. Great, just great. In trying to make it go away, I made it darker.

"Let's start with the name. We can't be The Boyz anymore. For obvious reasons," Blake continues.

Another thing that's obvious? Blake's inability to stop othering me. Jesus H. Christ, what is it going to take to make him stop?

I think about Griff's advice. *Make yourself indispensable.* How can I get Blake to see me as indispensable when he can't get over my appearance? It's not like I can wipe off my Asian features; it doesn't work that way. I'm staring at my lap, trying to come up with a diversion, when the stain from the Skittles catches my eye. If I was in the right headspace, I'd admire it because it's actually kind of pretty. Like an unintentional fashion statement.

Then it hits me. Maybe I'm looking at it the wrong way. Instead of trying to make myself invisible, maybe I should lean into it.

"Can I make a suggestion?" I say, surprising everyone.

It's pin-drop silent. Not because they're waiting with bated breath for what I'm about to say next, but because they're *uncomfortable* with me speaking up. I somehow manage to power through my uncertainty before I lose steam.

"What if—and I'm just spitballing here—we used our initials for our band name: RGB."

Bodhi lets out a *pfffttt*, letting his head dip back in obvious enjoyment of what he clearly thinks is my failed attempt at being relevant.

I ignore him and continue. "I've been thinking about what you said about branding ourselves. What if our image was diversity? Here's a clearly diverse band." I motion around to us and hesitate when I get to Griff. If I'm not mistaken, he seems to lean back, embarrassed even, of my suggestion. I pull my eyes away so he doesn't distract me from getting my point across.

"And RGB aren't only the initials of our first names; they're the initials of the primary colors of light and the source of all colors on the visible spectrum. And bam. That's our brand. It says we're an everyday band for everyone."

After I'm done explaining, no one moves. I can't decipher from their unreadable expressions what they're thinking. All I know is, I'm not super confident since Bodhi clearly won't support anything I suggest, but even Griff is avoiding eye contact.

Eventually Blake shifts in his seat. "I could work with that," he says, surprising all of us, especially me.

"You could?" I ask, more out of shock than anything.

"Well, hold up. Can I make a suggestion? Why does it have to be 'RGB'? Why does *R* have to go first?" Bodhi leans back in his chair and folds his arms across his chest.

It's the order of the rainbow, dickwad. Everybody knows it's red, green, then blue. Not everyone is a narcissist.

"I think it's the colors in rainbow order," Griff says what I'm thinking but in a *much* nicer way.

"RGB has a better sound," Blake says in his typical mince-no-words way. "Let's go with that for now. Next on our agenda will be to think of our sound."

The rest of class, we—or Blake, rather—makes a list of bands he thinks should be our band goals. One Direction or One-Republic . . . ? I'm not really listening because I'm still in shock. Not only did I somehow miraculously come up with the new name for our band but my name is an integral part of it. Or my initial at least.

"We'll hear song suggestions on Monday," Blake says, wrapping up at the end of class. "Have a great weekend. And Riley?"

"What?" I blurt, totally caught off guard. "I mean, yes?"

"Great job today."

After class is over, I run straight to my dorm, or maybe I float back. Hard to tell after Blake's words of praise. I believe his actual words were "great job," but coming from Blake, who pretty much tried to Asian me out of the group just yesterday, that's practically a glowing review!

I have a mound of homework waiting for me, but I can't focus. My brain is buzzing with too much feeling. So I do what I usually do when I feel this way: write it down. It's just a start, but I can feel it growing.

STARDUST

Capo: 4
G-D-Em-C

> *You made those colors in the sky*
> *And don't let the moment pass you by*
> *'Cause I can see it now*
> *You, me, them, us*
> *We could all be stardust*

TEN

Now that I'm getting acclimated to the school part, I'm figuring out how to navigate the boarding part—that is, the nonacademic time at Carlmont. Most of the day is spent either in classes or at meals, and in the evening there are two hours dedicated to studying, followed by an hour-long free period, then lights out. In the middle of the day, there's a small window of time after school and before dinner that's meant for extracurriculars, like sports, clubs, and tutoring.

The activities haven't started yet, but there's a table with information about each club offered in the student union. Before lunch, I head over there. Someone comes from behind me and hooks an arm with mine.

"What the—"

"Calm down, it's just me," Aerie says as Nari appears on my other side.

I calm down. "Sorry, no one's ever"—I look down at my arm linking with Aerie's—"done that before."

"Well, get used to it. 'Cause I'm an arm-linker." Aerie smiles wide, her face glowing like it usually does. Probably because of her nightly ten-step skincare routine, which she enlightened me about on my first night here. It's, like, nine steps longer than mine.

"What extracurricular are you signing up for?" Nari asks me. Her skin is equally as dewy, and she's got cute freckles sprinkled across her nose.

"I was thinking of getting tutored by Ms. Morales." Naturally I gravitate to hanging out with the teachers, even at Carlmont. What can I say? Old habits die hard. Plus Ms. M is cool.

"Tutored?" Aerie exchanges a glance with Nari.

"What's wrong with that?" Did I just reveal too much about myself? On a scale of one to ten, did I just rank myself dorktastic?

"Come on, Riley. If you continue at this rate, you'll be burnt out before the year is over," Aerie says.

"It's decided. You're joining ASA with us." Nari grabs my free arm. Apparently, she's an arm-linker too.

It's official. With Aerie on one side of me and Nari on the other, I'm a Riley sandwich. A strange sensation washes over me. Is this what it's like to have friends? I'm not trying to be weird about it and scare off my one chance at a friend group, so I clear my throat and ask, "What's ASA?"

"Asian Student Association," Aerie clarifies. "Jason and I are copresidents this year."

I stare at Aerie skeptically. "That's a real thing?"

Nari snorts. "Live under a rock much? Yes, it's a real thing."

I don't have to clarify that this was not a thing at my last school. They know.

"What do you do in ASA?" I ask.

"We talk about ways to raise awareness about the diversity of Asian Americans in our school and in our community, given the rise in Asian hate," Aerie explains.

"Don't you think that's messed up how people had to literally die for awareness about racism against Asians to gain traction?" Nari chuffs. "We've been complaining about microaggressions for, like, ever. No one took any of that seriously, which made us seem weak and passive. Which makes us easy targets for scapegoating when things get hard, like it did during the pandemic."

Aerie and Nari exchange a look that says *mhmm*, and I'm hit with a pang of envy.

Carlmont has so much more of everything than I'm used to—more industry knowledge, more cultural awareness, more social responsibility. I haven't experienced or witnessed violence, but racism exists where I live, and we don't talk about it. Or at least my parents don't.

"It sucks, but what can we do?" I ask earnestly.

"That's what we do in ASA. Sometimes we have suggestions and solutions, and other times we don't. But talking about it, acknowledging that it happens, sometimes is enough." Aerie squeezes my arm, and we walk to lunch together.

Five minutes ago, I may not have known what ASA is, but now I can't wait to be part of it.

After lunch, I head to the music room early and find Griff sitting behind his drum kit, practicing. He stops when he notices me.

"Don't stop on my account; that was seriously good." I sit in a chair, facing him onstage.

"Nah, I was just messing around." He sets his sticks down.

"Can you show me your signature move you mentioned yesterday?" Ever since he mentioned it, I've been curious.

The side of his mouth pulls up to a half grin. "Guess I could show you since we have a few more minutes before class starts." He resets, adjusting his position, then jumps in without a countdown.

He's intense and quick, like he's moving at the speed of

light. And the sound . . . It's the type of beat that gets your head bobbing before you even realize you're doing it. The type that makes you stop only to admire it, then get right back to head bobbing. It's the ultimate adrenaline rush. The second he's done, I applaud.

"Wow, that's more than a signature move. It's transcendental. I swear I just left my body."

He does a fancy bow, tipping his head and his hand to his stomach.

"Thanks." He wipes his brow. "What about you? RGB? That's not only the perfect brand for us, it's ingenious. By branding our band as a diverse and inclusive band for everyone, you have made yourself invaluable. The student has become the master."

It's my turn to do a fancy bow to him. We both laugh. "I couldn't have done it without your suggestion. Thanks for your advice."

"No problem. We've got to stick together, right?" He winks at me.

"Yeah, you're right." Bodhi may not be warming up to me, but it helps that Griff is. "Are you going to sign up for ASA?" I ask.

"Nah, not my jam." He shakes his head.

My brows furrow. "Why not?" It seems contradictory since he just said that we need to stick together. Why wouldn't he want to be part of ASA?

"Sometimes it's hard enough dealing with what we have. And at the end of the day, I just want to play music, you know?"

It makes sense what Griff is saying, and if I'm being honest, I hear echoes of myself in him. It was only a couple of days ago that I said almost the exact same thing to Aerie, Nari, Jason, and Brandon. Now part of me feels like it's hypocritical. Maybe it's because I'm the one who came up with the whole diversity brand, and I don't want it to be about lip service or performative bullshit. It reminds me of how Bentonville High would spend the whole month of February celebrating Black History Month. People would wear BLM merch and post photos with meaningful hashtags. Then when February was over, they would pack it up and not celebrate it again until the following February. It always felt wrong to pay attention to something one month out of the year when we should have been celebrating it year-round.

I don't want to be someone whose intentions amount to nothing more than an aesthetic. Like the "allies" and slacktivists who post a black square on Instagram but don't donate their time, money, or talents to Black activism. Or the people who prominently hang rainbow flags but still support anti-LGBTQ corporations by buying their products. Still, Griff makes me wonder, *Do I have to try and do it all?* When it comes to advocating for marginalized voices, is there only one way of doing it?

While I'm thinking, I'm still leaning toward Griff behind his drum kit. The door opens, and Bodhi's eyes widen at the sight of us.

"Don't let me interrupt," Bodhi says with a cocky grin. "I should've known," he says under his breath, loud enough for us to hear.

"Should've known what?" Griff asks innocently.

"That you two might start something up. You know, because you're both . . ." He lets the word hang, but Griff and I aren't stupid.

Griff shifts in his seat uncomfortably, and I lean back in mine. One Noah's ark comment from Bodhi and the loud energy from

Griff's drum solo is—*poof*—gone. Not surprisingly, the only person completely at ease in this room is Bodhi, setting himself up behind his piano, a stack of sheet music in his hands. Luckily, we don't have to sit in awkward silence for too long because Blake joins the Zoom. He looks tired today, more than yesterday, with disheveled hair and dark circles under his eyes.

Bodhi gets ready to share the song that he was being hush-hush about yesterday. By the way he was going on about it before class, I'm expecting nothing short of a brain explosion.

"Here's a copy of the music so you can follow along." He hands Griff and me copies of the music. "If you can," he says, only to me.

When Bodhi turns his back to us, I look to Griff, but he doesn't make eye contact. I'm not offended; I get it. It's the exact way I'd react if someone assumed I was dating the other Asian in the class. This is the type of thing Griff means when he says people like us have enough to deal with.

Bodhi starts playing the song, and Griff and I hold up the sheet music, which, for the record, I do understand. I mean, once he plays it on the piano for us, I do. I have to work backward to read the sheet music, matching the sounds to the notes and the different symbols as Bodhi plays. And it's not complicated. In fact, it's a pretty simple melody with a forgettable harmony.

When he plays the last note, he waits dramatically, letting the sound linger. Then he looks up at the screen expectantly.

Blake's reactions are usually pretty direct, but today he's unreadable. I can't tell if he's tired or if he's hungover or maybe both.

"Great job," he says, void of the emotion associated with the sentiment. I assumed he'd treat Bodhi differently because he's his son. To his credit, he doesn't.

"So is this our song? Our single that we'll perform for Marc?" Bodhi waits. Blake doesn't respond. The tension in the room grows exponentially with every silent second that ticks by. Bodhi's face turns ashen, and Griff shifts uncomfortably in his seat. Even I'm nervous for Bodhi.

"I mean, no one else has anything to offer," Bodhi says in the silence. "Right?"

"Actually, I've got something I'm working on." As soon as I say it, I realize Bodhi's question wasn't an actual offer to open the floor to suggestions. Merely a formality.

"What? *You?*" Bodhi isn't having it.

"Let's hear her out," Blake says, which shuts Bodhi up real quick.

"It's something I just started yesterday, and it's not complete. I can play what I have, though."

"You don't even have sheet music? How are we supposed to follow?" Bodhi's hands flail in a complete overreaction.

I'm not surprised Bodhi focuses on my weakness: technical knowledge. Low-hanging fruit seems like his type of MO. Of course, I don't say this out loud. There are already daggers in Bodhi's eyes, and I don't have a death wish. But I can tell Blake isn't completely sold either.

Blake rubs his chin. "Bodhi's right. How about you show us when you're finished?"

"In the meantime, we'll get started on my song?" Bodhi's face lights up with renewed hope.

"Sure. At least we have something to go on," Blake says. "And since it's the beginning of the year, we'll have time to work it into shape."

"What part needs work?"

"All of it," Blake says.

By the time we leave the music room, Bodhi's smile from earlier is shattered. I'd feel the same way if it were me. Showing your work to someone, not to mention someone you respect as much as Bodhi clearly respects his dad, is a vulnerable experience. It's a push and pull of wanting to share a piece of yourself with everyone and worrying everyone's going to hate it. I feel bad for Bodhi; even if he is an immature asshole, he's a person. So I offer up a sympathetic smile.

As soon as he catches my eye, though, he scowls. "Save your pity for someone who needs it. Like your TikTok account." Bodhi blows past me.

Like I said: low-hanging fruit.

ELEVEN

"Finding your voice in music is a concept that seems redundant," Ms. Morales says at the beginning of a new unit. "But voice in this context refers to you as a musician and not the tone of your vocal cords or musical notes."

She passes out papers with our assignment written on them. There are explicit directions to rearrange songs that are currently different from our sound and make them our own. Like how Johnny Cash took Nine Inch Nails' "Hurt," a voice completely different from his own, and made it something else entirely. Even Trent Reznor said that the song was no longer his after hearing Johnny Cash's version.

"Does this mean picking a song in a different genre than we normally play and rearranging it in the genre we do play?" a classmate with dyed blue hair who I think is in musical theater asks.

Ms. Morales makes a face as if to say, *Not quite.* "It's true that genre can be helpful to understand the roots of a song, but defining one's style by genre is, in my opinion, limiting, as it makes you declare what type of music—and only that, type of music—you are capable of playing. Instead, I advise you to hone into your natural abilities and let that set the tone." She leans against the edge of her desk and continues to explain. "For example, it seems common now for a rapper to also sing, but before 2009, there was a clear line between rapping and singing. In 'Empire State of Mind,' two separate artists, Alicia Keys and Jay-Z, brought their individual voices to one song—the rapper bringing a narrative style, and the singer bringing the emotional depth to accompany it. Drake is one of the earliest artists who showed us that it's possible for rappers to be singers and for singers to be rappers. Now more artists are coming out as rapper-singers. My point is, for you all thinking of pursuing music, don't get so caught up in genre and category. Focus on your sound and what's natural to you. That's how you'll find your voice."

Ms. Morales gets my head buzzing. She talks a language I didn't know existed and yet is familiar at the same time. Like I'm finally at home. When I get hit with a song idea, I'm not thinking about what genre or what category of music the song will fall under. It is what it is. It's refreshing to hear Ms. Morales encourage us to do what already feels natural to me. I waste no time after class ends and get lost brainstorming which song to use for the assignment. It feels like I'm working on the assignment for minutes, but the next thing I know, I worked right through study period and halfway into lunch.

By the time I get to the dining hall, most of the crowd already got their food and are finishing up their lunches at the tables. I get a plate and start filling it. It's fried chicken today (nom). I grab a piece and add a few greens on the plate for good measure. Probably not enough greens to balance out the grease. Still, it makes me feel better for trying. Before I can look for a place to sit, I hear my name being called out.

"Riley!" Aerie's waving me over to where she's at. Nari, Jason, and Brandon—her usual crew—are sitting with her. And I guess my usual crew now too?

"We thought you were skipping again," Nari says.

"I got caught up with an assignment and lost track of time."

"Putting in overtime on the second week of school? Someone's an overachiever," Jason says.

"Hardly," I say with my mouth full. After I swallow, I look to all of them. "Tell me something. Are you guys planning on pursuing music as a career?"

"I'm applying early decision to Juilliard. I want to play in the New York Philharmonic, which my parents refer to as *the Harvard of orchestras*," Aerie says, imitating her mom. The others laugh with her.

"Not me. I want to go to UPenn for business. I'm using my musical achievements to help me stand out when I apply," Nari says.

"Same. Except I want to go to medical school," Jason says. "Make my immigrant parents' dreams come true."

"Not sure what I want to do yet. I do hope that I can use the flute in something different from orchestra." Brandon nods thoughtfully. "What about you? Do you see music in your future?" he asks me.

If he had asked me last week what my plans for after graduation were, I'd have reluctantly said Bentonville U. But since I've learned that the band—and by association me—has a chance at being Blake's Next Big Thing, I choose Next Big Thing.

"Yeah, I do," I say, and the smile that stretches across my lips comes at once and without warning. It's the most honest thing I've said about myself in a while.

As monumental of a moment as it is for me, the group moves on from the subject as if talking about their future dreams is a run-of-the-mill conversation for them and not a mind-blowing admission like it is for me. People here, I'm starting to notice, actually grow up to be what they wanted to be when they were younger: actors, musicians, and filmmakers. It's wild.

Out of the corner of my eye, I spot Ms. Morales by the courtyard. She's leaning against the retaining wall of the next building over. I'm about to excuse myself to ask her about the assignment until I see she's talking to a camera. Behind the camera is a guy with dark hair, fair skin, and arms with a pretty insane amount of muscle definition. I don't know why that's important. It just is. I can't exactly see his face since the camera is covering it, not that I'd know who he is anyway. Aside from Aerie and her friends and Bodhi and Griff, I haven't had time to get to know anyone else here. And I'm pretty sure I'd recognize anyone with arms like his. When they finish, he and Ms. Morales exchange words before she leaves. The guy turns around to pack up his equipment.

At first glance, he seems like any other guy from Bentonville High. Athletic build and a hairstyle that seemingly defies gravity. With his black-framed glasses, he's got that nerdy-chic vibe going for him like a young Clark Kent. Then I notice he's wearing a Radiohead T-shirt, which really gets my attention. It's threadbare and frayed at the edges, and I briefly wonder if it's one of those manufactured-to-look-vintage shirts or if it's the real deal. Most of the guys back in Bentonville were only ever into sports. If it wasn't their favorite sports team branded all over their apparel, it was an athletic brand—Nike, Under Armour, that kind of thing. This guy, though, seems interesting. At least his choice of fashion makes me think he's different from the others. I wonder what his favorite Radiohead song is. It's probably "Creep." It's everyone's favorite. Which means we already have something in common. No way I'd approach him to ask, but I find myself thinking about it. . . .

I must've been deep in a daydream because I missed part of the conversation, and Aerie and Nari are getting worked up about something.

"My cousin seriously has issues." Nari shakes her head. "I swear, she has the worst case of white fever."

My ears perk up. Did I hear Nari correctly? "I'm sorry. Did you say *white* fever?"

"Oh yeah. She's totally got a thing for white dudes," Aerie confirms.

"Is that wrong?" I ask honestly.

I've only ever heard the term *yellow fever*, which makes me cringe every time I hear it. It was what the guys teased Harrison Slater for since it seemed like he only pursued Asian girls, zeroing in on the few that attended our school. First it was Tiffany, then Apurna. He tried with Pring, but she was an exchange student, so she peaced out before he could make his move. He never tried with me, though, since I iced him out before he even looked my way. But this thing with Asian women only dating white guys . . . that sort of thing happened all the time in my town. If you didn't date a white dude, you might not have had a chance to date, considering the pool was extremely limited.

"It's wrong if she's choosing who to date because she thinks white dudes are above dudes of other races. Like saying all white dudes are better-looking or more masculine. Or all Asian women are submissive. It goes both ways, and it's equally wrong," Aerie explains.

"You should see her on her dating app. When she showed me her profile, I noticed she swipes left on anyone with the slightest bit of melanin in their skin," Nari says.

"That's messed up. Way to dehumanize us," Jason says.

"Yeah, she's missing out." Aerie nuzzles her head into the crook of Jason's arm.

"I kind of feel bad for her. Maybe it's not totally her fault. She grew up in the middle of nowhere, Ohio, where there's no other options," Nari says.

This conversation makes me uneasy. Maybe it's because I am probably from where they consider "middle of nowhere" and just had mildly crush-y thoughts about a white guy. Which kind of makes shit-talking Nari's cousin sound a lot like they're shit-talking me.

The bell rings, and lunch is over. Maybe it's a good thing I didn't have a chance to ask them about the Radiohead T-shirt guy. I wouldn't want them to get the wrong idea.

After lunch, Aerie, Nari, Jason, and Brandon make their way to the theater for orchestra, and I head to the music room. On the way up, I notice Radiohead T-shirt guy. It's funny how you don't notice someone until one day you see that person in a cool band shirt, sleeves hugging his arms just so, and suddenly, he's everywhere. It's like the time my parents bought a Volvo. At first I was like, *No one has a Volvo*. Then I started noticing them everywhere. In the parking lots, at the grocery store, and on the highways. Guess it's like that with this Radiohead T-shirt guy, except he's way more pleasant to look at.

Crap. He noticed me staring at him.

Crap. He noticed me noticing him noticing me staring at him.

Crap, crap, crap.

I continue my walk up to the music room, fighting the urge to turn around and see if he's following me. I'll just have to make it a point to not notice him next time I notice him. Over time, he'll begin to wonder if I was the one who did the creepy stare or if he imagined it all along.

I open the music room door and walk into an empty room. Before the door closes, someone follows me in.

It's Radiohead T-shirt guy.

What the hell, did he misread my cues? Or worse, did he . . . *correctly* read my cues?

"You're Riley, right?" He cocks an eyebrow.

Face throbbing, I barely nod.

"I'm—"

"Xander McNeil," Bodhi says, walking into the room, Griff following right behind him.

"In the flesh," Xander says, holding his arms out to his sides.

At the mention of flesh, I stare at his arms because boy is there a lot of it.

Jesus, Riley. Get a grip.

"Hey, man. What brings you here?" Griff says. They exchange broey handshakes while I stand off to the side and watch.

"I'm getting a head start on the documentary I'm doing on your band for my final project." Then Xander turns to Bodhi. "My dad cleared it with your dad when he was over there last weekend."

Of course their dads are friends. Xander and Bodhi have that same effortless look of wealth and industry connections.

Bodhi's grin stretches wider than before. "Did your dad tell you about Marc?"

Xander nods. "Ms. Nelson thought it'd be a great idea to

capture it all on film, so here I am. Now that I'm wrapping up the *Day in the Life* series, I should get started on this."

"You're the one who does the *Day in the Life* series?" I blurt out, much too loud. So I dial it back down. "Those are great. Informative."

The three of them crane their necks to look at me like they're just now realizing I'm in the room.

"You watch those?" Bodhi makes a face, then turns to Xander. "No offense."

Xander laughs. "Offense taken, and thanks for watching," he says, first to Bodhi, then to me. He's got an undertone of humor. Like he's funny and not in your face about it.

"I really enjoyed it. Especially learning about the history of Carlmont and the inception of the contemporary band program. I don't know if you know, but there are some glitches in them. The first one had a skull flashing for part of it, and the second one had a link to a music video . . ." Oh my God, I can't stop the verbal diarrhea. I've gone full fangirl.

"He-he, yeah. That's not a glitch. Just wanted to have a little fun with it. Tell them how I really feel about some of the things I report on but, like, subtly. So far no one's picked up on it, so that's fun." He's doing that dry-humor thing again where he's funny but it's not a big deal to him.

"Cool, cool, cool. So about the doc." Bodhi just can't help himself. "Are you going to start filming us today? 'Cause I just dropped a new song the other day." He can barely contain his excitement even though Griff and I know it was hardly worth anyone's excitement.

Xander smirks, unfazed. "Relax. First I gotta work on a script. Then I'll get some footage during practices. After that I'll schedule interviews with each of you separately. You'll be seeing so much of me, you'll be sick of me."

Impossible, I think but don't say.

"Anyway, I'm just dropping off the release forms today." Xander hands them out to us.

"Are these standard release forms?" Griff asks, inspecting his copy.

"It means I own all the material I film during practices, interviews, anything that captures your likeness—basically you're signing over your life to me," Xander deadpans.

I suppress a laugh since no one else laughs. Bodhi wastes no time before scribbling his name at the bottom. Griff takes a little longer, reading each line carefully. I skim it, understanding not all but most of it. We all give Xander consent to film us for his documentary, which is by far the coolest thing I've been asked to be part of.

Xander collects the papers, then leaves, thanking us.

"I can't believe he's going to film a documentary on us," I say, watching Xander walk away.

Bodhi doesn't waste any time shutting it down. "It's just a school project. Don't flatter yourself."

Griff eyes Bodhi warily. Griff's been keeping his distance from me, lest anyone (ahem, Bodhi) get the wrong idea about us. I get kind of sad wondering if this is how it's going to be in the band. Stilted. Disjointed. Then eventually Griff leans over and says, "They do that kind of thing a lot here. Cross-collaborate for projects. The orchestra plays for the theater all the time, and we played the music for musical theater when they did *Hairspray*. And all the promotional stuff is recorded by the film department, so this is probably just one of those things."

Bodhi snickers, then starts playing Marvin Gaye's "Let's Get

It On" on the piano. For a second, I think Griff is going to recoil. Instead, he throws a notebook at Bodhi, which shuts him up.

Shocked, Bodhi stands up, arms stretched to his sides. "Bro, be cool. It's just a joke." Bodhi laughs at his own joke because no one else in the room thinks he's funny.

"Thanks," I say to Griff. I can understand why he can't always show his support, but I know he's got my back. And if I'm going to make it in a band with Bodhi, I'm going to need all the support I can get.

The first ASA meeting is the following week. After school, I meet up with Aerie, Jason, and Nari, and they take me to an empty classroom in the language arts department. When we arrive, the room is filled mostly with Asian students and even a handful of non-Asian kids. If we had ASA in my last school, it would have been a club of six kids, maybe seven while Pring was visiting. In fact, if there was something like this, I probably would've avoided it entirely. The mix of emotions swirling in me is overwhelming. On the one hand, it's like I've finally found My People. On the other, it's not something I'm used to, so I feel very fish out of water. Thankfully, Nari's there with me after Jason and Aerie take the podium, so I take the seat next to her when she sits down.

As soon as everyone's settled, Jason takes the podium with Aerie. After a quick introduction of themselves as the copresidents of ASA, they start talking about this year's initiative.

"Last year, we raised the concern of the lack of Asian American representation in our US history classes. As a result, we were able to work with the teachers to include a history unit on Japanese internment camps and address the causes and effects of the erasure of their occurrence in the US history curriculum. This project was spearheaded by Nari Hitomi." Aerie pauses for Nari to stand up. Everyone applauds. I applaud along with them. I've always heard about people wanting to make a change but have never actually seen the change. Here, it's not just *talk*.

"This year, we want to continue our efforts to bring more awareness and activism in response to the recent rise in anti-Asian hate crimes." Aerie looks to Jason to continue.

"Anti-Asian hate crimes aren't anything new," Jason begins. "As an example, Vincent Chin was a Chinese American man who was beaten to death in the eighties by two white men who blamed him for losing their jobs at an auto plant due to Japanese competition in the automotive industry. Vincent wasn't even Japanese, but that didn't matter. The point is, Vincent was a scapegoat, and what's worse is that the men who killed him never spent a day in jail. The judge who presided over their case said, 'These weren't the kind of men you send to jail.' In what world does murdering an innocent victim not make you a criminal?" He pauses for the wave of outraged murmurs to pass through the crowd before continuing. "The judge's ruling sent a clear message: Killing an Asian man isn't a crime. Flash forward more than thirty years later to the shootings at the Atlanta spa that killed six Asian women, among others, in a racially motivated attack. It's no wonder anti-Asian hate crimes are still happening, because history has shown us that when it comes to Asian lives, people can literally get away with murder."

"With social media and the pandemic, xenophobia and racism have become more visible. And if we don't do anything about them now, how is anything going to change?" Aerie adds.

The room is filled with energy. Some clap, some make sounds of agreement, and everyone is fired up.

"Now, I'm sure you're asking yourselves, 'What can we do? We're just high school students at a boarding school,'" Jason says, and heads bob in agreement, including mine. "We don't have to look that far to instill change. Like Nari's initiative, we can make a difference here. Violent racism stems from subtle biases and stereotypes rooted deeply all around us. Even at Carlmont."

Murmurs and looks reveal that some of the audience is wondering what he means.

"That's true." Aerie nods. "There is blatant racial bias and stereotyping right here in our classroom."

Really? It happened to someone else too?

Aerie zeroes in on me.

Oh no, wait. She's talking about me.

"We hear your frustrations, and we see you." Aerie gives me a look that says, *I got you*. "This year, we want to put the act in activism and put our talents to good use."

People clamor. They're fired up. They're outraged. And I want to get to that level with them, especially since that example of blatant racism Aerie was referring to was about what happened to me. But I can't seem to. I try to pinpoint my own feelings 'cause I'm definitely feeling something. Is it outrage? Am I fired up?

I'm *embarrassed*. That's what it is. Because this type of recognition feels like negative attention. It's the type of thing I actively avoided in Bentonville. And the fact that Aerie and Jason are trying to come up with an initiative, literally to call attention to it, makes me inwardly retreat.

For the rest of the meeting, we're directed to come up with

ideas and suggestions to address anti-Asian hate. There's a group of kids focused on creating materials about "knowing your rights" and another that is focused on making an infographic for bystanders to know how to intervene. I latch on to a group with Nari and Brandon, but I'm not really present. There's too much going on in my own head, competing for my attention.

Did Aerie and Jason compare the murder of innocent Asian American victims to *my* pain? It seems outrageous, and I can't really grasp the connection. Instead of making her point, it trivializes mine. Maybe I shouldn't have said anything to Aerie or Nari. Maybe I made it a bigger deal when I told them how Blake treated me, or maybe they did. Either way, I'm feeling *this small* that I even whined about it in the first place.

Maybe Griff is right. Maybe we can't do it all. Trying to make it in the band is hard enough. And if I have to choose, I'd rather focus on the music.

VISUAL	AUDIO
Text on-screen: *A Day in the Life of a Monty* Episode Three: The Boarding Life (more like The Boring Life)	
Wide shot of Ms. Susan Morales outside the dining hall. Text on lower third: Ms. Susan Morales, Head of Music Department at Carlmont	Hi, I'm Susan Morales. I head the music department at Carlmont and teach music and composition. I also am a chaperone and a dorm head. In fact, as a boarding school, Carlmont understands that students are away from home, but we're committed to creating a homelike environment for the staff and the students. In doing so, we faculty have many roles.

Montage clips of Ms. Susan Morales teaching in a classroom. Cut to: a clip of the orchestra performance. Cut to: a clip of a group of students singing. Cut to: a clip of a performance by The Boyz.	Ms. Susan Morales voice-over: My professional background is in music composition, with a special interest in piano and violin. My role is to oversee the orchestra, vocal, and, most recently, the contemporary band program here at Carlmont.
Wide shot of Ms. Susan Morales.	When school is over, there are designated times for the rest of the day. Students are required to attend an extracurricular activity before dinner. After dinner, it's study hours, followed by an hour of free time, and then lights out. The weekends are also a full-time job for the faculty. We have events, scheduled shuttles, and volunteer days.
Stock image of a house party. Source: Shutterstock	Ms. Susan Morales voice-over: Once a month, there's a weekend designated to off-campus visits. We call them *open weekends*. This is the time when students can spend an extended time off campus with their family or relatives.
Image of Norman Rockwell's painting "Freedom from Want," also known as "The Thanksgiving Picture."	Ms. Susan Morales voice-over: During breaks and holidays, we realize that it's not always possible to find accommodations, especially if students don't live within a reasonable distance. We want to remain open for those who can't leave campus during the shorter breaks, so the faculty take turns being on duty for

	holidays. During the breaks, the same safety rules apply; however, we make sure to have activities throughout this time to ensure the hardworking students get the much-needed break they deserve.
Wide shot of Ms. Susan Morales.	In addition to rules for the students, the staff are committed to creating a safe and happy environment for your kids. We hope they feel like Carlmont is a home away from home.
Text on-screen: **Producer: Xander McNeil**	

TWELVE

It doesn't take long for me to settle into a routine at Carlmont. Even though the classes here are more interesting than any class I've ever taken, it's still a lot of work. Between general-ed subjects and my music, I've got homework for days. Add that to my already hefty workload of trying to play catch-up with my bandmate who never ceases to point out just how behind I am, and I'm swamped.

On the plus side, my hard work is paying off, and I seem to be making some progress. I'm not, like, playing any of my own songs, and there's hardly room for creative input from anyone who isn't a Collins. But at least I'm playing my guitar now. Even if it is only a basic melody with an uncomplicated chord progression, it gives me the fuel I need to carry on. And Griff gets it. Every now and then, when Bodhi spends much too long explaining the reason he chose a particular note or the way a song makes him feel, Griff gives me this subtle look like he's screaming on the inside. So that's something.

My parents and I keep missing each other's calls because of the time difference and our conflicting schedules. I've missed an ungodly amount of calls from Elise and have received an equally ungodly amount of texts from her. Elise's texts are not only amusing; decoding them is like trying to figure out the question in a *Jeopardy!* category, emoji edition. The latest one is a string of food emojis, followed by a clock, then a sleeping emoji, then a question mark. What is *I'm hungry, but I'm also tired?*

I hang out with Aerie and her friends when I can, but she's busy too. Every day, breakfast, lunch, and dinner is spent in the music room practicing, the sound booth practicing, or in the library, thinking about practicing. We see each other at the end of the day in our room, but by that point, our internal batteries are drained, and all we want to do is sleep to recharge ourselves for the next day. Lather, rinse, repeat.

The irony here is, now that I finally have a life, I don't have time for it. I've hardly even had time to spend on "Stardust." It's not like me to not finish a piece when I get inspired. It's also my first time at Carlmont, where things are always go-go-go. It's a good kind of busy, but sitting on an idea for this long is making me antsy.

I haven't been to an ASA meeting since that first one I attended. I could probably make time for it if I wanted to. I just . . . don't want to. The thing is, at the last meeting, things got heated. And I got the distinct impression that Aerie expected me to be at the same level of heat as everyone else, if not more. Maybe that's how Aerie would deal with it if her advisor treated her the way Blake treated me. But it feels unfair to automatically assume that I'd go about it the same way just because we're both Korean American. She should know more than anyone here just how different we are. Anyway, I just got Blake to see me as part of the band. I'd very much like to keep it that way.

I just want to play music and get along with my band. I also don't want to hurt Aerie's feelings because I know she's coming from a good place. And she's been a friend from day one when she didn't have to be. So when I skipped the next few meetings,

I told Aerie I was swamped with work because it was not only believable, it was also kind of true.

Weeks turn into months, and pretty soon it's November. With flights being so pricey and Carlmont being a onetime thing, I've convinced my parents to let me stay on campus with the few students and faculty that are staying behind.

During the break, the campus feels like a ghost town, which is good. No distractions. I only emerge for meals and spend the rest of the time finishing "Stardust." Carlmont has an endless wealth of resources, and Ms. Morales even helped me learn how to use the music software on the computers to figure out how to transcribe my music. Now I can edit in percussion and textures to make it sound like it would if the band played the song. The old me returns, and the energy from creating my own music comes flooding back like a memory. I get carried away with it, and without lights out during the break, I stay up way later than usual.

"Happy Thanksgiving!" Mom, Dad, and Elise FaceTime me super early on Thursday morning.

"Thanks," I croak, still in bed.

"You're still sleeping? Ry, it's almost 10:00 there."

"Were you up late partying?" my dad says, and we all laugh. Only with me would this question be considered a joke.

"I was working on my song," I say, patting my unruly hair down.

"That reminds me. College apps are due in January. Maybe you could get a start on them now?"

I'm trying really hard not to think about why working on my song reminded her of college apps. Especially when I'm expected to go to Bentonville U.

"It's one app; it won't take too much time."

My mom and dad exchange a look.

"What's that look about?" I ask, calling them out.

"Last time we talked, I got the sense that maybe you weren't happy with applying to just one college," Dad starts explaining.

"So that got me thinking," Mom continues. "Maybe it would be good to apply to another school."

"Really?" I jolt up to a seated position. If my parents are open to other schools, then maybe I could apply to Wesleyan or Luther. Maybe I could even stay in LA.

"I know I said it's a pretty much guaranteed acceptance with your grades and my connection to the school. But just in case it isn't, I think it would be a good idea to apply to another school. You know, as a backup. And Hartfordshire U is Bentonville U's sister school. We'd get the same perks there, and it's only an hour away, so we can talk about commuting later. It's your choice."

I deflate. If I had my choice, I'd stay in LA because as far as I know, Hartfordshire is not much different from Bentonville. At least I don't think it is.

After we end the call, I do a little more research and find out that Hartfordshire has a small yet established music department. Okay, fine. I was wrong. Hartfordshire U and Bentonville U are not the same. Which is something.

All day long, sports play on the big screen projector in the student union, and at night the dining hall serves a traditional turkey dinner complete with carb-heavy sides. I'm not big on turkey, and I definitely don't care about football, so I plan on using the extra time to finish my song.

On my way to the editing building, I spot someone familiar. Or kind of familiar to me. I slow my step next to Xander, who seems to be watching something through the screen of his video camera.

He looks up at me from behind his camera when he notices me. "Oh, hey."

"I thought that was you. Didn't realize you were here this week." I am pretty certain I would have noticed him even if I spent most of my days working on my song.

"I wasn't. Just got back today."

"You spent Thanksgiving break with your family and decided to come back on the actual holiday?" My eyes widen. "Sounds like drama."

He lets out a small laugh. "Nah, it's nothing like that. Although I can see why you thought that." He rubs his chin. "Chris Pembrook's film premieres tonight, and he's a client of my dad's, so instead of a family gathering, my parents are going to be there."

"Wow, that sounds unreal." I mean that in every sense. I can't believe this is how people here spend their holidays. The craziest it gets in the Jo household is when we go Black Friday shopping before it's officially Friday. (Woo-hoo.)

"Yeah, it's pretty cool. I guess. That's not really my thing, though."

Movie premieres aren't his thing? Guess when you grow up in the entertainment industry, you can take it for granted.

"I saw the last *Day in the Life* episode. Insightful as always. Especially the glimpse into what people here do on the weekends. Was that photo from a party you went to?" I thought it was a joke at first, like the flashing skulls and link to Blake's music video in the other episodes. But now that I know he actually does get invited to A-list celebrity parties, it's making me wonder.

A smile tugs on his lips. "Not even close. I found it on Shutterstock."

"I noticed it's been a while since the last episode. Is that what you're working on now?" I point to his handheld camera.

"Nah. When I realized no one noticed my Easter eggs, I got bored with that." He shrugs. "Besides, Ms. Nelson keeps reminding me that I need to get started on my final project. The documentary on RGB."

Hearing Xander say the name of our band makes my stomach flutter. "I can't wait for that to start up. What are you doing now?"

"Just filming cinema verité." Probably noticing the confused look on my face, he follows up by saying, "It's a fancy term for B-roll."

"Ah, got it."

"Figured it's easier filming while the campus is empty."

"Right. I'll let you get back to it, then. Your arm's probably sore from holding the camera like that." I point to the camera in his hand.

"This is nothing. Wait 'til you see the gimbal." When my brows furrow, he says, "It's a metal box frame around the camera that acts as a stabilizer. It's not only an intense arm exercise; the way I have to balance the thing engages my whole body. On the plus side, I don't have to go to the gym anymore. It's a full-body workout." He pats his abs.

Ah. That explains the muscle definition in his arms. I try not to imagine what he means by full-body workout, which is harder to do than you'd think.

"You want to try?" he asks, noticing my stare lingering on his camera.

"What, me?"

"Here, take this." He gives me his handheld camera.

My hand dips as I take it from him. It's heavier than Xander makes it seem. The camera is shaky as I pull the lens up to my eye. I can't tell if it's because I'm not used to the weight of it or because of how close Xander suddenly is. I can feel the warmth from his body.

"Everyone's a storyteller," he says in a low and soft voice from behind me. "We just use different mediums."

"What am I trying to see through this?" I try my best to focus on the lens. It doesn't help that Xander's completely at ease being *this* close to me.

"It's not about what you're trying to see," he corrects me. "It's about what you're trying to show us. How do you, Riley Jo, see the world?"

I keep a steady hand on the camera in front of my face even though my heart is beating out of my chest. No one's ever asked me what I see. And the way he says my name . . . Goose bumps.

I point the camera around me aimlessly, then spot a snail on the side of the paved path. I zoom in and watch through the lens as it makes its way on the path. A random student who happens to walk out of the editing room and down the path almost steps on the snail. I'm about to yell out to the student to watch his step. Then I remember I'm still filming. The unknowing student narrowly misses the snail, and it makes it safely to the other side of the path, blending into the grassy lawn. This whole encounter reminds me of Elise. We could be escaping a house fire or an avalanche, and she'd stop for this. You could say she's like the snail—so wrapped up in its own little world, it doesn't notice big, giant feet stomping all around it.

"It's stupid," I mutter, handing the camera back to him.

"Why would you say that?" His brows arch. "You showed a snail's journey that revealed how harrowing its life can be. And on a macro level, you showed us how our journeys, depending on whose vantage point you see things from, can either be the hero's or the villain's." He smiles approvingly, and my insides swell. "Or that snails as a species are completely clueless."

I've either unearthed a hidden talent for filmmaking, or Xander's really perceptive. Obviously I'm not some filmmaking genius. Is it possible I make sense to Xander?

"You saw all that from this?" I point to the snail, now barely visible in the sea of grass.

"You'd be surprised how filmmakers tend to gravitate to the same story ideas. People are more similar than you'd think."

Are they? Most people point out the differences, not the similarities, in one another. Guess Xander isn't like most people. It's making me feel all sorts of things.

When we part ways, Xander off to the main campus and me to the sound editing room, a familiar crackle of energy pulses through me. I don't hear lyrics quite yet. Just a faint melody.

Interesting development.

THIRTEEN

The Sunday after Thanksgiving, students come back to campus. While Aerie is unpacking, she's filling me in on what she did over the break.

"Oh my God, the filing was endless. I swear, my parents are more excited for me to organize their paperwork than to see me over the holidays."

"You should tell them about the paper cuts," I offer, remembering how her parents don't make her do anything to jeopardize her violin-playing fingers.

"I tried. Their policy is no blood, no broken bones, no excuse."

"That's cold."

She laughs. "They mean well, though. You should come with me next time. Maybe my parents would give me a pass if I brought you home."

"Yeah, right." I wave her off.

"No, I'm serious! You should come over during winter break if you don't want to go home. They've been dying to get to know you."

"What, me? Really?"

"In the four years I've been here, you're the first Korean roommate I've had. Of course they want to meet you!"

"But staying at your house for an extended period of time? That's a lot to ask."

"Just think of them as long-lost relatives." She swats a hand at me. "I guarantee they'll treat you like that anyway. They tend to overfamiliarize themselves with random Korean people. They have zero boundaries."

"Good to know." I laugh. I'd love to meet them. Except ever since I missed Thanksgiving with my family, Elise has been nonstop bugging me about coming home, sending me enough prayer hands and home emojis to fill an entire book and then some. There are only three weeks before winter break begins, and I don't have the heart to bring up the idea to stay with Aerie during break, so it looks like I'll be going back home for the holidays.

Before I know it, it's the week before winter break. We're making progress on the song Bodhi came up with. It still sounds a little uneven, though. I can't put my finger on what's not working, and even if I did, I'm not sure I'd have the technical terms to explain it—a base requirement when talking to Bodhi. Which is why months of playing together have amounted to a handful of one-sided conversations about mundane small talk that no one really cares about, like the weather and dining hall food. Which, for the record, is better than I expected.

While we're waiting for Blake to join our Zoom meeting, Bodhi wants to run through the latest version one more time. Usually he's confident—too confident if you ask me. But today he's noticeably on edge. I don't know what that's about. And I don't really care. By now I've learned to peacefully coexist with him. Why rock the boat? I still get to play music, and you can't put a price on that. So we start playing, and I drift into autopilot.

In the middle of the song, Bodhi abruptly stops playing the piano.

"Wait." Bodhi waves a hand in the air, signaling me and Griff to stop. "What the hell was that, Riley?"

"What the hell was what?" I ask in all sincerity. Coming from Bodhi, it could be any number of things.

"That change-up in the chorus. Don't think I didn't notice. You're doing it on purpose." He points a finger at me.

"First of all, I'm not doing it on purpose." My hand grips my guitar. How freaking dare he accuse me of intentionally messing this up. "And second, my subconscious just does things without thinking."

"Well, learn how to control that. This isn't amateur hour." His face is puckered, like the pressure is building and he's about to combust.

"Hey, listen. It's been a long day/week/month. Why don't we take a break?" Griff offers. He's usually quiet and only speaks up when he has to. I'm glad I'm not the only one realizing Bodhi's being extra, even for him.

Bodhi manages to calm himself down, heeding Griff's words. He covers his face with his hands, then rakes a hand through his messy bed head, which I think is a stylistic choice.

"Sorry," he says. It's hard to know if he's saying sorry to me or to both of us since he says the apology looking at the floor. "We've got the Spring Concert coming up, and Blake hasn't mentioned it to Marc yet. This song needs to be perfect, and it's nowhere near that."

I cut him some slack because it's important to me too. And if what he's saying is true, that Blake hasn't mentioned us to Marc yet, then that's concerning for not just Bodhi but for all of us.

It's almost halfway through the year; there isn't a lot of time left before the Spring Concert.

"Can I . . . make a suggestion?"

Griff looks to Bodhi, who waits a beat before he shrugs.

Oh, hello. Bodhi is giving me an opportunity to voice my opinion? Things must be more dire than I thought. I try to piece together the words to describe the changes I hear in my head so they deign to live up to Bodhi's standards. I hate that he has such impossibly high standards, but it would be a shame to lose his interest now.

"Here, let me play for you what I have in mind. It'll be easier." Without giving him an opportunity to protest, I start strumming the intro, putting the emphasis on the down chord. Then, when it comes to the verse, I slow it down. Way down. The fast and loud intro juxtaposed with the slow and drawn-out verse acts as an amplifier. The intro grabs your attention, and right when you're at the edge of your seat, it surprises you with an unexpected softness, putting emphasis on the words.

> *Gonna break it, gonna reshape it*
> *Gonna take it to a place where I can't fake it*
> *Now I'm even more of who I am*
> *Yeah, yeah, yeah*
> *That's who I am*

The just-okay lyrics have more impact this way, and it sounds so much better. I let myself go. I freestyle the bridge, even go an octave higher in falsetto. I get lost in it, letting the sound run through every part of me. I haven't let myself be this free with music in front of them. Tension I didn't know I was holding on to melts away, and I'm going, going . . . gone. For precisely ninety seconds, I forget everything. When the last note hangs in the air, I teleport back to the present.

Bodhi and Griff stare, open-mouthed, at me. And I can't tell if it's a good stare or a what-did-we-just-hear stare. Griff blinks first, then looks to Bodhi.

"Not sure about the falsetto. I could never reach that note, but"—Bodhi rubs his chin, then his face, and when his hands get to the top of his head, he stands up and blows out a breath—"it's aight," he reluctantly concedes.

"Seriously?" I can't help the surprise in my tone. Coming from Bodhi, that's high praise indeed.

"Bro, what?" Griff nods his head up at me. "That was dope. I didn't know you could play like that. What else you got?"

The adrenaline still pumping, I jump at the chance to show them "Stardust." It isn't quite complete, but the song has been living in my head rent-free for days/weeks/months. I start plucking at my strings in the notes I know like the back of my hand. It's a complicated yet understated arrangement that keeps my fingers constantly moving up and down the neck of my guitar. I sing the first verse of what I have, and then I stop after the chorus.

> I've always wanted to be your light
> Always wanted to dream my dreams up high
> And when my shine ain't so bright
> I'll fall gently and pass you by
>
> And when you find your place on the ground
> You can let your head live within the clouds
> I can hold you while

You let your heart soar
Watch it sparkle into so much more

You made those colors in the sky
And don't let the moment pass you by
'Cause I can see it now
You, me, them, us
We could all be stardust

Even though it's only a verse, it's such a rush.

"That's all I have so far." I'm catching my breath like I've run a marathon.

"Sorry to interrupt." Blake's voice cuts through the speaker, and our heads whip up to the screen. I got so lost in my song that I didn't—I mean, *we* didn't notice him. "Is that something new?"

"Nah, we're still working on the old stuff. Riley was just showing us something really rough," Bodhi's quick to respond.

"Okay," Blake says. He's got that look in his eye like he's thinking.

"We should probably get started," Bodhi says eagerly. "We can play for you the changes we've made."

The three of us get in our ready position and start playing Bodhi's song. When we finish, Blake is quiet, digesting our latest version.

"It's good," he says, and Bodhi beams. "But in this market, good isn't good enough. Songs have to offer something new, and I'm just not hearing it." He sighs, raking a hand through his thinning hair. "During the break, let's try and come up with a fresh take at the song."

"And then you'll talk to Marc about us. Right?" There's a

nervous edge to Bodhi's tone, as if he doesn't believe Blake is actually going to go through with it.

"Don't worry about Marc; I'm working on it. Which reminds me, I'm having a little get-together at my house next Saturday. Bodhi's going to be there," Blake says, and the smile on Bodhi's face returns in full force. "Why don't you come, Griff? And you, too, Riley."

Whoa, this is a serious development. I'm not just being invited over by my advisor. I'm being invited over by *the* Blake Collins. I bet his house is massive. I bet he has a pool that looks over the Hollywood Hills. I bet it'll be the coolest place I have ever been to in my entire life.

"Dope," Griff says, all chill. So I take his lead and be whatever about it.

"Cool," I say like it's no big deal, even though it's a *very* big deal.

First thing's first. I have to think of a way to get to Bodhi's house during the break.

"Is the invitation to come to your house still open?" I ask Aerie in our room after school.

"Does that mean you're coming?" Her eyes practically bulge out of their sockets.

"If my parents are cool with it, I'd love to stay. The band is having a get-together at Blake's house."

I might be imagining it, but Aerie does a slight eye roll at the mention of Blake. It's so subtle, I don't know if it actually happened.

"What are you waiting for? Call your parents already!" Aerie's back to being excited, shoving my phone in my face.

It's study hours, so instead of calling from my room, I head to the sound booth. I tell my mom that plans have changed and catch her up to speed. She's not as enthusiastic as Aerie.

"You're not coming home again?" my mom says. "You know you're going to have to come home sometime."

"Yeah, like when I go to Bentonville U and will be there for four more years?" I'm not exactly planning for this to happen, but using it as a reminder helps my argument here, so I'm going with it.

"Guess you're right." She mulls it over, unconvinced. "What about presents? You love opening them on Christmas morning together."

"Consider this my present!" I accompany that with a giant smile, hoping to convince her. "And I'll give you . . ."

"Finishing your college app?"

"Deal!" I say, more enthusiastic than I'd normally be when agreeing to finish the application to the school I have lukewarm feelings about. "I should be able to fit it in during the two-week break."

"You only have to do one app since Hartfordshire is Bentonville's sister school. They accept the same common app."

"I know, but Hartfordshire requires a supplemental essay for the music department, so I'll have to write another paper and include an audition video."

It gets real quiet when I mention the music department. I don't know what to make of that. I thought she just didn't want me to go to an out-of-state college. Her reaction tells me otherwise. I want to ask her what the deal is with music because clearly she has an issue with me pursuing it as a career, whether in LA or in Arkansas. But I just got my get-out-of-Bentonville-for-the-holidays card, and I don't want to jeopardize that, so . . . I don't say anything more about it. And neither does she.

After Mom talks it over with Dad, they both agree to let me stay. I let Aerie know when we're washing our faces in the communal bathroom. Now that I'm coming, she's positive her parents won't make her work during the break.

"Oh, don't forget I have plans the Saturday before Christmas," I say, patting my face with a towel after washing it. "I'll take an Uber." I don't remind her where I'm going because I sense she's got feelings about that.

"'Cause you're going to Blake's?" She side-eyes me before washing her face.

Okay, I'm definitely not imagining her tone change.

"Yep." I nod.

"Can't believe the school didn't do anything after you reported him. I hope they at least keep it in their records." She looks at me through the mirror. I don't look back.

I don't have the guts to tell her I didn't go through with reporting him. It's the kind of thing I think she'll make a big deal out of. And after all the progress I've made with the band, it's hardly worth mentioning now.

"He's not so bad," I say, deflecting. "You know, once you get to know him."

"Oh, I see how it is," she says with a smirk once we're back in the room. "You drank the Kool-Aid, and now you think you're one of them."

"Okay, that's a stretch."

"You know what I mean. What he did to you was inexcusable, and until he understands why he can't treat people like a statistic, he won't change." She proceeds to pat some kind of a solution on her face—step two in her ten-step skincare regimen.

"My point is, things have gotten better. I was even able to come up with a new angle for our brand." While she applies steps three through six of her skincare routine, I explain to her the idea behind RGB. I hope it gets her to understand the shift in the band dynamics. "Now that we've solidified our brand as a diverse band, I have cemented myself as an integral member." And, not to mention, I've made myself indispensable, like Griff suggested.

"If you say so," Aerie says. "All I'm saying is, I know Blake's type. They string people along with crumbs of praise while taking all the credit and keeping POC as part of a 'colorful' backdrop."

I wouldn't say I drank the Kool-Aid like Aerie claimed. But she's right in thinking that the few months I've been in the band have changed my perspective. If the music labels are the ones who dictate what's hot, and Blake is trying to give us the best chance at getting signed by a label, then it's the industry, not so much Blake, that's messed up. Knowing this makes it possible to not take Blake's K-pop comment personally. If I'm able to move on from it, Aerie should too. Honestly, I just want to play music, like Griff said. That way we'll get signed by Ruby Records. Then it's goodbye, Bentonville, for good.

Even though I know she's not convinced, I don't push it. Besides, it's only one night I'll be at Blake's house. The rest of the time I'll be at Aerie's.

"What do you want to do over the break?" I switch gears, which seems to do the trick.

Aerie's face lights up. "Oh my God, I don't even know where

to begin. I have a crap-ton of K-dramas I'm so behind on. We have a persimmon tree, and I bet they're all ripe right now, so we can gorge ourselves with those. Oh, and we definitely have to meet up with Nari, Jason, and Brandon since they don't live too far."

"I can't wait," I say. We'll be having too much fun for her to make a thing of me going to Blake's.

FOURTEEN

The last day of school before break is a half day, and since Aerie's parents are at work, we take an Uber. It's about a forty-five-minute drive to her place, which she said is an "old" home. When we get there, however, I realize she means *old* as in *historic*, not *old* as in *run-down*.

"My house isn't nicer than any of the other homes in the neighborhood," she says when she notices me gawking.

"Only because the houses in this neighborhood, you have to admit, are *all* nice." I'm kind of glad that we don't live close enough for Aerie to visit my home. Not that I've ever been self-conscious of that sort of thing. In Bentonville, we live comfortably. But the filigree etched into the wall panels and doorframes in Aerie's house is a whole other level.

She laughs it off and shows me around. There are three stories in her house. The first floor is where all the main rooms are, plus the master bedroom, which is palatial. The middle floor is where the other bedrooms are, plus a game room. Aerie's brother decided to do some fellowship on campus over winter break, so we have the top floor all to ourselves. It's one giant open-spaced room that looks like a page right out of Pottery Barn Teen. There are two beds, a dresser, and a vanity table with a cute faux fur rug, twinkle lights strung over the bedposts, and a hammock hanging from the ceiling in the corner. It's a dream.

Later, it does become a dream because I end up falling asleep after we zone out on our phones. It's been a long week/month/semester. My body must have shut down the second we had downtime. The next thing I know, Aerie's shaking me awake.

"My parents are here. Come down now," she says with urgency.

I pat down my bed head, wipe the drool off my face, and follow Aerie downstairs to the kitchen. Or at least I try to. My feet are heavy and I haven't fully come to my senses yet, so I stumble through her hallway and massive stairs. By the time I reach the first floor, I see Aerie's parents standing side by side in the foyer, waiting. Aerie's dad is dressed in a black suit jacket, sporting a houndstooth flatcap, and her mom is in an elegant sweater with a bedazzled neckline. Immediately, I can see where Aerie gets her looks. With her slim nose and wide-set eyes, she's a mirror image of her dad, minus the frown he's currently giving me.

"Hi, Mr. and Mrs. Jung. Thanks so much for having me." I walk over to them with my hand out, ready to shake theirs.

They don't extend a hand.

Instead, they stare at Aerie and say something in Korean. Aerie says something back.

"You don't speak Korean?" are the first words that come out of Mr. Jung's mouth. No *hi* or *hello*, just, you know, an accusation.

"Sorry, no. My mom was born in Arkansas, and my dad came here for college." I don't know why I feel compelled to offer up an excuse for my lack of Korean language, but here I am. Offering.

After an awkward silence, her mom chimes in. "It's okay. Don't worry. You don't have to speak Korean."

Well, thanks. I didn't realize it was a prerequisite for staying at the Jung household.

"Umma, Appa, Riley is from Arkansas. There are no Korean

people there." Not entirely true, but I get what Aerie's doing, so I don't correct her.

"Ahh." They both accept this response and then proceed to prepare dinner without another word to me.

Later, while Mr. Jung is sitting at the dining table and Mrs. Jung is plating the rice, I pull Aerie aside.

"What was that all about?"

"Sorry, I forgot to tell you about my parents. They're really traditional."

Before I can ask what that means, Aerie's mom calls us to the dinner table. I follow quickly behind Aerie since I get the feeling I didn't make the best first impression. I'm not sure what I did wrong exactly. But I'm hoping things will blow over by the time dinner is over.

Dinner is over, and things did not blow over. Not at all.

"List of Faux Pas (A Sad Song)" by Riley Jo:

> *- Wearing shoes inside the house, a big no-no (in my defense, I only did it once, to get to the backyard)*
> *- Not greeting them when they came home (an honest mistake!)*
> *- Not speaking Korean (apparently growing up as a third-generation Korean American is no excuse not to speak the mother tongue)*
> *- Offering up a handshake when I clearly should have bowed*
> *- Eating before they eat*

*- Using one hand (instead of two) to pass a plate of food/
napkin/drink*
- Telling them I don't like fish
- Not eating second helpings
*- Unintentionally blabbing about Aerie dating Jason (I
didn't know it was a secret!)*

I wouldn't be surprised if the list was longer than that, considering I didn't know half of these things were thought to be offensive. But since there were so many (OMG), Aerie only told me the major offenses. The point is, my first, second, and third impressions were not good ones.

"It's just the way they are. Don't take it personally. They like things done a certain way," Aerie offers a week later when she can tell I'm still feeling way out of my depth with her parents. This time, I accidentally mentioned I'd be going out on Saturday night, and apparently Aerie's not the only one who has feelings about it. On top of being super traditional, they are super strict as well and have a firm 10:00 p.m. curfew. Thankfully, Aerie covered for me and said Blake is a family friend I have to meet. A lie I'm willing to go along with if it means I can go without getting any more heat from her parents.

I have a mild heart attack when Aerie's parents seem disappointed when she mentions meeting up with school friends on Friday. But after doing the dishes, cleaning the tables, folding our laundry—all the things my parents remind me to do when I talk to them—they finally agree to let us go to the mall to meet up with Jason, Nari, and Brandon. Thank God for that. I could use a break from Aerie's home, as nice as it is.

The Grove is an outdoor mall about twenty minutes away from Aerie's home. It feels very LA even though I've hardly experienced the city. Four months here and I've spent most, if not all, of that time either at Carlmont or at Aerie's house. Everywhere you look, the mall is decorated with lights and ornaments, which makes it feel like it's the holidays despite it being in the midseventies and sunny in December.

We meet up with Nari, Jason, and Brandon in the parking lot. I hug Nari and slap hands with Brandon and Jason, and the tension from my shoulders immediately melts away. It feels good to be here. Despite the awkwardness this past week, there's a familiarity with this group that feels close, like family.

We take turns going into random stores, not really looking for anything. Aerie and Nari try on dresses at Anthropologie, and I wander to the section with housewares. I realize I've been staying at the Jungs' house during the holidays, and yet I haven't bought them one present. What to get people who have everything? They even have a separate kimchi fridge, which is something I never knew existed.

In the houseware section, I spot a ceramic picture frame with whimsical flowers on the edges. I realize the best thing to get someone who has everything is something sentimental. So I buy two—one for Aerie's parents and one for Aerie. I stuff them into my bag just as Aerie and Nari emerge from the dressing rooms. Nari buys a boho-chic dress, and Aerie buys a headband, saying her parents would nag her for spending money on clothes when her parents have a textile company that makes clothes.

"Oh my God, right?" Nari says. "That's so something my mom would say. 'Nari, why are you paying for napkins when you can get them for free at McDonald's?'" She laughs.

"My dad says that about the condiments at the Costco food court. He thinks it's a buffet." Brandon rolls his eyes.

I laugh because it sounds kind of ridiculous. I can tell by the way they're reacting, nodding in vigilant agreement, that they're laughing in that too-real type of way. I dial it back so it doesn't seem like I'm laughing at their parents.

"Yo, I'm starving, Marvin," Jason says.

"Should we go somewhere else or stay here?" Aerie asks, pulling out her phone and searching her maps.

"Let's eat around here," Nari suggests. "They have an 'international' food court." She snort-laughs.

"I'm guessing that means they have a Panda Express and a Taco Bell." Jason snickers.

"And an 'authentic' boba shop owned by a Filipino family," Brandon says.

"And that's bad?" I'm asking honestly because the last time I checked, Filipino would constitute as *international*. I can't tell exactly what it is they're mocking. In Bentonville, it's common for an ethnic restaurant to be a hodgepodge of foods. For example, the sushi restaurant near us has Korean barbecue, orange chicken, and other Asian foods that aren't sushi, let alone of Japanese origin. I didn't think anything of it because that's the way it is in Bentonville.

I might be imagining it, but Aerie exchanges a subtle glance with Nari at my comment.

"What?" I ask them.

"Nothing, it's nothing," Aerie says dismissively.

"Boba is Taiwanese. You can't just insert a random Asian

nationality and call it authentic just because boba originates from Asia." Jason shakes his head.

"Oh yeah. That is so . . . wrong." It's not that I don't agree with them. It's that I didn't realize it was a thing that was offensive.

"But we're still going, right?" Brandon asks.

"Oh, hell yeah. I mean, Panda Express isn't exactly authentic, but I do love their orange chicken." Jason nods.

"Oh my God, right? If I don't cough from the vinegary sauce at first bite, then it ain't right." Brandon fist-bumps Jason.

I'm fascinated by the way they can joke around about the nuances of racism. Is it weird that I envy this type of awareness and at the same time wish I didn't know? Like, do I really want to feel guilty about drinking inauthentic boba?

Despite the shit-talking from before, we each get a plate of food from Panda Express and a boba from the "authentic" boba shop. I eye Jason's giant cup of boba milk tea with a slight smirk.

"What?" He shrugs. "It's not the Filipino couple's fault that they immigrated to a consumer-capitalist country only to find out that boba, not halo-halo, was trending. They're not appropriating; they're surviving." Then he adds, in a lower voice, "Besides, I had a craving, and this is all they have here."

We laugh and take turns teasing him for being a hypocrite. It's fun hanging out, making playful digs at one another. And there's good music playing in the outdoor mall. The latest AJR song comes on, and it has a pop-y melody that's infectious. It's not long before we start singing along. With this many performers in our group, I should have guessed where this would head. Jason begins rapping beats, and Brandon makes a high-pitched synth-like sound, and Nari taps a utensil on the cups. Aerie and

I give each other a look before she starts tapping on the table, adding a textured layer of percussion to the song. It doesn't matter that we play different instruments in different genres. Our instincts take over, making a cohesive sound. Pretty soon our entire table is loud enough to gain traction. It's not, like, a performance that could win American Idol or anything. But it's pretty damn good. Like street art, it's unconventional and just as catchy, with a unique sound.

When the song ends, we get a smattering of applause, which prompts Jason to stand up and bow. We laugh, then Aerie tugs at his sleeve, urging him to sit. "Oh my God, Jase, could you be more embarrassing?"

He laughs, totally not embarrassed. In fact, he's living for the attention. We laugh at him while he tries to milk the audience for more claps. I'm not as bad as Jason, though I do feel the same rush of excitement when I perform, so I get where he's coming from. I'm starting to feel more and more comfortable with this group. We're different and, at the same time, similar enough to get it.

An older woman with white hair and thick glasses keeps staring at us. She eventually steps toward us and says, "Excuse me."

After taking turns looking around, we notice she's addressing us. She's not talking to anyone in particular, so there's a lull in our response.

"Yes?" Aerie eventually speaks up.

"I'm really impressed by your performance. Where are you guys from?" She blinks innocently, waiting for our response.

I can sense everyone's gut clenching. Without looking around, I know we're all thinking the same thing.

"It's just that I know there's a music school not too far from here. I'm wondering if y'all are from there." She peers at us over her glasses that are sitting at the edge of her nose. And I swear there's an audible sigh as soon as she says this.

"Yes, we're from Carlmont," Nari confirms with a smile.

"How lovely." The lady clasps her hands together, seemingly pleased with Nari's answer as much as she is with herself for making the correct assumption. "I'm here visiting colleges with my daughter. We happened to notice Carlmont when we were at UCLA. It's a boarding school, right?"

"Yes, it is." I nod.

Her smile stretches wider. "You're all quite talented, and your English is really good too," she says. "How long have you been in America?"

So close. We were *so close* to having a pleasant conversation with this perfectly nice stranger. I can sense the collective cringe.

She waits expectantly for an answer, and I find myself offering one. Or trying to. My throat closes up like it does when I'm expected to answer anything too difficult. It's too much for me; I'm overwhelmed.

If I were in Bentonville and this sort of thing happened, I'd start talking real loud, leaning into a deep Southern accent that some people have in the parts of Arkansas that border Texas and Oklahoma. You know, to prove a point that I'm not only from here, I'm *from* here. My typical passive-aggressive approach, the only-way-I-can-cope approach.

"We speak fluent English because we're American," Jason says, enunciating the word *American*. He says it so loudly, people crane their heads to see what the commotion is. Suddenly, I see eyes everywhere. I feel them watching with their metaphorical popcorn, just waiting for a scene to break out.

"I think you should know that all of us were born in this

country," Aerie says to the lady. She's gearing up to say more, but the secondhand embarrassment gets to me.

"We should probably get back," I say to Aerie. "Your parents will be worried." I go to throw the trash away and start walking toward the parking garage. After a second, the others follow me. I glance back and notice the lady turn back to her table and shrug to her partner as if she has no clue why Jason and Aerie were getting worked up.

"How come you're in such a rush all of a sudden?" Aerie asks when I slow down at the entrance of the parking garage.

"I sensed a crowd forming, and I didn't want people to get the wrong idea, that we're the ones causing trouble." I feel like a coward saying the words out loud.

"Don't you see? That's just playing into the model-minority myth. That we'll just take it," Jason says to me.

"Trust me, I wanted to say something. But only angry words came to mind, and I just thought it would make things worse," I say defensively. Part of me feels like they're blaming me when I'm just as much stereotyped as they are.

"Riley's right," Aerie says, putting a hand on my shoulder. "We shouldn't assume everyone knows what to say in these instances. Maybe we should work on making a script in ASA so that we have the words to educate people on why it's racist to assume we're not from this country."

"Is that our job, though? To educate people to not be racist? Isn't that what the internet is for? They can just google that shit on their own," Brandon says.

"Problem is, they don't. And if this is still happening in a diverse city like LA, I can't see things changing in the rest of the country. I mean, my family's been in California for four generations, and that lady thought I came from another country, no hesitation." Nari gestures with a frustrated hand. "I'm just so tired."

"Me too," Aerie says. "But we can't just give up."

I'm envious of Aerie. She can so easily put herself out there without being afraid of backlash from that lady or anyone else. She's brave, proud, unapologetic. I wish I could be more like her. At the same time, though, I wish I didn't have to want to be like her. Why do any of us have to worry about being asked how American we are? Because when someone asks us when we came to this country without assuming we could be from this country, it makes us feel like we don't belong. And for me, who feels even less connected to my Korean heritage, it means that I don't belong anywhere. Like I'm some kind of unassimilable alien.

"You okay, Riley?" Nari asks.

"Yeah," I say, blinking a few times. "Sorry, I'm still processing."

"It's because Riley's from Arkansas." Aerie tilts her head as she says this to Nari, Jason, and Brandon. "And her parents are pretty Americanized." Aerie *comforts* me by putting an arm around my shoulder.

What is happening? Why is Aerie making me feel deficient for growing up differently from her? When I don't know not to wear shoes in the house or I use one hand instead of two to hand a dish to Aerie's parents, I feel like I'm playing a game I don't know the rules to. Except this isn't a game; it's real life.

Both my parents are Korean American, and yet their cultural differences are hard to miss. For example, my dad eats pickles with spaghetti because he misses the sour-and-tangy taste of kimchi with every meal. My mom flip-flops between putting cheese in everything and fad-dieting because that's how she grew up in Little Rock. It's making me wonder . . . is there only one way to be Asian American? Is there not diversity within diversity? Because Aerie's making me feel like the "wrong" kind of Asian American every time she points out the fact that I'm from Arkansas.

My go-to reaction is to do something to prove Aerie wrong for accusing me of thinking I'm more white than I am Asian. Only I can't. Not this time. No one has ever assumed I was "too white" or "not Asian American enough." And even if I wanted to prove Aerie wrong, what would I do? Eat more kimchi? Take a crash course on Duolingo and start speaking Korean to her?

It's just the way they are, I recall Aerie saying as she told me I'd get used to her parents. Well, maybe this is the way I am. Why can't she accept me the way she expects me to accept her parents for the way they are?

FIFTEEN

By the time Saturday rolls around, I can't wait to go to Blake's house. Things have been weird with Aerie since, well, I got here. And now it's even more weird since the mall incident.

Whatever. Maybe there's such a thing as too much time together. I wouldn't know since this is my first time having a close friend, my first time having a roommate. I'm sure we'll get over it eventually, but right now we could do with some space between us.

Aerie offered to drive me to Blake's house. I politely declined. It's almost an hour away by car, and honestly, that might send us over the edge. So I take an Uber.

Blake's house is in Calabasas, a city just north of Hollywood, where I naively thought everyone in the entertainment industry lives. Even though the house isn't *where* I thought it to be, it looks exactly how I imagined it to be.

As the car approaches, there's a wrought-iron gate that's opened up, leading us through a long, curvy path with a circular driveway at the end. When I get out, it only gets better. The house has pillars (pillars!!!) in front of ornate double doors leading to the sweeping staircase inside, with a massive chandelier hanging from the ceiling. In the back is a vast, tiered backyard with a patio above an iconic rich-people pool overlooking the hillside. Everyone here, I notice, has that airbrushed-spray-tan-and-plumped-lip look. To me, they exude entertainment-industry wealth. I feel way out of place, not because this is not remotely my scene but because I'm at least twenty years younger than most of the people here. Honestly, though, what did I expect? That Blake would throw a party for a bunch of teenagers?

Okay, yeah. That's exactly what I expected.

I venture outside by the pool, where I finally spot someone I recognize. Griff is sitting by the pool, lying on a lounge chair. When I get near him, he sits up.

"Finally, someone I know," Griff says.

"Same," I say, taking a seat in the lounge chair next to him. "I almost didn't find you in this castle. I knew Blake's house was going to be nice; the Zoom meetings we had showed some pretty high-end furniture. I didn't expect this." I gesture around.

"Yeah, he made some good investments with Ruby Records."

"I checked on the website, and according to Blake's bio, he hasn't signed any big bands yet. This can't all be from 'Clubbin'.' can it?"

"Blake gets a cut of profits from all the bands the label represents. It's where he made most of his money. Now he wants to be more involved, hence this party. It's his first time proving himself to Marc and the people in the industry. At least that's what I gathered from overhearing conversations."

"Isn't that Xander?" As one of the few people our age, I can easily spot him from across the pool. He's wearing another T-shirt that catches my eye. Today it's The Who.

"Yeah, his dad is Blake's manager. He's probably here too."

"Ah, so that's how they're connected. They seemed very familiar with each other. Like they grew up together or something."

"Apparently Bodhi lived with Xander for a short time. They don't really talk about it much, so I don't ask. Different circles and all." He motions to Xander, who is comfortably mingling with the crowd and carrying around a handheld camera.

"I thought this was going to be, like, a house party with other high school students. You know, beanbag chairs, someone's playlist connected to a portable speaker, beer pong—that sort of thing. Not *this*. There's even a live band playing. Wait, are they"—I squint my eyes at the pair—"famous? They look familiar. I just can't place them."

"Yeah, that's Skye Lander. They're an up-and-coming brother-sister duo that Ruby just signed."

"That rings a bell. Probably saw them on TikTok."

He smirks at me. "Look who's caught up."

"Shut up." I nudge him. I notice he's dressed in a pair of designer jeans and a sports coat. "I would've tried harder if I'd known what this party was about." I look down at my leggings and oversized sweatshirt.

"This old thing?" He tugs at his jacket, laughing at himself. "Nah, you're good. Bodhi said Marc might be here, so I wanted to make a good impression. So far, no Marc sighting."

"Speaking of Bodhi, where is he?" I scan the crowd, looking for the familiar beanie-clad head I'm still not used to. Apparently in California, people wear winter gear ironically.

"Don't know." He shrugs.

"You haven't seen him yet?"

"Nah. He's probably busy."

At that moment, we see Bodhi come from the double doors leading out to the backyard. He makes eye contact with me and

Griff, I'm sure of it. I raise a hand to wave at him. Instead of waving back, he quickly looks away. He spots Xander across the patio and goes to clasp hands with him.

"What was that all about?" I scrunch my nose.

"What was what all about?"

"Bodhi saw us, then ignored us for Xander."

Griff shrugs, completely unbothered. "I don't know if you've noticed, but there's a hierarchy here. People who are in the entertainment industry are at the top, and people like you and me are at the bottom."

"Um, ouch?"

He lets out a sharp laugh. "I don't mean that in a pitiful way. It's facts. Even the students whose parents are doctors, lawyers, tech gurus ... they rank even lower than the families who work in the entertainment industry," he says casually.

"And that matters?" Ranking people based on anything, let alone their careers, feels ... I don't know, wrong.

"Matters to some people." He nods up at Bodhi. "They may not be tight, but in Bodhi's mind, that's where he belongs. And until we become an established band, we're still at the bottom of the hierarchy, and Xander's at the top."

"You're okay with that?" It strikes me as odd that Griff is so casual about this system of unfair proportions. As if he has no sense of self-worth, which I know isn't true.

He does a subtle headshake, seemingly annoyed. "Of course I'm not okay with it. A lot of things in the entertainment industry are messed up—shadow banning, Hollywood so white, nepo babies, not to mention the wage gap between men and women. It's just the way it is." He holds his hands up as if to say, *What're you gonna do?*

"I know about the other stuff you mentioned, but nepo babies? What's that?"

"That's nepo babies." He points to Bodhi and Xander chatting it up with drinks in their hands, mini replicas of their dads. "People who have an extreme advantage over people like us due to their parents' famous names."

"I don't know," I say, unconvinced. "Helping one's child break into a notoriously difficult industry? Doesn't seem too bad." I'm having trouble lumping Xander and Bodhi in the same category. Xander sees the similarities in people, whereas Bodhi is determined to focus on the differences. They're nothing alike.

"Maybe. But let's say there's an audition for a lead role in a film, and they've narrowed it down to two people. One is an aspiring actor who's working two side gigs, living in a two-bedroom apartment with three roommates in the bad part of town, just to make ends meet in the five years they've been trying to make it in Hollywood. And the other is Bruce and Demi's kid. Who do you think the industry execs will choose?"

"Bruce and Demi's kid," I say, deflated.

"In a heartbeat." He sighs, raking a hand through his hair. "It's a bigger issue than parents helping kids. Diversity becomes an issue because nepo babies perpetuate more of the same, which is rich white privilege. And if you're counting, it means that the odds are stacked way against people like you and me."

If that's the case, what am I doing here? What is the point of any of this?

"Hey, no," Griff says, probably noticing the defeated look on my face. "It's not like that for us. Not after you suggested RGB, which is clutch."

"You think?" I bite my lower lip.

"No, definitely. You made it work, and I can tell Blake is all in."

Right then, a full-grown man does a flip off the diving board and into the pool with his suit and sunglasses on. Griff and I duck on reflex. We mostly avoid the splash and are only sprinkled with a few drops.

"The hell?" Griff looks over to the guy, who's living for the attention. He calls over a waiter, demanding another drink, and tries to coax others to join him.

"Guess some people never grow up." I smirk.

"Seriously," Griff agrees. Then, a second later, he says, "Wait, why are we just sitting here? We're the 'kids' in this group. We should be the ones jumping into the pool and enjoying ourselves, not watching from the sidelines."

I can tell he's not just referring to the pool. He's referring to the fact that too often, he and I spend time talking about others getting the opportunities we don't. So I say something so un-Riley-like.

"Let's explore," I say, looking around the massive property.

"Sure, why not?" Griff shrugs and stands up. We walk to the main house, passing a full-service bar on the way.

"Should we get a drink?" I ask him.

"Nah, I'm driving home tonight. But don't let me stop you."

I realize he thinks I meant an alcoholic drink. "Oh, I meant ... like a Sprite or a Coke." A blush reaches my cheeks. "It sounded less uncool in my head before I said the words out loud."

Griff laughs with me. "You're good. Let's be uncool together." He orders a Coke and a Sprite and offers me first pick. I choose the Sprite. "If anyone asks, you're drinking a gin and tonic, and I'm drinking a rum and Coke."

"Deal," I say.

The double doors into the house are propped open, and clusters of people go in and out of them. Inside is a large living room with an oversized sofa facing a white grand piano.

"Wow. Do you think this is where Bodhi learned to play?" I ask, running a hand across the glossy piano.

"I don't think so. Anytime Bodhi refers to his training, he only ever mentions playing in Florida when he lived with his mom."

I look around the room. "How come there aren't any photos of Bodhi or him and his dad together?"

"Bodhi never talks about it." Griff shrugs. "Like I said, different circles."

There are frames hung everywhere, mostly of Blake when he was in Boyz Club. Candids of the group on tour, album covers, press photos. There's even a framed copy of the record that went double-platinum. It's like he's living in the past.

"Okay, but this is seriously cool." I point to the framed double-platinum record.

"I know, right? Can you imagine having one of these?" Griff stares at it longingly.

"I literally cannot." Thinking about having a career as a music artist is a stretch as it is.

I wander into the other rooms, looking for more evidence of Bodhi's presence in Blake's life. Call it morbid curiosity, but the way Bodhi goes on about Blake, as if he's God's gift, makes him seem like he's father of the year/decade/century. And now that I'm here, there's something not adding up. I'm consumed with trying to find evidence that Bodhi means as much to Blake as Blake means to Bodhi.

Every room has some kind of memorabilia framed and on display. Ticket stubs, venue flyers, and posters of the boy band. When I get to the game room, there's something that makes me stop in my tracks. A large frame mounted on the wall with an actual suit inside.

"Oh my God, Griff. You have to come see this." It's the white suit from the music video. I'd recognize it anywhere.

Griff appears seconds later, drink still in hand. "What in the nineties hell?" He snickers.

"Didn't you see the music video for 'Clubbin''? It was posted in the *Day in the Life* series about him."

He snorts. "No. Did you?" He eyes me accusingly.

"So, don't judge, but I've watched his music video for 'Clubbin'' an unmentionable amount of times."

"What? Are you serious? How many times are we talking about?"

I blush, realizing I've revealed more than I bargained for. It's too late now, though. At this point, I just have to own it. "Let's just say enough to memorize his dance routine." I do a tame version of his choreographed moves. "You've got to admit. He's got some dope moves."

He coughs, choking on his drink. "Oh my God. Coke just went up my nose, but it was so worth it. Did you say *dope* or *joke*?" He puts a hand to his mouth to cover his laugh, but it's no use.

"Come on." I hold my hands out to my sides. "Pop-and-lock is making a comeback."

"Never." He shakes his head.

I do the signature move, starting with the wave that begins

at one arm and flows through the body to the other arm. Then I bust into the jerky motions of the dance routine that aren't as smooth as Blake's in the music video but are pretty good for a novice like me.

"Admit it. You wanna try."

After hesitating, Griff eventually rolls his eyes at himself and follows along.

"See, it's contagious!" My smile stretches across my whole face.

"Fine. You got me." He gets the routine pretty easily and quickens his pace. I try to catch up with him. Pretty soon, we look like a sped-up, warped version of Blake's music video.

Just then, Blake appears in the room. "There you guys are." A cocky grin takes over his face as soon as he recognizes the familiar dance moves.

"Still got it," Blake says to a guy next to him. Which is a weird flex since we're basically doing a parody of his old moves. As long as he's not offended, though, I'm not about to point it out. "This is who I've been telling you about: Riley Jo," Blake says to the man.

I instantly recognize the face. It's Marc Rubinstein. Griff straightens up as soon as he recovers, and it makes me stand at attention too. The first thing I notice is how much shorter Marc is in person than I thought he'd be. We're almost at eye level.

"It's such an honor to meet you, Mr. Rubinstein." Oh my God, did I just curtsy? I try to play it off by pretending to wipe something off my knee, but I'm not sure they bought it. Wow, I have managed to out-dork myself.

Griff straightens his jacket and extends a hand. "Mr. Rubinstein, I'm Griff, the drummer of RGB."

Marc doesn't glance at Griff's direction. Instead, his eyes focus solely on me, making me sweat.

"I hear you're the one we can credit for RGB. I love it. It's very on-brand for what young people are gravitating toward. There's this New Age–hippie resurgence thing going on—love is love, that kind of bullshit."

The way he says it makes my brow quirk. Is this a compliment or a dig at me?

"No, it's a good thing. Trust me," he says, reading my mind. "And you're smart for leaning into it." He does this weird wink-and-finger-shooter combination that is super Hollywood-cliché. People really do that here? Guess that tracks since he's everything I imagined he'd be—tight T-shirt, velour jacket, and gold jewelry. Lots of it.

"You should hear the song she's come up with. Riley, why don't you play for us?" Blake says, putting me on the spot.

"What, now?" I look around at the party. Still going on. Still very Hollywood.

"We have guitars and a mic set up," he says, as if that's what I was worried about.

"Um, okay," I hear myself saying.

A few minutes later, I'm in a closet the size of our dorm room. Instead of clothes, there are rows of guitars on display. A lot of them are electric, flashy, and from high-end brands, and some are older and delicate, which makes me think they're probably a rare breed that isn't made anymore. I'm tempted to try an older-looking acoustic guitar with an unusually flat top, but with Blake breathing down my neck, waiting for me to choose one, I'm hyperaware that this is no time to experiment. I opt for a Taylor-made acoustic guitar that's similar to the one I own.

By the time we go back outside, the stage is lit and there's a mic stand. My nerves start acting up.

"Bro, you okay?" Griff asks me.

"Would *you* be okay?" I peer over at him.

He chuckles, which puts me slightly at ease. "When you're up there, and you think you might hurl all over us or something, just think about Bodhi's face." He points at Bodhi standing next to Blake poolside, an obvious frown on his face.

"That thought never entered my mind. Is Bodhi going to lose his shit on me even more?"

"No, that's not what I mean." Griff shakes his head. "I know it's not easy for you, and I can sense you wanting to have more creative input. In all the years we've been playing together, Blake's never asked his own son to do what he's asking you to do. Here's your chance."

In a sobering moment, I hear what Griff's saying. This is a huge opportunity. Not a time to second-guess what I've been trying to assert in the band this whole time—that I belong here.

"Thanks, Griff. You're a real friend."

He nods at me.

I get onstage, overlooking the swimming pool, and when the spotlight finds me, I shield my eyes with a hand. After my vision adjusts to the light, I notice there are so many faces staring at me. Most of them industry people. Their expressions aren't ones of anticipation. They're ones of judgment, waiting to see if I can measure up to the quality of talent they're expecting. It's the moment when they'll decide whether I'm worth their time or not. As my fingers find their place on the guitar, a calmness overcomes me. I am Zenner than Zen.

I slip into another world as my fingers drift up and down the neck of my guitar, strumming, plucking, and ripping into crazy chord progressions. I'm here, but I'm also not here. And the second the first word comes out, relief hits me like I've been given a lifeline.

Lately, it's been feeling like I haven't been able to express myself properly. To my parents, to Aerie, to random white ladies at the mall . . . Music has been the only way to let it out, but I haven't been able to even do that with school and band taking up most of my time. These past few months, I've been feeling like I've been holding my breath. And I wasn't planning on performing my song when I got here, but I'm glad I am. I need this like I need air.

I sing the complete song, ending with the additional verse added after Blake heard me play "Stardust" the first time.

> *I always held my heart on my sleeve*
> *Always thought goodness came from belief*
> *But when you set yourself free*
> *You can find out who you're meant to be*
>
> *You made those colors in the sky*
> *And don't let the moment pass you by*
> *'Cause I can see it now*
> *You, me, them, us*
> *We could all be stardust*

Blake, not surprisingly, has a seriously good sound system. I let the last note echo in the air with my eyes closed, and before I can open them, I hear it. Loud applause.

Marc must've been close by because I see him approach me on the makeshift stage, a close-mouthed smile stretching across his face.

"Riley," Marc says, approaching me like we're pals. Then he holds out his hand to shake mine. I must've handed mine to him, because next thing I know, I'm shaking his. "I like your sound—a folksy yet accessible pop-rock vibe that's got mass appeal." Marc turns to Blake, who nods in agreement, standing behind him. "There's a raw confessional quality to your style of writing that listeners gravitate to. It's honest and also has an optimistic musical undercurrent that looks toward a brighter future."

"Thanks," I say. It's not always easy accepting compliments. But his words describe exactly what I intended with the song. For once it feels good to be able to express myself fully and be understood. I always knew music was the only thing I never had to explain. I blink away the tears.

"What did I say?" Blake holds his hands out to his sides, all proud. It makes me fill with pride knowing he was this confident in me.

"You did good, Blakey. It's got legs. She's a talented songwriter." Marc taps Blake on the cheek in a brotherly way. "Just a few more tweaks. You know, make it more commercial. Maybe add some synth beats. We'll talk later, 'kay?" He shares a broey handshake-hug with Blake and leaves.

"Riley." Blake turns to me, holding his hands out. "You did

good." He comes in for a hug, an actual hug. I just stand there frozen, not knowing how to react. I won't lie, though. The hug feels good. Not in, like, a pervy way or anything. More like a mentor way. "We'll talk more about it next week, but . . ." Blake leans in and says, "I think we have our song."

When he turns on his heels to leave, Blake gives Bodhi a look. I can't tell if it's a you-better-step-up-your-game look like a parent would give him. Or if it's a hope-you-can-work-it-out look like an advisor would give him. Either way, once Blake leaves, Bodhi approaches me.

"Nice job there, Jo." Bodhi pats me on the shoulder awkwardly. Now, this is seriously unexpected. Even more than Marc's compliment. Bodhi's never said a nice word to me, let alone congratulated me.

"Thanks, Bodhi." Even though the words come out just as stilted as his, this is good. We're making progress. At least he's acknowledging me. He lingers as if he's going to say more.

"I think we got off on the wrong foot. I'm really sorry for, you know, being an asshole." He throws his hands up as if to say, *My bad*. "There's a lot riding on this, and it made me not want to take any new chances."

Plot twist. I did not see *this* coming. "Oh wow. That's really big of you," I say genuinely. "And I get it. Insecurity makes us act in ways we normally wouldn't."

"Wait, what? *I'm* not insecure." The familiar cut in his tone returns with the subtext that says, *Who are you to call me insecure?*

"I meant about the band's prospects not being secure, not about your abilities," I stammer. Okay, well, now that it's established that Bodhi's *definitely* insecure, I know never to bring it up again. Ever. *Jeez.*

"Yeah, that makes more sense." Bodhi nods, vaguely accepting my explanation. "Anyway, I hope we can work on this song together."

"Yeah, of course. We're a band. It's a group effort."

"I'm glad we sorted that out," he says before strutting offstage.

SIXTEEN

On Christmas morning, my family FaceTimes me.

"That doesn't look like your dorm room at *Chalamet*," Elise says. My parents and I crack up.

"I'm at Aerie's house, remember? And it's *Carlmont*," I correct her for the dozenth time. After all this time, how is she still getting it wrong? Although sidenote, a school where Timothée Chalamet is the headmaster? Where do I sign up?

"We got the present you sent us." Mom beams with her phone in her hand, showing me her email confirmation.

"As promised, I submitted my college app*s*." I make sure to enunciate the *s* at the end. No reaction.

"Best present ever," Dad says.

"Okay, my turn. Where's my present?" Elise looks around the tree.

"Aw, Lise. I'm sorry about not getting you anything this year. I'll make it up to you when you come to LA."

"I'm coming to LA?" she shout-talks.

My parents look at each other funny.

"Aren't you coming to the Spring Concert?" I ask.

"It's during the middle of school for Elise.... We didn't think it was a big deal.... Is it a big deal?" My mom's string of excuses strikes a nerve.

"It is a big deal," I say definitively. "If it does well, then it might open some doors for us to keep playing together." I don't know why I can't actually say the words *record deal*. Maybe because it feels too big for me to even say, or maybe it's because I don't want to be disappointed by their reaction. Like right now.

"If it's important to Riley, we should look into it, shouldn't we?" Dad suggests. I wish I could leap through the phone and hug him. Except we both know my mom's the one who has the ultimate say.

Mom hesitates. "I don't know. We're already planning on coming for graduation the month after. It's a lot of traveling," she says. My heart sinks, knowing her mind's made up.

"Please, Mom!" Elise gets in her face, rubbing her hands together.

Mom shushes Elise. "We'll talk about it later," she says to me. Which I know is code for *We'll talk about it never.*

Later, I join Aerie and her parents for their Christmas-morning ritual of opening presents in front of the indoor plant that they've decorated. It's a tall succulent-looking thing with hardly any leaves. So, like, the exact opposite of a Christmas tree. Aerie told me they usually put in more of an effort, but this year, since her brother, aka the Golden Child, didn't come home for the holidays, they are keeping it low-key. Patriarchy one, Aerie zero.

Since Aerie's been touchy about me leaving for Blake's, she doesn't ask how it was, and I don't bring it up either. After my performance at Blake's, I'm feeling on top of my game for once with the band, and I don't need any negativity to derail me. And lately, Aerie's been pretty obvious about her feelings when it comes to anything associated with Blake.

It helps that I'm preoccupied with trying to make things less awkward with her parents. Except without knowing exactly how I've offended them, it's not really working. We're polite and skirt around one another when possible, but there's definitely tension there. Hopefully I can show them with my gift how grateful I am to be here.

Earlier, I brought down the presents I wrapped, which I'd kept hidden in the closet upstairs. We sit around the plant, opening up gifts. Aerie's parents give her a box of clothes from their store, and to my surprise, they give me a box of clothes too. Aerie's not as thrilled as I am to get samples of clothes her parents' textile factory produces. To me, these outfits are way trendier than anything I've ever owned.

"Thank you so much! I can't wait to wear these," I say.

Aerie's parents smile wide, probably the widest I've seen them smile at me since I got here.

Aerie's brother sent her a heart rate monitor and a metronome because apparently he's dorktastic like that. I give Aerie a framed photo of our first selfie together. It's kind of blurry, but it's not about the quality of the photo that counts. Aerie gets it.

"Awww, this is so special. I'm going to put this next to the poster of Sarah Chang, my other cherished photo." We both laugh. I'm glad we're still able to joke with each other even though things have been weird. Aerie gives me my present, which is a T-shirt that reads *Eat. Sleep. Play.*

"I love it," I say. "Also: accurate." I point to the words.

We share another laugh. I get all warm inside. It feels good to laugh like this. It almost makes up for the lukewarm festivities I had with my family on FaceTime earlier.

It's time to give Aerie's parents our gifts. Aerie goes first and hands them an envelope. They open it and read slowly.

"Juilliard?" Aerie's mom and dad say in unison. They gawk at her with their mouths hanging open. Aerie nods, and they jump up and down for joy, hugging one another.

I let them have their moment together even though I am just as excited for Aerie as her parents are. I knew she was expecting to hear from them since she applied early decision and she was checking her mailbox religiously. I can't believe she was able to keep it a secret for so long.

"Seriously?! You didn't tell me you got in!" I say when the hugging/dancing circle concludes.

"I just found out a couple of days ago. Apparently it got sent to Carlmont, and the school forwarded it to me, so it took an extra week to arrive. Anyway, I thought the timing was perfect and I'd surprise everyone."

"It's definitely the best surprise." I look to her parents, who are wiping tears of joy out of the corners of their eyes.

"Aerie, you work so hard. We're so proud of you," her mom says. Her dad nods, still too choked up for words.

A pang of envy hits me like an electric shock. Aerie's parents are different from mine in every way possible, even this. There's no way that my mom would say those words to me. In fact, she could barely say any words of encouragement when she knew I was applying to the music department at Hartfordshire U.

After they have their moment, I'm about to clean up when Aerie stops me.

"Oh, wait, we forgot one more present," Aerie says.

"It's nothing, just a small token." I already felt insecure about my present. Aerie's acceptance letter is a tough act for anyone to follow.

Instead of grabbing the present I bought for them, Aerie goes to grab a giant box that was hiding in the corner. I'm about to correct Aerie and say she's got the wrong present when she gives me a look. *Trust me*, she mouths.

I watch, utterly confused, as her parents unwrap the present and reveal a box of Asian pears. To my even bigger surprise, her parents are genuinely grateful. *Over a box of fruit?*

"You shouldn't have. Too expensive," her dad says.

"We'll eat these tonight after dinner." Her mom pats me on the back.

My smile probably seems modest, like a humble-brag. Really, though? I'm baffled.

"What was that?" I ask Aerie when we're back in her room.

"I just wanted to help, so I bought you a gift to give them."

"I already bought them a gift."

"Yeah, I know. I saw it the other day. The framed photo of me performing at the Winter Concert."

"You knew, and you still bought the box of fruit?" I'm part confused, part annoyed. I still don't get what Aerie's intentions are.

"Look, I know you didn't get off on the right foot with my parents, so I was just trying to help. They're not sentimental; they're practical. They wouldn't appreciate a photo of me."

"But fruit?"

She sighs. Is *she* frustrated? *At me?*

"I know you don't get it. It's a Korean custom." The way she has to explain our culture to me cuts deep. "Fruit is really expensive in Korea, and even though my parents can buy whatever fruit they want here, it's not something they can easily forget. So to them, it means a lot when someone brings fruit, okay?"

I wish I understood her, but I don't. And the more I think

about it, the more I get worked up about it. Like why I'm expected to know these things when my parents didn't live like this. Or why my parents didn't choose to pass on their culture to me. My mom was born here, but my dad wasn't. He could have taught me more of the traditional values, and he chose not to. And then there's the part of me wondering why, if the intent of the gift came from the heart, any of this matters at all. Is respecting a person's culture more important than acknowledging people's good intentions?

The swirl of emotions is overwhelming. Partly because I can't pinpoint who it is I'm upset with. Am I mad at Aerie for getting a gift on my behalf? Or at her parents for judging me for not being Korean enough? I understand respecting elders, but does it have to come at the cost of disrespecting myself?

It's like that lady at the food court who made the assumption that we're foreigners and not from this country. Her intentions were to compliment us, and I get that people shouldn't make assumptions, but is it right to be angry at her? Whose fault is it if people don't know they're doing something wrong? I'm not, like, condoning microaggressions, but in these instances, I'm not sure who I'm frustrated with.

Later, Aerie's extended family is going to come over for dinner, so we don't talk about the present anymore. Instead, we get the house ready in silence.

Then her family comes one by one. Aunts, uncles, cousins, cousins' kids. The spread is 100 percent Korean-catered, right down to five different types of kimchi, and no pickles in sight. Even though all her relatives are nice, most everyone speaks in Korean, and I feel lost and removed from the group. Aerie's busy with her familial obligations, so I hardly spend time with her either. I end up helping out in the kitchen, feeling more comfortable cleaning up left-behind plates and wiping down tables.

"That was more work than you probably bargained for," she says to me once we're in her room. "Hosting for the holidays means all-hands-on-deck. Sorry you got roped into it."

"It's fine." I wave off her apology. "I'm literally mooching off of you for two weeks; it's the least I can do." This part I don't have to fake. I do feel indebted to them even though it's been super awks.

"Look, I'm sorry about my parents." Aerie brings up the elephant in the room. She plops herself on her bed.

Lying on our separate beds, facing each other, it sort of feels like we're back in the dorms. The familiar comfort of being me returns.

"No, I'm the one who should be sorry," I say as a reflex. "It's just that I don't know what I did wrong."

"You didn't do anything wrong. I probably should have given my parents a little more context before you came. When I told them you're Korean like me, they took that literally. They didn't know you would be so American."

Her response throws me off for a couple of reasons. One, I didn't think there could be a thing as "too American" for Americans. And two, how is that a bad thing?

"What I'm trying to say," she says, noticing the blank look on my face, "is that my parents are old-school. They still like to do things the way they did when they were growing up."

"I totally get that that's how they want to do things. But to expect me to be that way too?" I shake my head. "Doesn't make sense."

She snorts. "You want my advice? It's easier to go with it than to try to make sense of it."

I'm not sure I completely agree with what Aerie is saying. It seems like a shade away from being fake with one another. But I know that families are complicated. Mine definitely is. And even if I don't agree with her approach, I respect that Aerie is trying to help me understand her family better. At the very least, I know Aerie cares about me enough to take the time to explain it to me. Which is more than what most people would do.

By the time New Year's Eve comes around, things are somewhat back to normal between us. Aerie's parents, not surprisingly, aren't budging on their 10:00 p.m. curfew, even on New Year's Eve. So we decide to spend a low-key night watching a *Die Hard* marathon.

"I'm glad you're here," Aerie says during a lull in the movie.

"Me too," I say. And I mean it. Things got weird between us for a minute. But I can't remember the last time I rang in the new year—or any special occasion for that matter—with a friend. That's something I'm not about to take for granted.

Aerie's parents drop us off at Carlmont, and I decide to take Aerie's advice. *It's easier to go with it than to try to make sense of it.* So I go with it.

I make sure to take my bag with two hands as Mrs. Jung carries it to me. I bow at a ninety-degree angle when they're about to leave. And say *gamsahabnida* instead of *thank you*.

Aerie's right. It's not hard to do those things even if they're not natural to me. And I can tell it means so much to Mr. and Mrs. Jung; their smiles at me today stretch wider than in the entire two weeks I was with them. It still feels fake-adjacent, like I'm putting on an act for the sake of someone's happiness. But I also believe in good intentions, and my intentions are genuine, like Aerie's.

When school starts the next day, there's no gradually easing in. We jump right back to it. There's something about the second semester that gets everyone amped up. It's our final push before the end of the year. Even though it's my first year here, I can sense how important it is for everyone, not just the band. Aerie's already doing extra practices in the classrooms after school because the sound booths and theaters are all booked up. Blake mentioned we'd be finalizing our song to present to his marketing team, and even Xander is finally starting to schedule his interviews with us for his documentary. We have our first one scheduled today.

VISUAL	AUDIO
Wide shot of Riley Jo sitting on an empty stage in the auditorium.	I'm Riley Jo. I play the acoustic guitar and sometimes write songs. I'm from Bentonville, Arkansas. I'm new this year. And so far we're doing pretty good. At least I think so.
Wide shot of Bodhi Collins sitting on an empty stage in the auditorium.	Introduce myself? Seriously, bro?
Wide shot of Griff Torres sitting on an empty stage in the auditorium.	I'm Griff Torres, drummer. I'm from a small town just outside of Bakersfield, California. Yeah, there's a whole lotta nothing there except a bunch of Torreses.
Wide shot of Bodhi Collins.	Okay, fine. I'm Bodhi Collins, lead singer, keyboardist. I sometimes play bass, rhythm guitar—basically I can do anything that can be played. Including your mom. Whoa, hey. I'm kidding. Calm down.
Wide shot of Riley Jo.	What was it like our first day together? It was probably typical . . . as far as first days at a new school go.
Wide shot of Bodhi Collins.	Oh man. The first day I met Riley, I was not expecting that. What kind of confusing name is *Riley Jo* anyway? With a name like that, I was thinking this person was going to look more like me. You know what I'm saying, right?
Wide shot of Griff Torres.	It wasn't just that Riley was Asian. I mean, look at me. [Gestures to himself.] I'm sure people don't know what the hell I am when they see me. It was that Riley turned out to be a *she* and not a *he* that threw me off.

Wide shot of Riley Jo.	It happens all. The. Time. People are always confused when they meet me, asking me, "You're Riley Jo?" As if I somehow don't know my own name. Or, even worse, suggesting that I don't live up to their expectations of what I should look like based on my name alone. [Rolls her eyes.] I should be used to it, but ... Anyway, after the name thing got cleared up, it got ... [Pauses, looking up.] Actually, I think it got more awkward.
Wide shot of Griff Torres.	As soon as Blake got on the Zoom, he didn't waste any time telling Riley she didn't fit the look of our band. Which was, well, I'll just say it—messed up. I mean, Asian people don't just play K-pop, but far be it from me to correct anyone, let alone Blake Collins. And to be honest, it wasn't completely his fault. He was only trying to look out for us, especially after what happened last year.
Wide shot of Bodhi Collins.	Never thought I'd say this, not after they bailed on us, but I started to miss Jeremy and Jake. I don't know what happened that made them leave. Anyway, they left right as Blake was about to present us to Marc Rubinstein—you know, head of Ruby Records. The plan was, we'd spend the summer getting our single ready for Marc so that as soon as school started, we could play for him. Except that never happened. The day after school ended last year, we got word that they transferred out. Just like that. [Snaps his fingers.] No explanation, no nothing.

Wide shot of Riley Jo.	I had heard about Jeremy and Jake leaving. I got the feeling they left some pretty big shoes to fill. I sensed the band's hesitation, especially when it came to, um, our look. They didn't even want to hear me play any of my stuff, which I thought was weird at first.
Wide shot of Griff Torres.	It wasn't just the look; she didn't have a fan base. I mean, TikTok followers didn't make me an overnight star, but they helped me get the attention of Blake, who is going to help us become big. When Riley said she didn't post her music online, there was a moment of panic in Bodhi's eyes.
Wide shot of Bodhi Collins.	Right off the bat, she asked us how soon we could cut a record. On the first day of school. [Leans in and laughs.] I knew right then, this girl is as green as they come.
Wide shot of Riley Jo.	Oh God. I cringe thinking back to that. I knew nothing about the business side of music; it's true. So when they started talking to me about Blake's ties to the A&R at Ruby Records and how he might even get Marc Rubinstein to sign us, I couldn't believe what I was hearing. I just thought this was a music school. I didn't realize we were gearing up to be pop artists. That's why I hadn't posted any of my stuff online. Because I didn't think it was possible.

SEVENTEEN

"Any chance you can cut that last part out?" I ask Xander as he's packing up his equipment. His T-shirt today is the Ramones, which helps distract me for a minute. Fun fact: the Ramones got their name from Paul McCartney, who used the pseudonym *Paul Ramon* when he checked into hotels. First Dee Dee adopted the last name, then all the others in the band followed suit. I love how they became a family through music.

"What part?" He stops wrapping a cord around his arm. I get momentarily distracted.

Focus.

"The part where I mentioned I didn't think we would be an actual band with a record deal." Something about Xander must have made me comfortable—*too* comfortable. Because I'm realizing now that I admitted just how inexperienced I was when I first got here. And not just the music stuff. The industry stuff too.

"I wouldn't worry too much about that," he says, continuing to wrap the cord around his forearm.

Okay, cool, so does that mean he's going to cut that part out, or—

"For what it's worth, it won't matter once Marc hears you perform at the Spring Concert. I heard you play at Blake's."

Ohhhh. He's complimenting me.

"How do you know Marc will come to the Spring Concert?"

"He'll come." He raises a brow like he knows something.

"You're, like, really good." The blue in his eyes stands out even more in contrast to his dark hair. He stares questioningly at me.

Wait. Is he . . . *flirting*?

The old-timey bell rings, signaling lunch is over. We break our stare, and whatever was there (or not there) between us is now gone.

"We worked through lunch. If you want to stop by the dining hall, I can tell everyone you'll be late since I'm headed up there to get some cinema verité." He starts to walk over to the music room next door.

"I'm fine." I'm starving. "I had a big breakfast." I did not. "I'll get something at the student union later." I probably won't because I'll get distracted by practice or homework or Aerie.

"Cool," he says. And boy, is he.

My stomach chooses to call me out and make the growliest sound ever known to man.

"So you like the Ramones?" I say quickly to cover up the fact that I'm capable of making a sound that gross. Plus I tend to talk about music when I'm nervous, and being with Xander without him being behind a camera makes me nervous.

"What?" He looks down, then realizes what's on his shirt. "They're okay."

"Yeah, I don't really play punk, but I like listening to it. Did you know that Joey and Johnny liked the same girl? And Johnny ended up marrying her, causing a huge rift in the band? They still kept playing together, though. I can't imagine what that was like."

What is happening? It's like confession. Make it stop.

Bodhi and Griff show up just in time to stop me from another bout of verbal diarrhea. We go into the music room, and they all exchange bro-hugs. I'm about to find my chair on the stage in the back of the room when I get stopped.

"Riley, what is up?" Bodhi comes at me with a hand. Is he coming in for a bro-handshake?

I go through the motions, clasping hands with him, and he does a head nod at me before sitting at the piano.

"What's up, Riley? How was the rest of your break?" Griff, who seems just as weirded out as I am, asks. He sits behind his drum kit.

"It was good," I say, still confused by Bodhi's unusually friendly greeting. "How about yours?"

"Crowded." Griff smirks. "But it was good seeing my family."

While Griff continues telling me about the things he missed about home (his parents' cooking and catching up with old friends) and the things he won't miss anytime soon (sharing a room with his two brothers and being startled half to death by his dog, who barks at its own reflection), Xander sets himself up in a corner of the room where he can film all of us, including the screen we talk to Blake through. Right as Xander finishes setting up, Blake joins the Zoom.

"Welcome back. It's good to see everyone." And a beat later, he adds, "Especially you, Riley."

Me? Why me?

"I just got off the phone with Marc, and he gave me the go-ahead to proceed with 'Stardust' after he heard your performance over the break. We have until the Spring Concert to get it ready for him. If he likes the final product, then . . ." He holds his hands out for us to fill in the blank. So that's what we do.

"Oh my God, no way!" Griff stands up with his hands on his head.

"You think we'll be ready by then?" Bodhi doesn't seem as

completely surprised as the rest of us, which explains the bro-handshake earlier. Still, he does seem caught off guard by the timeline.

Blake nods. "Everyone's socials are getting good traction. If you guys keep it up, it's definitely possible. Riley, how soon do you think you can finalize the piece?"

"Give me a week?" I say.

Blake nods again. "Once Riley finishes the composition, we'll get started on practicing. The last thing we need to finalize is our image. I'll be working on coming up with an album cover design," Blake says. "Something that fits your overall image."

The three of us share excited looks.

"An album cover? That's, like . . ." Griff says, miming a bomb exploding in his head.

"I have some ideas if you want to talk later," Bodhi offers.

Blake smirks. "The album cover you debut with is supposed to set the tone for who you are, so it's going to take a professional team. I'm working with the marketing and design departments at Ruby Records. They have all the info and are already working on coming up with some mock-ups. Thanks to your ingenious branding idea for RGB, Riley." He tips his head at the screen, but I'm pretty sure it's meant for me. "You guys worry about the music. Let me worry about the business side. I'll share the proofs with you when I get them," Blake says. "I'm sure you have a lot to practice, so I'll leave you to it."

As soon as the meeting is over, Xander starts packing up his equipment.

"Marc is coming to watch you perform at the Spring Concert. That is shocking news," he says to me, deadpan.

For some reason, my cheeks flare. I can't believe I completely forgot he was in the room with us. And he heard everything Blake said.

"Guess you were right." I try but fail to bite back a smile.

Xander gives me another look as if to say, *Duh*. I roll my eyes at myself.

Once he finishes packing up, Xander leaves us to practice, which, not gonna lie, is a downer. I could get used to seeing more of Xander in our class. Bodhi, Griff, and I ready ourselves onstage to do a run-through of what we have so far, and suddenly Bodhi stops me.

"Riley," Bodhi says as soon as the door closes behind Xander. His voice catches me off guard. Probably because I've never heard him say my name so . . . pleasantly.

"Yeah?" I peer up skeptically.

"You think you can show me that chord progression in 'Stardust'?" He asks the unthinkable.

Doth my ears deceive me? Is *the* Bodhi Collins asking *moi* for help?

Bodhi must have mistaken my shock for hesitation, because he starts backpedaling. "It's cool. I'm sure I can figure it out," he says, arranging the sheet music on his piano stand.

"No, no. I can help." I stop him.

"No, really. It's not that big of a deal." He turns his back to me and faces the piano. Griff watches from behind his drum kit, his eyes ping-ponging between me and Bodhi.

"Come on," I say. It might not be a big deal to him. But it is to me. "Let me show you the chord progression."

He stops with his back facing me. Then, after a long pause, he twists his body to reveal the side of his face to me.

"Okay, fine." He shrugs.

Somehow Bodhi managed to make it sound like I'm begging to help him, not the other way around. But I'll take it. He probably had to force down a sizable chunk of humble pie to ask me for help in the first place, all things considered. And I know I should think it's messed up that Bodhi's only being nice to me because I have something to offer. But I don't know. I feel pretty good about it. Maybe it's the interview with Xander that reminded me of how far I've come, or maybe it's something else.

The thing about the Ramones that gets me is that even though they played great music together, Joey and Johnny couldn't stand each other. In the twenty-two years they played together, they hardly spoke to each other. When Joey died and the Ramones disbanded, Johnny said that he wouldn't want to play without Joey despite the fact that he was the most difficult person Johnny ever worked with. They were in it together.

When I envisioned my first day with the band, I thought it was going to be all rainbows and butterflies. Like one big, happy family. I'm lol-ing at how naive that was of me because I know now that bands, like families, are complicated. They don't always get along, and they don't have to be friends to be in it together. That's why today means so much to me. Bodhi may not be the easiest person to get along with, but him asking me for help is his way of saying we're in it together.

On the way out of the room, Griff gives me a wide grin with his brows arched real high like he's saying, *I told you so*. I tip my head back at him, saying, *Yep, you sure did*. If it wasn't for Griff, I wouldn't have put my head down and my earmuffs on. And if I hadn't done that, I wouldn't have made it this far.

Now that school's back into the swing of things, ASA starts up again too. At the end of the day, Aerie and Nari link arms with me, and we walk to the room together. Guess I have no choice but to go with them today.

"What's on the agenda for today?" Nari asks Aerie.

"I've been thinking about what happened over winter break with that lady at the food court."

"You have?" I literally haven't thought about it since we've been back. I'm surprised it's still on her mind.

"How can you not? It's frustrating how some random white lady assumed we weren't from this country. Jason and I were talking about it, and we decided instead of talking, we should do something."

Even though I was frustrated at the time, too, I feel a little called out for not thinking about an incident that happened over a week ago.

"You, especially, will appreciate today's meeting." Aerie says this like she's being helpful.

Since the beginning, Aerie's been so helpful. With school, friends, and even the music stuff. And I know she doesn't mean to, but lately, Aerie's "help" is feeling less and less helpful.

As soon as the classroom is full, Aerie and Jason take their spots at the podium in front of us while I find a seat next to Nari and Brandon. We slap hands and catch up with one another until Aerie settles us down.

"Now that it's officially second semester, we'll be dedicating the rest of the school year to coming up with a legacy project. As a reminder, it's something that we contribute to the school as a representation of progress."

"Over winter break, something happened that gave us an idea,"

Jason continues. "A few of us experienced a seemingly harmless encounter at a mall when a well-intentioned white lady asked us how long we've been in this country. Like it wasn't even a possibility that we could be from this country. Some of us have been here for many generations. How are we still seen as foreigners?"

Heads bob, and random chatter spreads through the audience.

"After the incident, we didn't know how to react. Some of us wanted to get angry while others didn't want to cause a scene. So in the end, we did nothing. The worst kind of action—*inaction*." Aerie dips her head and sighs.

"This is a problem that's too real for most of us," Jason says, taking over. "Sometimes the issue seems too big, too complicated for us to do anything about. And even though it's a normal response to not know how to respond, we can't expect change if we don't enact change.

"So what can we do as students at a boarding school for the arts?" Jason looks to Aerie, and they both nod. "We started looking up ways ASA could participate in the Stop Asian Hate movement and stumbled upon a Chinese American photographer from San Francisco. He was born in the US and experienced his first racial slur when he was called a chink as a teenager in New York City, of all places. So what did he do? He didn't retaliate or get angry or fight. This individual used another way to respond: his art.

"With the rise in the post-pandemic anti-Asian hate crimes," Jason goes on explaining, "this artist has been inspired to use his medium to respond to the heightened awareness of the misconception that Asians are perpetual foreigners. He was inspired to create a collection of photographs portraying Asians occupying spaces that are usually occupied by white families and individuals."

Aerie holds up a photograph of an Asian dad at the beach carrying a toddler in one arm and a baby in the other, staring out to the sea. In another photograph, a young Asian woman is lying comfortably in front of an American flag. And the last photograph is of an older Asian couple dressed in denim, basking under the glow of sunlight on a picnic blanket. "His collection of photographs is aptly titled *Perpetual Foreigner*. What he showed us with his photographs was a way to channel his frustrations into something beautiful."

"Since we're from an arts school, this resonated with us. We cross-collaborate with different departments. The orchestra provides background music for theater, the film department provides stage lighting and sound equipment, and so on. We're a well-resourced, not to mention extremely talented, group. As we think about our end-of-the-year project, we want to focus on the community we live in. What talents of ours can we use? How can we turn our frustrations into something beautiful?"

Everyone's excitedly chattering, with some scattered hands popping up.

"For the next few weeks, we'll be taking suggestions." Aerie puts out a shoebox and paper and pens to the side of it.

People are crowding around the suggestion box with their ideas for ways to use art to combat hate. For the first time, I can see a way that I can contribute to ASA in a genuine way.

I haven't seen eye to eye with Aerie lately, and if it was up to me, I'd never come to another ASA meeting. It's what I usually do when something gets too difficult—I avoid it like the plague. Not Aerie, though. When she cares about something, she goes at it in full force, like her music, ASA, and even her friendships. She's been looking out for me since the first day I got to Carlmont. I feel bad for getting prickly about her "help-ful" comment earlier.

VISUAL	AUDIO
Riley Jo sitting on a stoop on the set of Fake Hollywood on the backlot of the Carlmont Campus.	Once I came up with RGB, it was like something clicked in Blake. He might not have been able to place us as a band, but the idea of being a band for everybody really struck a chord in him. Since then, my acceptance in the band hasn't been an issue.
Griff Torres sitting on a stoop on the set of Fake Hollywood on the backlot of the Carlmont Campus.	RGB was such a smart move by Riley. To be honest, I kind of wish I came up with it myself. [Chuckles.] Anyway, I'm glad she went for it.
Bodhi Collins sitting on a stoop on the set of Fake Hollywood on the backlot of the Carlmont Campus.	Riley got lucky with RGB. I mean, diversity and inclusivity are super trending right now. I can see the appeal, and yeah, it helped her position in the band. She still had a lot of catching up to do, though. A lot. I mean, I'm not blaming her or anything, but we were working on a song I had written called "I Am Me." Would've fit so well with the brand of shattering expectations since I know what it's like to have so many obstacles in my way. I mean, Blake's my dad, but he doesn't give me any special treatment for being his son. Anyway, Riley, she just kept slowing us down.
Wide shot of Griff Torres.	Bodhi's definitely the most technically trained in the group. I read somewhere that Blake's been training Bodhi since he was thirteen, so it makes sense that he and Riley keep butting heads. She's unconventional.

Wide shot of Bodhi Collins.	The most basic knowledge of songwriting is structure. And the foundation of song structure is simple. Most usually have an intro, followed by either an AABB or ABAB pattern, *A* representing verse and *B* representing chorus. You could throw in a bridge, though it's not necessary, but that's about it. It's a formula that works time and time again. And if it ain't broke ... you know? Riley's new, and I tried to give her some grace, but she kept trying to do things like add two bars or a key change-up just because she felt like it. Anyway, it was clear she had no idea what she was doing.
Wide shot of Riley Jo	I knew exactly what I was doing. I played the music the way it should've sounded, not what was written on some stupid piece of paper. Music is a natural part of me, like a feeling or a reflex. Before I came to Carlmont, I used to rearrange pieces to fit my vocal range all the time. Ms. Morales, our music teacher, told me that was a form of composition. And after hearing Bodhi mansplain it to me, it dawned on me that he was telling me everything I already knew. He just put technical terms to it.
Wide shot of Griff Torres	You ever watch those old-timey cartoons where Tom chases Jerry or the Coyote chases after the Road Runner? It was kind of like that watching Bodhi try to outwit Riley. Every time he tried to teach her something, she'd beat him to the punch line. [Laughs.] I think Bodhi got the hint

	after, like, the four-hundred-and-ninth time Riley surprised him. Either that or he was hitting a roadblock and he actually let her help him with his song.
Wide shot of Bodhi Collins.	I'm just saying, the timing of her "impromptu performance" [using air quotes] of "Stardust" was pretty convenient since Blake just happened to join the Zoom at that moment. I'm not saying she planned it, but . . . [Shrugs.] Anyway, that's not what's important. What's important is that Marc thinks we're ready. And the song's not bad either.
Wide shot of Riley Jo.	So anyway, I've been working with Ms. Morales on getting the arrangement onto sheet music, but while I work on finishing it out, I've been sharing with the rest of the band what I have so far. Even though Blake liked it, the others had some pretty strong opinions.
Wide shot of Bodhi Collins.	I was listening to Riley's song when it dawned on me. This is a love song; it's ripe with emotion and tension. So naturally I thought, *Why not make it a duet?*
Wide shot of Riley Jo.	It's not a love song. I'll say that much.
Wide shot of Griff Torres.	I couldn't get involved with whatever was going on between Bodhi and Riley. I had my own shit to worry about. Every drummer knows they're replaceable. It's my job to add some kind of trademark move that is irreplaceable. Ergo, I'm irreplaceable.
Wide shot of Riley Jo.	I knew what they were doing. I also knew that if *we* were going to work as a group, *I* had to make some changes. So I spent the next few weeks trying to incorporate all their requests. It took me

	an extra week, but I edited the pronouns from *I* to *we*, added a male harmony bit, and created an extra bar of drum fills to make sure Griff made his mark on the song as well.
Wide shot of Bodhi Collins.	It sounds way better as a duet. There's this part where she says, "*I can hold you while you let your heart soar, / Watch it sparkle into so much more.*" Really drives home that angsty-love vibe.
Wide shot of Riley Jo.	Really. It's not a love song.
Close-up of Griff Torres.	I'm not sure what "Stardust" is about. [Chuckles.] I mean, I'm sure I could just ask Riley. But that takes the magic out of it. There's a line in the chorus: "*There's no sense without trust. / That's the beauty of stardust.*" That line gets me for different reasons on any given day. It could be about first loves, but also it could be about hopes and dreams. I mean, that's the beauty of music, isn't it? Songs mean different things to everyone. Which, I guess, tracks with our band's overall message.
Close-up of Riley Jo.	The thing I love most about music is that it's open to interpretation. It can be what you want, when you need it. And there's nothing wrong or one-sided about it. It doesn't lose its relevance or importance to anyone else who has a different take on it. It's up to each listener to make it what they want.

EIGHTEEN

"So you're really gonna leave us hanging like that?" Xander asks, packing up his equipment. Today his shirt is the Beastie Boys.

"Like what?" We walk through the backlot of Fake Hollywood together.

"How about just telling me what 'Stardust' is about. I won't tell, I promise." He puts a finger to his lips.

"A magician never reveals their secrets."

"Wow, I thought this was about music. Is there more to Riley Jo than meets the eye?"

The moment my name rolls off his tongue, there they are again. Goose bumps.

"It seems limiting, like saying this song means one thing, when really it could be meaningful to someone else in a completely different way. Like other forms of art, I think songs should be open to interpretation."

"I don't know. People want to know what they're getting into. I don't think that's bad."

"You sound like you speak from experience. Is that how it is in the filmmaking world?"

He pats his camera bag. "I stick to a script."

My brows furrow. "Isn't the nature of a documentary inherently unscripted since it's a collection of factual events?" Then a second later, I add, "Unless you're telling me that the Matrix is real." I stop in front of a fake flower shop and turn to Xander. "Is it? Is this a glitch? Would that make me Neo and you . . . Trinity?"

"You're funny." He laughs.

He thinks I'm funny.

"Not the Matrix. At least I don't think it is." He scratches his head, continuing to walk. "I applied to USC's film school, my dad's alma mater," he says, like he's a shoo-in. "And I've already got an internship lined up with J. J. Abrams." He glances sideways at me, expectantly. When I don't react, he says, "*Mission: Impossible, Star Trek, Star Wars* . . . ?"

"Oh, *that* J. J. Abrams. I thought you meant . . ." Yeah, I can't come up with anything remotely believable, so I don't even try. Luckily, Xander doesn't seem to notice.

"Anyway, I'm not trying to win the Oscars or anything, just trying to finish high school. Second-semester senior, you know?" He shrugs like I should know what he means. "Besides, I got a foolproof script—a high school band's meteoric rise to fame . . . yadda yadda yadda. I can't lose."

When he puts it that way, our achievements don't sound special at all. My mood shifts. It reminds me of what Griff said to me before, how Xander and Bodhi are nepo babies. Xander's life seems like a fairy tale compared to mine. The right family connections in the right schools and an industry ready to accept him. And his physique is perfect in every way, shape, and—not the point. Guess it also means when you have parents like Xander's, you can take these once-in-a-lifetime opportunities for granted.

"Adam Horovitz said, 'A good path to creating something mediocre is having rigid rules for what you're making,'" I can't help myself from saying. Maybe it's envy, maybe it's disappointment, or maybe it's something else altogether. I just need to know he's not as shallow as he's coming off.

"Adam who?"

This time, he strikes a nerve. I don't hold back. "Come on. Beastie Boys?" Like, I'm not a music snob or anything, but he's literally wearing the freaking merch, and he doesn't know who they are? I never pegged Xander for being a poser. He usually hangs out with a group from the film department, and when he's not filming his doc, he's in the editing room. Not that I'm, like, stalking him or anything. Just saying that something doesn't add up.

"Oh, that Adam Horovitz. I thought you meant . . ." He stares sidelong, trying to hold in a laugh. And as much as I want to be irritated with him and his perfect life perfectly mapped out, I can't.

"Touché." I laugh at myself. "I know squat about filmmakers. Musicians, on the other hand . . ."

"Yeah, let's talk about that. How do you know so much about musicians?"

I give him a funny look. "Hi, I'm Riley." I hold out a hand like I'm meeting him for the first time. "I play the acoustic guitar for the band RGB. You may have heard of us? We're a high school band on its meteoric rise to fame . . . yadda yadda yadda." I have to say, for my first time, I do a pretty spot-on impression of Xander.

A chuckle escapes him. "You're funny," he says for the second time in this conversation.

As far as compliments go, being funny is not, like, objectively the best compliment in the world. It's not as if Xander is telling me I'm the most beautiful girl he's ever seen or the most talented musician he's ever heard. But *daaaaamn*. It's pretty close.

"I mean, it's not just the music. You know a lot about their history, their lives, their *direct quotes*." He raises a brow at me. "What's that all about?"

"It's because . . ." *I learned everything about the guitar on the internet. Because I didn't have real friends and for a long time considered music my only friend. Because I'm a loner.* ". . . I must've read about it somewhere, and it stuck with me." A lie. But also self-preservation. So I give myself a pass.

"Can you explain the T-shirts at least?" I ask. "Why are you wearing the shirts of musicians you're kinda meh about?"

"Who says I'm meh about them?"

I give him a look.

"Okay, fine." He smirks. "But before you call me out on my BS, let me explain." We reach the end of Fake Hollywood. From the edge of the campus, looking down at the backlot with the fake palm trees lining the sidewalks in front of the fake storefronts, it's cinematic, like Xander and I are real costars in a movie. We're even standing under a streetlight shining on us as if it's our very own spotlight.

"They're my dad's shirts from his touring days. Before he started his own management firm, he used to manage bands, and he'd go to a lot of concerts. I hardly saw him growing up. But he'd always bring back a T-shirt. They didn't make kid-sized shirts, so he got the smallest one they had. I probably outgrew these in middle school. I just can't bring myself to get rid of them."

Nor should you, I think but don't say. "Your dad sounds cool," I say instead.

"He is. He's been through some stuff," he says, thinking out loud.

"Your dad? Blake's manager?" I find that hard to believe.

"It wasn't always like this. He and my mom fought a lot when he was on the road. So he quit managing bands and started working on the business side. It was better hours, but I could tell he gave up a piece of himself. Then he decided to start his own company, and that wasn't easy either. They used their entire savings, so we lived paycheck to paycheck—nothing like what we have now."

"I had no idea."

"How could you, though?" he asks sincerely. "Things were different back then. I still remember him, nose to the grindstone, day in and day out, without complaining. It was his eyes that told a different story, though. Defeat. I'd always wondered why he chose to keep working in a business that he didn't seem to like. Then, over time, the business grew, and he got to do what he loves best: work with music artists. And I always admired that about him. He never quit on either of us—his family and his passion. Guess I didn't realize how much it meant to me until now." He shakes himself out of a stare. "Why am I telling you all this?"

"Because . . . I asked?" Not sure if it's a trick question or if he was asking himself.

He gives me a funny look that I can't read.

"What?"

"Maybe you are a magician or something. Because that's not a story I've said out loud since . . ." He blows out a breath, searching the sky for an answer. "Ever," he says, finishing his sentence. "Anyway, that's the unabridged response no one asked for about the origin of my fashion choices. A documentary short by Xander McNeil," he says, trying to lighten up the mood.

I smile. "Don't sell yourself short. That's a film I'd definitely watch." I'm glad he's not just some kind of privileged nepo baby who takes his position for granted. His story about his dad is all heart. I can root for a guy like that. Not that Xander needs me to root for him. As we part ways and leave the set of Fake Hollywood, I can't help but think that this is the most real conversation I've had since . . . I don't know when.

Back in the dorms, Aerie and Nari are in my room, soaking their fingers. I've noticed they've been doing it more in the short time we've been in school since the break.

"School's been out for hours. Where were you?" Aerie asks.

"I got caught up with the documentary interview."

"Ugh, what a time suck." Nari makes a face. "I mean, I can't imagine having to do that on top of everything else. It's not like you're not busy as it is."

Because I don't fully feel like it's a time suck, I don't respond. Instead, I ask them about how things are going with orchestra.

"It's an endless grind. Like the shirt I got you, it's eat, sleep, play. Eat, sleep, play. Eat, sleep—"

"Play? I think I get the picture."

"I was going to say, 'Soak my hands, then play.'" Aerie points to her hand, and we laugh.

"You already got into Juilliard." I point to Aerie, then look to Nari. "And you're applying to business schools. Why are you killing yourselves over this? You're second-semester seniors; you could be coasting," I say, pretty much quoting Xander. I realize I'm being hypocritical. Aerie's eat-sleep-play routine is pretty much my routine. But it's different. Unlike hers, my future is not clear-cut.

"Our performance here still counts. Going to Juilliard doesn't guarantee my future. If anything, there's more competition there than here. If I want to audition for the New York Philharmonic one day, then making first chair in Carlmont's prestigious orchestra is one of those things that might distinguish me from another candidate. It's like building a résumé."

"I never thought about it that way," I say. "What about you, Nari? What's your excuse?"

"I'm just competitive like that. I can't turn it off, even if I tried."

"It's true. You should see her at a sample sale. God help you if you're the same size as her," Aerie says, and we all laugh.

"Besides, my parents are coming to this thing. I don't want to embarrass them; they're so proud of me," Nari says.

Nari's words poke at a bruise. My parents haven't brought up the Spring Concert again, not since I told them about it. And unlike Nari's, my performance is pivotal in determining my future. I wish my parents cared a fraction of what their parents do.

As Nari packs her things up, including a series of Japanese erasers that are in the shapes of foods—a bowl of ramen, a sushi set, that sort of thing—I being to wonder how she's so strongly rooted in her Japanese culture as a fourth-generation Japanese American. So I ask her.

"My parents are big on keeping the traditions alive at home. We make a lot of the traditional foods from scratch, even though there are Japanese restaurants on the corners of every street in our neighborhood. We bow when we greet other Japanese people, and respect for your elders is a big deal in our home. Also a big deal, not talking about our feelings. There's a lot of sweeping things under the rug, and they don't believe in therapy. I'm trying to break that habit by oversharing about menstrual cramps and when I have *feelings* about someone special. It makes them super uncomfortable, but it's worth it."

"Wow, sounds awkward," I say. "Also brave." I could barely tell my parents about applying to the music program at Hartfordshire U, let alone period pain.

"You know, you can always talk about your *feelings* with me. I won't be super uncomfortable about it." Aerie nudges Nari.

"Nice try," Nari says.

"You have to tell me your crush at some point; might as well be now." Aerie and Nari go at it while I'm still thinking about what Nari said. Unlike Aerie, who is content with maintaining her parents' status quo, Nari is pushing her parents to believe in something they don't believe in. I haven't even brought up the fact that my song was handpicked by Marc himself. The truth is, I've been avoiding the subject because it's too uncomfortable. Maybe Nari has a point. Some things are worth being uncomfortable about.

It isn't until we're about to fall asleep that night that Aerie turns to face me from her bed.

"Nari still won't tell me who her crush is."

I wait a beat for her to say more only to realize there isn't more. "Oh, that's"—I search for the right word to convey my support—"annoying" is the best I can come up with.

"It *is* annoying. She usually tells me everything." Aerie goes on about how this is so un-Nari-like to not confide in her about something this big, and now Aerie's questioning what she could have done to compromise her trust with Nari, and she knows it'll make Nari close up even more if she keeps asking, but Aerie can't help herself from asking because she desperately wants another couple in the friend group for her and Jason to do couple-y things with. It's exhausting.

Honestly, I'm finding myself in uncharted waters. Not having had a friend group before means not having had to deal with these types of issues. I don't want to be fake, but I can tell Aerie's spiraling, and it's getting late. So I say as many things I can think of to comfort her. "Don't take it personally." And "I'm sure she'll tell you when she's ready." And even "It's not you; it's her." I think that works in this case, right?

"I mean, you'd tell me, wouldn't you? If you had a crush on someone?" Aerie asks me.

"Yeah, of course." It's a good thing it's dark in the room. Otherwise, she'd see the guilty expression on my face.

Not that I don't trust Aerie.

Not that I like Xander.

Or maybe I do like Xander. I don't know.

NINETEEN

I've been thinking about Nari's strategy when dealing with her parents, and it's time I push pass the uncomfortableness. Maybe then will I make actual progress with my parents. During lunch, I call my mom.

"Look what I got today!" she sing-songs, derailing me. She's holding up a bumper sticker that reads BENTONVILLE U PARENT.

"Wait, what month are we in?" I ask. It's possible I practiced straight through January and February.

"It's still January. I know you won't get the official letter until March, but I saw them at the bookstore when I passed by today, and I just couldn't help myself. Next year you'll be here with me. Can you imagine it?"

No, I literally cannot imagine it. And I've tried. I know it was part of the deal to go to Bentonville U after graduation. But things have changed.

"I've been thinking, Mom. . . . I'm grateful to be given the opportunity to go to a college—"

"Tuition-free, I might add."

"Yeah, that too. And I'm grateful, I really am. But it doesn't seem fair that I could be taking up a spot from someone who might really want to be there." It may not be my dream to attend Bentonville U, but I might be taking away someone else's dream. And that hasn't been sitting well with me.

There's a pause. "What do you mean?" Mom eventually asks.

"I guess what I'm trying to say is that maybe I won't have to give up music at the end of the year." It takes a monumental effort to get the words out. It's not everything I want to say, but at least I managed to say something this time.

"Oh, hon, is that what you're worried about?" she says. "You don't have to give up music."

"I don't?" I startle. Wow, Mom is being way more cool about this than I gave her credit for.

"Absolutely. There are tons of people here wanting to learn how to play the guitar. You could teach them and make a really good side income. Especially after your training at Carlmont."

I take it back. She's not being cool about it at all.

"No, I mean an actual career. Not a side anything." I tell her about how I performed my song at Blake's house, how Marc's coming to see us perform at the Spring Concert, and how if he likes what he hears there, he'll offer us a record deal.

"You went to your advisor's house? *Alone?*" Of course she focuses on the wrong thing. "As an academic advisor myself, I can tell you that this is a major violation of ethical conduct."

"Mom, relax. I went with my bandmates, and it was a casual holiday party. He only asked me to play the song because Marc Rubinstein, the head of Ruby Records, was there. And he pretty much said the song is a hit. If we can nail our performance at the Spring Concert, he might even offer us a record deal!" In my excitement, the words come spilling out.

"Oh, okay. I'm relieved to hear you weren't there by yourself."

Again, she is focusing on the wrong thing.

"Haven't you heard anything I've been saying?"

"Oh, Riley. It's not that I'm not excited for you. These things sometimes don't pan out. I don't want to celebrate before anything's official."

"I don't get it. You were precelebrating before I got the offer to Bentonville U." I can't help calling her out. This seems hugely unfair.

"That's different. You have a better chance of—" She stops herself, but not soon enough.

"I knew it. You don't believe I can do it, do you?" I always suspected it, even though I've never had confirmation. Until now.

"Of course I believe in you. It's the entertainment industry I don't believe in."

My voice retreats like it usually does when I feel like I'm being backed into a corner. It's hard enough when I'm trying to prove to others I belong here. But my own mom? It's too much.

It's silent for a while before she says, "I don't want you to get hurt, that's all."

That's all? She says she doesn't want me to get hurt, but she is the one hurting me.

After my call with Mom, I get to lunch late. People are already leaving the dining hall, and I don't see Aerie or Nari anywhere. It's pasta day, so I slather marinara sauce on a pile of spaghetti and find a seat. On my way, I pass by the sandwich station, and the vinegary smell of pickles assaults my nostrils. Thinking of my dad makes me stop to grab a few before I find a table to sit at.

Mouth full of pasta, I take a bite of pickle. It's tangy on both fronts—from the brine of the pickle and the zest of marinara sauce. Even objectively I know that it's an acquired taste. And definitely weird. Wonder if the kimchi-spaghetti combo would taste better or if it's equally an acquired taste.

Imagining my dad eating pickles instead of kimchi makes me sad. It's like he's suppressing what's natural to him in order to conform. I understand that he's trying to do what he thinks is best: assimilate to the American way. But hearing how Nari and her family preserve their culture by carrying on their traditions makes me wonder why he felt like he had to choose between his past and his future. Why couldn't he have both?

"Something wrong with your lunch?"

I must have been deep in thought because Xander is standing right in front of me, staring at me like I'm malfunctioning.

"I lost my appetite," I say, which is pretty much the truth.

He looks at my plate. "Probably because you're eating . . . *that*." He makes a face.

"It's not so bad. It's a Jo family recipe. You should try it." As soon as I say it, I have a change of heart. "On second thought, don't. My dad introduced it to us when we were younger, so it's an acquired taste. Doubt it'll live up to the hype."

"Yeah, I wasn't going to. Interesting story about your dad, though. Do tell." He pulls up a chair and sits down. So I tell him the story about kimchi and pickles, and he kind of gets it.

"My dad made me squirt ketchup packets straight into my mouth when I ate French fries in his car. Now I can't eat fries any other way."

"Um, elaborate please." It's my turn to lean in.

Xander chuckles. "When my dad's company started taking off, he bought himself a car. And not just any car—an Aston Martin. Said it was a necessary business investment because he was starting to meet with important clients, but my mom wasn't fooled. None of us were. Not that we gave him crap for it. He worked so hard for it; we were happy for him. Anyway, he loved that thing almost as much as he loved us. Which is why he let us eat in the car but only if we left no trace of it behind. Hence ketchup packets in the mouth." He laughs. "Our house was a disaster, but you couldn't sneeze in his car without permission. Whatever. People have their things, and my dad's is music and cars."

"I respect that," I say.

"Yeah, me too." We share a smile.

Talking with Xander is freeing. We don't talk about what it means to be in a band or what it means to be Korean/American/Korean American. I can imagine Aerie saying that Xander having the luxury to not talk about race is a privilege afforded only to people like him, but maybe it's what I like best about him. We can be who we are without worrying about what it means. When did everything get so complicated?

A second later, we're still sharing a smile.

Now we're just staring at each other.

Okay, what is happening?

"There you are," Aerie says with Nari next to her. Xander and I break our stare as Aerie and Nari slow their steps, approaching us. "Oh, we didn't mean to interrupt."

Xander clears his throat. "No, that's cool. I have to get to class." He smiles at Aerie and Nari. "See ya, Jo," he says in a super casual way that makes me think I imagined our lingering stare a second ago.

"Yeah, see ya." I watch him walk away.

Aerie and Nari waste no time and take his place in front of me.

"So what was that about?" Aerie sing-songs.

"We were just talking about the doc." I avoid eye contact.

"*Okaaayyy.*" Nari eyes Aerie in a super-obvious way.

"What's up?" I ask, desperate to move this conversation along.

"We were coming to check up on you since we didn't see you at lunch. I've been dying to tell you what Jason just told me," Aerie says.

"Yeah, Aerie and Jason were whispering about it all throughout lunch. They wouldn't even tell me what it was about. Not until she told you first. It was super annoying," Nari says, nodding her head at me. "Anyway, we found Riley. Now spill." Nari leans in, resting her head on her hands.

"Okay, well, don't tell anyone that I told you, but someone's got a crush on you." Aerie points to me.

Wait. *Me?*

"Who?" It can't be . . . Xander? My face burns thinking about it. How would Aerie know? I mean, she hardly talks to him. They barely acknowledged each other.

"Oh my God, just say it already," Nari says.

I brace myself for it.

"It's Brandon!" Aerie's face looks like it's going to burst, she's so thrilled.

"Brandon Lee?" Nari says, confused.

"Brandon-who-plays-the-flute-Brandon?" I clarify, even though it's the only Brandon I know.

Aerie's brows furrow. "Okay, what is going on here? This is not the reaction I was expecting."

I snap myself out of it. "Not that I'm not flattered or anything. I mean, no one's ever had a crush on me before. And I like Brandon. Just not like that."

"What's not to like? He's good-looking, smart, and talented.

He's the number-one flute player in orchestra. Just imagine what he can do with his lips." Aerie puckers up.

I roll my eyes playfully. "I'm sure he's a catch, but I don't know. I just don't feel that *it* factor with him." I might have been more open to it if I didn't have whatever it is I'm feeling for Xander. And I can't seem to put it into words either. It's kind of like trying to explain to my parents why music means so much to me. I don't know why I like being around him; I just know that I do.

"Do you mean you don't *feel* it with Brandon or that you don't *see* it?" Nari snorts.

I'm caught way off by Nari's comment, and apparently so is Aerie.

"Oh my God, Nari!" Aerie gasps. "You can't say something like that. It's offensive." Aerie swats a hand at her. Even though Aerie knows it's wrong to say it, she seems to know what Nari meant by it. I'm still not following.

"What did you mean by that?" I ask sincerely. It reminds me of the way Nari eyed me suspiciously the first day of school. Like there's more to it than that.

"Nothing, it was just a joke," Nari says. The way she and Aerie exchange looks, trying to keep themselves from smiling, tells me it's more than a joke.

Later in the week, Xander's in the music room with us filming cinema verité during our practice for his project. I do my best to pretend he's not there, but it's not that easy. Then Blake comes on-screen and announces he's got proofs of our album cover, and he's got my full attention.

"This album cover is going to set the tone of who you are, and we wanted to break you out in a big way. We had a few different options and then had marketing take a poll with a test group that would be your target audience, and this is the one that was the most popular."

Bodhi, Griff, and I exchange an excited look before Blake shares his screen with us.

There's an audible gasp that escapes us. My initial reaction is positive. There are three circles—one red, one green, and one blue—overlapping with one another like a Venn diagram. The overlapped areas are what the colors would be if they mixed, and in the center it's white. Superimposed in the three circles is a faint outline of our faces.

"Marketing felt that this is very pop but also edgy," Blake continues. "What do you think?"

"I love it," Bodhi says right away. "The colors make it pop— excuse the pun." He snorts.

"Yeah, and there's also a kind of artsy thing going on with the whole RGB color vibe," Griff adds. "What do you think, Riley?" I know Griff well enough to know that he's sensing something and wondering if I sense it too.

"It's very eye-catching. I think the marketing team did a great job," I say hesitantly. Something's off. I just can't quite put my finger on what it is.

"I told them about your idea behind RGB, and they loved it," Blake says with a catch in his voice. "In fact, they pointed out how at the center of where the colors overlap, you see how it's white?" He points his mouse to the white area in the overlapping space of the three circles. "They really liked how it really drove home the point that we don't see color, we see individuals."

What? No. That's not what I was saying.

"Which leads me to the next point on the agenda," Blake says before I can say anything else. "As soon as you turned in the sheet music to 'Stardust,' I decided to poll some marketing data on it since we were already doing the album cover. And what we found was interesting."

VISUAL	AUDIO
Wide shot of Riley Jo standing out in front of the music room at Carlmont.	I knew there was something off with the album cover. I just couldn't place it right away. And then ... [Shakes her head.] Well, you heard what happened.
Wide shot of Griff Torres standing out in front of the music room at Carlmont.	First glance? I liked what I saw. The colors are vibrant in a minimalist way. The white space drew me in right away. When I noticed the outline of the colors that vaguely resembled people were actually us, I started to get ... uncomfortable.
Wide shot of Bodhi Collins standing out in front of the music room at Carlmont.	Blake is only trying to help us be the best versions of ourselves so that when Marc sees us perform at the Spring Concert, he'll want to sign us on the spot. I trust Blake.
Montage of an inebriated Blake Collins surrounded by girls at a nightclub in the nineties. Source: TMZ	Blake Collins voice-over: Being a musician is not as glamorous as it seems. Sure, there's plenty of partying, girls, booze, etc. But it was also a lot of hard work.
Video clip of Boyz Club's music video of "Clubbin'."	Blake Collins voice-over: I spent hours learning how to act, dance, and sing. The music industry is cutthroat, and if it's that competitive for someone like me, well ... [Holds out his hands and shrugs.]

Wide shot of Blake Collins on Zoom.	Believe me, I want to see RGB succeed. As part of the process, all artists go through a marketing analysis that polls their popularity with a sample market of their audience. In this case, we're looking to target the twelve-to-twenty-five-year-old age group in big cities and rural towns. We poll them on a number of things we have to take into consideration, like album cover, song titles, band names, and even the artists themselves....
Wide shot of Griff Torres..	Blake had some interesting data he shared with us. He ... [Pauses, rubbing his hands together.] I want to make this clear that this is coming from Blake, not me. [Long pause.] Anyway, according to "market research," Blake said an overwhelming majority preferred the song to not be a [clears his throat] duet.
Wide shot of Riley Jo.	Blake then followed it up by adding that Marc wouldn't know how to market a band with an Asian female lead because, get this ... there is no market for a band with an Asian female lead. [Shakes her head.]
Wide shot of Bodhi Collins.	The key thing to understand is that it's not personal. I know this because I'm used to being around the industry. This sort of thing happens every day. You can't let ego get in the way.

Wide shot of Griff Torres.	It's fucked up for sure. In fact, I almost walked out of the room. On principle. Then I thought about it. He could have rejected us if it was a race thing. But he didn't. Instead, he explained it to us from a marketing standpoint, and I'm ashamed to admit, he's probably right. I can't tell you the last US pop band with an Asian American lead that hit the top forty. But we need to look ahead and focus on the positives. He's willing to work with us, and if we want a chance at getting a record deal, I think we should listen to him.
Wide shot of Blake Collins on Zoom.	Listen, you can be mad at the numbers—that's totally valid. Just don't be mad at me. I'm only telling it how it is. As their advisor and a music artist with a double-platinum record with Ruby Records, it's in our best interest to look at it from all angles. Bottom line is, I'm doing this for them as much as I'm doing this for me. And if the numbers say Bodhi should sing the lead, then I say Bodhi should sing the lead.
Wide shot of Blake Collins on Zoom.	There's a reason why a lot of bands don't make it big. Sometimes you have to put your ego in a bag and move on, and this, unfortunately, is one of those times for Riley.
Wide shot of Riley Jo.	I mean … [Stares off camera.] [Long pause.] [Shakes her head in frustration.] What more can I say?

TWENTY

As soon as class is dismissed, I'm out of there.

"Riley, wait," Xander calls out after me.

I don't stop marching off in the direction of my dorm. A few more minutes and I can unleash the tears building up in the privacy of my dorm room. Crying in public will only make this a bigger deal. And it's already bigger than I want it to be.

"Hey, you want to talk about . . . ?"

"Nope." I keep marching. He keeps following.

"You're obviously not okay. Just stop."

I stop. "Why do you care?" I'm never this direct, but in all the years people have been treating me like I'm invisible, Xander is the only one who's ever cared this much to follow after me. It's making me wonder . . . what the hell is wrong with *him*?

"Just let me explain," he says. But before he can, I hear Bodhi's voice. The scratchiest record scratch there ever was.

"Am I interrupting something?" Bodhi wriggles his stupid eyebrows at us. "Xan, you dog. Didn't know you had it in you."

"Bro, what?" Xander holds WTF hands out to his sides, horrified by the accusation.

I'm pretty sure if Aerie and Nari were here, they'd know just what to say to Bodhi. That he's treating me like some hypersexualized or fetishized Asian woman stereotype. I can't find the words, so I just say, "Is it impossible for you to think that a guy would talk to me with any other purpose than to just talk?"

"Whoa, Xan. Better keep your girl in check. She's a wild one," Bodhi says, completely unfazed.

I know how this goes. Xander is going to get uncomfortable being associated with me in a romantic way and is therefore going to repel me like I'm some virus. So I save him the trouble and rush off to the dorms while he's still arguing with Bodhi.

"What happened?" Aerie asks me as soon as I step into the room. It's confirmed; I look as bad as I feel. "Oh my God. Sit."

After I sit and she offers me some water, I gather enough strength to tell her what happened in band. Before I can finish my last sentence, she gasps in horror.

"First he tells you they don't play K-pop, and now he tells you that you can't sing the lead because you're *Asian?*" Aerie is fuming. "That's, like, beyond a microaggression. He's being openly racist. And you said Xander has it on film?" Aerie points to me.

I nod.

"Then you definitely have grounds to get him fired. You have to report him. Again," Aerie demands.

When my brows quirk, revealing a guilty expression, Aerie gasps again. "You didn't report him?!"

"I thought— I didn't think he would do this to me again." I bury my face in my hands. "I've been so stupid."

"It's okay," Aerie says, putting a hand on my shoulder. "It would have proven a pattern, but it's going to be fine. This offense of blatant discrimination is bad enough. So what are you going to do?" She stares down at me, wide-eyed.

If I get him fired—if I even *could* get him fired—it means we won't get signed by Marc, and that means goodbye, record deal, and hello, Bentonville U for four years. I don't say this out loud because Aerie already seems to have a misconstrued version of Bentonville as it is. She doesn't need to know all the details.

"You don't understand; I need this opportunity. They don't come by that often, and I don't know if I'll get another one if I do something rash like try to get him fired." I feel guilty admitting that I need Blake, but it's the truth. And to my surprise, Aerie seems to understand.

"There have to be other ways of breaking into the industry. What about social media? Lots of famous artists got their start online, like Justin Bieber, Shawn Mendes, Charlie Puth...." Aerie stops, then cringes. "And now that I'm hearing all the white-boy names come out of my mouth, I'm realizing that's not a realistic alternative for you." We both groan in agreement.

A beat later, she lights up with an idea. "You know, there's this artist named Kim Woo-sung. He's from LA and couldn't make a name for himself as a musician here, so he relocated to Korea and became a famous K-pop star there. After he became an established artist in Korea, he's performing in the US as a Korean American solo artist, and his fan base is starting to rise," Aerie says, giving me a hopeful look.

"So you're saying if I go to Korea and become a K-pop artist first," I say, processing out loud, "then I can come back and have a chance at being an American music artist here?" I finish with a raised eyebrow.

"Yeah, I know that's not ideal." She sighs, considering more options. "You can always fund your own album," she says, kind of like a question.

"I definitely can't do that." My head dips lower. If coming to Carlmont for a year is a stretch, funding my own album is out of the question.

"Maybe it sounds ridiculous, but you should think about going to Korea," Aerie offers. "You can audition for one of the big music companies in Seoul and join a pop music training program. It's super competitive and it might be a long shot and it might not be the most direct way to become an American pop star, but at least they can't discriminate against you because you're Asian. Isn't it better than being in a band that wants you to be invisible?"

I'm speechless. It's not that I don't agree with Aerie. Going to Korea to be a pop star is better than being invisible in my own band. My question is, are those *really* my only options?

The next day, I'm still deciding how to proceed before continuing with the song. As much as I wanted to take the wait-and-see approach, with the Spring Concert coming up in a mere three months, I don't have that luxury. I don't think going to Korea to be a K-pop star is the answer to my problems, but neither is staying in the band under such repressive conditions.

I head over to the administration building. I'm trying to gain enough courage to actually walk in there and tell them about Blake. Nope. Can't do it.

Before I turn back from the door, I notice Griff walking out.

"What're you doing here?" I ask, wondering if Griff is here for the same reason I am.

"My parents are providing lunch for Campus Beautification

Day tomorrow. I was just finalizing the details with the office."

"I see," I say, making a mental note to find out what the hell that is later.

"Are you coming in?" Griff is holding the door open for me.

"I was going to. Now I'm not so sure."

"Okay." He rubs the back of his head, confused. "What's going on?"

"So about what Blake said yesterday," I start.

His head dips. "Sorry, man. That was, like, so many levels of fucked up."

I figure if anyone understands, it's Griff.

Wait. If he understands me, then why is this the first time I'm hearing it from him?

"If you knew it was fucked up, how come you didn't say anything to Blake yesterday?" I ask.

He pulls his head back, shocked by my tone. "You think Blake is responsible for making Bodhi the lead singer?"

"Who else would it be?" I can't tell if this is a trick question or not.

He shakes his head. "Blake's just doing his job. It's the system that's fucked up. As much as you want to blame Blake, he's just the messenger."

"So you're saying that Blake is a *good* guy?"

He holds up his hands at me. "I won't go that far, but he's not the bad guy here. He's just A Guy, okay?"

"Okay, fine, whatever. So Blake is not *the* bad guy. How does that make it better?" I scoff. "If the system is broken and the music industry isn't willing to produce songs with an Asian American female lead because there currently isn't a market for an Asian American female lead, then how will anything ever change?" I ask, frustrated. "What does any of this mean"—I gesture around us—"if I'm not able to sing the songs I write?"

"Look. I don't have all the answers. All I know is that Jeremy and Jake didn't like the way they were treated, so they left. Guess where they are now?" He doesn't wait for me to answer. "They're in junior college playing local dives for pennies. How is that sticking it to Blake?"

As much as I want to prove Griff wrong, I can't. So I don't say anything.

"Sometimes you have to play the game, and this is part of it. I mean, look around. There aren't many bands with Asian American members, not just leads. As fucked up as it is to say this, we're lucky to even have this opportunity with Marc." His gray eyes tense, revealing a deep crease in the space between them.

Griff's right. I think back to Blake's party. When I first got there, no one noticed me. I was as good as invisible. It wasn't until I performed my song for everyone that people, Marc especially, noticed me. And I have to be honest, if it wasn't for Blake, that wouldn't have been possible.

"Doesn't it bother you, though? Doesn't it tear at you, piece by piece, knowing that we're being told to stay in the background, to be invisible? Like we don't matter? All just so you can be *white-famous*?"

"Riley." He tilts his head. His expression, though, is void of sympathy. "I'm a drummer. Being the lead was never my dream. My dream is to be part of a band, a good one. And yes, hopefully become *white-famous*. Because that means security. And security means my parents won't have to worry that they used their restaurant as collateral to take out a loan for me to be here." He sniffs, shifting his stance. "So you can judge all you want, but

I'm not doing this just for fame. People like you and me"—he points a finger to me, then himself—"our path to success isn't as clear-cut as it is for the Bodhis of the world. We have to be creative and look for our opportunities. It doesn't mean it's any less legitimate. Saying yes to playing backup for now doesn't mean you need to stay in the background forever. Once we have a record deal, we'll have a fan base, which means leverage. We can break out and be our own artists."

"Guess when you put it that way . . ." If I'm understanding Griff right, his advice is similar to Aerie's. Sometimes we have to take the indirect path to becoming big, and going along with Blake's "marketing plan," a thinly veiled excuse for a public display of discrimination, is much like Aerie's suggestion to be a K-pop star.

"All I'm saying is, don't do anything rash. Just think about it," Griff pleads.

I still don't know what I'm going to do, but I can at least agree to that much.

TWENTY-ONE

It's Campus Beautification Day, and I realize I forgot to ask what that means.

"Wear clothes you don't care about," Aerie says, throwing on an old sweatshirt over a pair of equally old sweatpants.

I raise an eyebrow at her. "You're scaring me. Do we have to, like, paint houses?" Then, a second later, so as not to sound like a priss, I follow it up with "Only because I'm incapable of coloring within the lines. I'd bring down the value of the house or anything I have to paint, for that matter."

"Don't worry, we're not painting anything," she says as we're walking out of our room. "Have you thought of any suggestions for our ASA final project?"

"Um, no. I couldn't really come up with anything."

"Really?" The lilt in Aerie's voice tells me something's up.

"Why do you ask?" I can't help myself.

"Oh, nothing. I mean, I just thought you might have some suggestions. You're so creative," she says.

Well, I've been kind of busy on the creativity front, trying to work my way through a shitty system to break into a notoriously racist industry so I can do what I love and get the hell out of Bentonville. I'd say I'm maxed out of creativity at the moment.

"I'm sorry. I'll try to carve out some time later today," I say instead.

She squeezes my arm that's locked around hers, seemingly happy. Which makes me happy.

When we get to the entrance of the school, we're told to pick a task around the campus. Replanting flowers around the administration office and front entrance, scrubbing the insides of the fountains, raking leaves—those sorts of things. Jason meets Aerie with a cup of coffee.

"Shit, Riley. I'm sorry I didn't get you a coffee. I only have two hands, and I can't, like, risk getting scalded, not this close to the Spring Concert."

"It's okay, really. It's the thought that counts," I say.

"He really is thoughtful." Aerie gives Jason a hug.

"And look, I even got you the special gardening gloves. The heavy-duty ones." He pulls them out of his back pocket and hands them to her.

"Aw, you guys are so cute." Seeing Aerie with Jason makes me envious.

"We are, aren't we?" Aerie looks up at Jason extra smiley.

Jason smiles back in the same extra way. "I can get you a pair too," he says to me. "Here, take mine. I'll go snag another one from the bin before they're all taken."

"No, it's all good. You take them. I'm going to join my bandmates," I say before even confirming they're around. Aerie and Jason accept my excuse, and they go off to the front entrance to replant the flowers there.

Truth is, the two of them are so cute I don't know if I can handle a whole morning with them. They don't get people commenting on how she's got white fever or he's got yellow fever. Why can't people just like each other and not think about what message it sends to the world? Why does everything have to mean something? While I'm thinking about it, if I'm being honest, I didn't come up with a suggestion for the ASA project because it feels forced. How can I come up with a plan to raise awareness about racism against Asians when I can't even advocate for myself?

I eventually end up finding Griff by the fountain in front of the library. It's been drained, and he's already got a brush in hand.

"Can I join you?" I ask.

He nods, grinning, then hands me a brush from the bucket next to him. We climb into the empty fountain and start scrubbing but don't talk. I think we said enough yesterday. At least it's not awkward. It's actually comfortable with Griff, knowing he feels the same challenges I do. At the same time, though, I feel an extra layer of added frustrations because of my position in the band. Like Griff said, he's the drummer, and being a lead singer is not something he wants. And if what Blake is saying is true about Asian American female leads not being marketable, then why am I even bothering with any of this at all?

I get lost in my thoughts and take it out on the fountain. It's like the time I didn't get the part of Cosette in *Les Mis*. Can I not aspire to go for roles that are traditionally played by white people? I feel very much American, but the opportunities I'm presented with tell me I'm "other." It doesn't seem fair that I can't dream the way others do. I can't figure out who I'm most upset with. Is it the system for being broke? Bodhi and his dad for perpetuating the system? Or people like Griff for their complacency? It's all too much.

I get distracted by a commotion coming from the gate of our school. Judging by the sound the engine makes coming up the hill, it's massive. When it gets closer, I see that it's a food truck.

On the side, there's a rainbow with a sign that reads ALOHA

EATS. The truck slows down as it approaches us, and eventually it comes to a stop. Griff stands up to make his way over to it. The man driving it gives him a firm handshake and pulls him in for a hug. A woman appears from the other side wearing a T-shirt with the restaurant's logo on it and goes to wrap Griff in a bear hug, rocking him from side to side before releasing him. They get back in the truck and park by the student union.

"I'm guessing you know them?" I say to Griff when he returns.

He laughs. "You can say that. They're my parents, and that's the food truck I was telling you about."

Ah yes. Part of the restaurant they put up as collateral for your tuition, I think but don't say.

"Griffy!" His mom comes running toward him and gives him the same bear hug she gave him earlier, as if she didn't just see him a few minutes ago. Griff's dad pats him on the back while Griff's in his mom's embrace.

"Okay, Ma. I'm happy to see you too." Griff gently gets his mom to release him from her grip. "This is Riley Jo. She's the guitarist in our band I told you about." His mom is taller than his dad, with broad shoulders and kind eyes that light up when she smiles, like she's doing right now.

"Hi, Mr. and Mrs. Torres." I simultaneously wave and bow to them. After the fiasco with Aerie's parents, I'm not sure how to act in front of Griff's parents. Clearly. They don't make a thing of it and take turns greeting me. His mom pulls me in for a hug.

"Riley, you are so pretty," Mrs. Torres says once she releases me from the hug, generously eyeing me up and down.

"Ma," Griff warns.

"What?" She puts her hands out to her sides. "I can't comment on a girl being pretty?"

"Okay, Ma." Griff laughs, unconvinced.

"You hungry?" Mr. Torres says, taking inventory of me. "Of course you're hungry. Too skinny!" He tsks and goes straight to the food truck and hands me a plate before they officially start serving others.

"What about me, Tay-Tay? Your own flesh and blood." Griff holds his hands out, giving them puppy eyes.

"You can wait with the others." His dad swats a hand at Griff. "This is the first time Riley's having Aloha Eats."

I laugh and thank Mr. and Mrs. Torres for their generosity. After they leave, I raise my eyebrow up at Griff. "You call your dad 'Tay-Tay'? After . . ."

"Yes, we call him the same nickname as Taylor Swift because the resemblance is uncanny," he deadpans.

I bust up laughing. "I don't know why I asked."

"I'm just playing. T-a-t-a-y is 'dad' in Tagalog. It's supposed to be said like *ta-tie*, but I learned to speak Tagalog by reading it, so I kept saying tay-tay instead of ta-tie. Anyway, my family thought it was hilarious, so naturally they wouldn't let me forget it, and the nickname stuck." He laughs.

I laugh, too. "Your family sounds fun."

"They are." He smiles fondly.

"So, you speak Tagalog?"

He looks up thoughtfully. "I know how to say 'mom,' 'dad,' and all the bad words. You know, the essentials," he says, and we both laugh.

Griff's parents aren't who I expected. The way he talks about them, they sound like the Kris-Jenner-level-momager type. So I imagined them to be shrewd businesspeople in uptight clothing and overly Botoxed faces, similar to the industry people I saw at

Blake's house party. The smiley-eyed folks in front of me who make me feel instantly comfortable are the complete opposite.

Soon a line begins to form in front of the truck, and Griff's parents start serving plates of food. It takes some effort for me to wait for Griff. The aroma wafting in my face while I hold the plate is tempting me to ditch him right now. I somehow manage to power through the urge. As soon as he gets his plate, we take a seat on the steps in front of the library and dig in.

"Oh my God," I say with my mouth full. The kalua pork is smoky and tender, and the pineapple in the fried rice gives it the perfect combination of sweet and savory. For dessert I try haupia for the first time, which Griff says is coconut pudding. It's creamy, not too sweet, and the coconut flavor is not too overpowering.

"I'm sorry about the other day," Griff says during a lull. "I know it doesn't seem like I'm supporting you, but I am. I'm giving you the same advice I'd give myself if I were in your position."

It's not that I think Griff and I should have the same reaction to racial bias just because we're both Asian. I'd be no better than Aerie thinking there's only one way to be Asian American. I guess I just expected Griff to be more understanding since he's in the band, unlike Aerie.

"What I don't get is, why is Bodhi so hard on me? Is it because I'm a girl? Because he doesn't do that to you." I can't let it go.

At first Griff seems startled, then he sets his fork down and looks thoughtful for a solid minute.

"It's probably because you're more of a threat to him," he finally says.

"Me?" I almost choke on my fried rice.

"Yeah, because you both have lead-singer qualities, only you have more talent. Isn't it clear?" He looks over at me as if to say *Duh*.

"What? Then why am I being asked to sing backup?"

"Don't take this the wrong way, but ... are you that naive? Do you really think the music industry is a meritocracy?"

"Um, if you mean that people who are talented enough and work hard enough can achieve their dreams, then yes. I do think that."

"I hate to break it to you, but it's not. Everyone trying to make it in the music industry is hustling. You think Skylar Twist is a star because she works harder than others?"

I stare quizzically at him. Is this a trick question?

"Everyone works hard. Not everyone rises to the top. It's up to the gateway in the music industry. That is, the record labels."

"Isn't it the fans who make musicians popular? Don't they control what's hot?"

"Sure, fans create lasting power. But you first have to be on the fans' radars, and in order for that to happen, you need a platform large enough to reach them. Bottom line is, you need industry professionals to become big."

I see what he's saying. Doesn't mean I like it. I don't know why I keep trying to make sense of it. Maybe Aerie's onto something. Maybe instead of trying to make sense of it, I should just give in to what they want. Which is more of Bodhi, less of me.

I get distracted from my thought when Griff's mom comes jogging up to us when the line dies down.

"Griff, before you go, sign these for us." She hands him a folder and a Sharpie. When she looks over at my plate, her eyes grow wide. "You didn't tell me your friend has such a big appetite. I like her even more. Griff, you should bring her to the restaurant, eh? That way we can treat her properly."

"Yeah, you should come sometime," Griff says.

"Any friend of Griff's is a friend of ours," she says, her smile so big it reaches her eyes.

"Thank you, Mrs. Torres," I say with a hand shielding my mouth. I know it's rude to talk with your mouth full, but it seems even ruder not to acknowledge Mrs. Torres.

She waves at me before going back to the food truck to help Mr. Torres clean up.

"Your parents are adorable," I say once my mouth isn't stuffed with food.

"Yeah, they're pretty cool." Griff sets his plate of food aside and opens the folder, revealing a stack of headshots.

"Whoa."

"Don't be too impressed. These are for the loyal customers at Aloha Eats. My parents have been managing my career since I was little. It hasn't stopped even though I'm at Carlmont." He holds up a headshot as proof. "I'm just a local celebrity. But in my parents' minds, I'm a *celebrity* celebrity."

"I can see that." I hear in Griff's voice the weight of the burden he feels. Support like the kind Griff has is a double-edged sword. I'm still envious. Not everyone is fortunate to have that kind of support.

It's time for us to continue beautifying the campus, so we toss our plates in the trash on our way to say goodbye to his parents. Inside the food truck, Mr. and Mrs. Torres are wiping down the stations and closing food containers. While we wait for them to finish, I notice the inside of the food truck is wallpapered with photos of Griff at all ages. In each one, he's behind a drum kit. Griff onstage, Griff at a school performance, Griff at an open mic . . . Griff, Griff, Griff. Even the candids with his siblings are of him on the drums.

"So what did you think of the food?" Mr. Torres asks, stepping out from the food truck with Mrs. Torres.

"It was delicious," I say.

"She ate the entire plate." Mrs. Torres nudges Mr. Torres.

"I gave her double portions too." Mr. Torres eyes me impressively. "Do you have a boyfriend?" he asks, and my cheeks instantly flare.

"Tay-Tay!" Griff's mouth hangs open.

"What? I can't ask an innocent question?" Mr. Torres looks genuinely appalled.

"If only that's what you were doing," Griff says, shaking his head.

Mrs. Torres comes and wraps a loving arm around Griff's shoulders. "I don't worry about your future in music. Your relationship status, though . . ." She tsks, patting his head.

"Damn, that's cold, Ma." He side-eyes his mom with a smile.

"I'm just saying, she's cute, and she likes our food. Besides, she seems okay with your bean-shaped head."

"Ma!" This time, Griff's cheeks flare.

"When he was born, he had a funny-shaped head," Mr. Torres explains, ignoring Griff. "The doctors said he would grow out of it." He purses his lips. "He didn't."

"Oh my God." Griff rubs a hand over his face, then looks to me. "Any chance you can forget you heard that?"

"Nope." I shake my head, laughing.

"Let's leave the lovebirds alone, Cher," his dad says.

"Oh my God." Griff rolls his eyes. "Sorry," he says to me.

"Don't be. Watching you feel this uncomfortable is way too much fun."

"Thanks," Griff says, shaking his head.

We say bye to his parents and watch as the truck putters out of the campus's main gate. I didn't understand it at first, how Griff seemed so cavalier about telling me to play backup to my own song, but I get it now. When there's this much at stake and the odds are stacked up against you, what else can you do?

VISUAL	AUDIO
Wide shot of Cheralynne Torres in the kitchen of the Aloha Eats restaurant. Text on lower third: Cheralynne Torres, Mother of Griff Torres	Our Griff was always a natural-born musician. When he was only two, he would grab the spoons at the restaurant and bang on pots. All kids do it, yeah? But when Griff did it, oh my, did it sound good. Made everyone in the kitchen dance. [Dances in her seat.]
Wide shot of Thomas Torres in front of the Aloha Eats restaurant catering van, pointing to items. Text on lower third: Thomas Torres, Father of Griff Torres	We have the Griff T-shirt, the Griff apron, the Griff posters . . . he's a celebrity in our restaurant. Everyone is very kind. When they come, they ask about him. How he's doing. Does he have an album out yet? And we tell them, "Not yet. Soon, though. Very soon."
Wide shot of Cheralynne Torres in the kitchen of the Aloha Eats restaurant.	After the pandemic, people began blaming Asian people for the virus. As if it wasn't hard enough for our business to survive. We had a few challenges at our restaurant. Some windows smashed in and people spray-painting mean things. Thankfully, no one was hurt. [Whispers to camera.] Don't tell Griff. He assures me it's not like that at school, and with business getting slowly better, I can finally sleep at night. Now, all Griff has to do is focus on becoming a big star. Then it will be better for everyone.
Wide shot of Eunice Jo at her kitchen table. Text on lower third: Eunice Jo, Mother of Riley Jo	Riley's so different from our other daughter, Elise. Elise has many interests and can easily be diverted if needed. She's a free spirit, and I want her to stay that way for as long as possible. But Riley, she's singular and gets tunnel vision when it comes to her interests. She was really into musicals,

	and then after her last audition, when she didn't get the part, she stopped altogether. I think it's because she tends to put all her eggs in one basket. She's creative and also cerebral and introspective—there's so much going on in that mind of hers, I just don't understand her sometimes. Maybe that's why I don't understand her obsession with music.
Wide shot of Eugene Jo behind a desk with a placard that reads ACCOUNTANT. **Text on lower third:** **Eugene Jo, Father of Riley Jo**	When did Riley start the guitar? I don't know exactly when she started playing, but it was probably during middle school. During the pandemic, Riley got really into it. All of our other friends were complaining their kids were playing too much video games or YouTube twenty-four seven. [Shakes his head.] Not Riley. Morning, noon, and night, she was playing the guitar. It was great. Riley's mom doesn't get it, but I do. I know that spark in Riley's eye. The one she gets when she plays. I had the same when I used to write poetry. I'm glad Riley has a hobby that's similar to mine. It brings me so much joy, as I'm sure it does to her.
Wide shot of Eunice Jo at her kitchen table.	When the pandemic ended, I thought she'd go back to her normal life. [Shakes her head.] She didn't. We agreed to let her go to Carlmont, but honestly, I didn't think she'd get in. Not because she's not talented. We share walls with her; we know she's good. The website said that with very few spaces in the junior and senior classes and with a high volume of applicants, it's hard

	to get in. And it's a parent's job to worry about their child's future. Still, I'm glad she got this opportunity. You know, before she has to put her hobbies aside and focus on college.
Wide shot of Carly Rae Blake at her kitchen counter. **Text on lower third:** **Carly Rae Blake, Mother of Bodhi Collins**	I met Bodhi's dad at the Fort Lauderdale County Fair. He was doing one of those reboot tours, trying to relive his glory days. [Snorts.] It was a sad showing, and everyone who was there was either too old or too young to even know who he was. My girlfriend Jenna was a big fan of Boyz Club in the nineties. She dragged us there, and *Looooord*, she made such a spectacle. Even if she didn't, I'm sure they would have noticed us. We were the only ones between the ages of twenty-five and forty-five; true story. Anyway, after their set was over, Jenna made us go over there. She was trying to get with Blake. Ended up sucking face with Dex Then Blake did his signature eye thing he does with the camera where he squints, kind of like a wink, then nods. Yeah, it's cheesy, but it totally got me. We made some small talk about my last name being his first name and how if we got married and he took my last name, he'd be Blake Blake. Which, I know. It would have never happened. But you say stupid stuff when you're flirting, and boy, was that flirting. Nine months later came Bodhi. I hadn't kept in touch with Blake, so I didn't think I needed to when Bodhi came. When shit got hard— [Puts a hand to her mouth.] Oh, my bad. Is it okay if I say "shit"? Damn it, I said it again. Sorry.

Wide shot of Blake Collins on his patio, sunbathing. Text on lower third: Blake Collins, Father of Bodhi Collins	If you want some advice, kid, take it from me. You can't believe everything you hear. If I had a dime for everyone who talked shit about me, I'd be rich. I mean, richer than rich.
Wide shot of Carly Rae Blake at her kitchen counter.	So where was I [pauses] Oh, right. When Bodhi was five, I was in the middle of moving out of my mom's. Suddenly, I had to pay for rent and childcare, and it was too much. So I called him, and he remembered who I was as soon as I said, "Remember me? Blake Blake?" He was all too excited to hear from me. Then, as soon as I mentioned Bodhi, he couldn't get off the phone fast enough. Then he ghosted me completely. It wasn't until years later when I got one of those DNA-test thingies that he would talk to me again, and even then he wasn't willing to recognize Bodhi as his son. So I had to get a lawyer to send it to his business manager. That got his attention. Then he finally recognized Bodhi as his son. Poor thing.
Wide shot of Blake Collins on his patio, sunbathing.	Does it look like I'm being a bad father? I'm busting my ass trying to get him a record deal. Hell, I even invited the kids to my house to get them under Marc's nose. All I'm saying is, actions speak louder than words.

Wide shot of Carly Rae Blake at her kitchen counter.	I love my kid, but he was so quick to embrace Blake, even after the whole paternity scandal. It's almost insulting. Sure, Blake pays for Bodhi's fancy school tuition and music tutors, but Blake hardly sees Bodhi. Twice a year, three, tops. And always when the press is guaranteed to be around. That's not a dad. That's PR. I think deep down, Bodhi knows this, and I worry he's too infatuated with THE Blake Collins, famed music producer and former pop star. It's a lot of pressure Bodhi's putting on himself to get his dad's attention.
Wide shot of Blake Collins sitting on his couch at his Calabasas home with a grand piano in the background.	I'm invested in Bodhi, clearly. I mean, what kind of a dad would I be if I wasn't? Even still, I can't let nepotism cloud my judgment, so I've made myself clear to Bodhi. I'm not going to present them to Marc unless everyone in the band can show me they're ready.

TWENTY-TWO

By Monday I've had time to digest Blake's "marketing plan"—well, *digest* is a bit of an overstatement. More like vaguely chewed the suggestion, then swallowed it whole and crossed my fingers it would eventually come out the other end.

Surprisingly, what confuses me the most is talking to Aerie and Griff. They're both telling me to focus on the long game, only with very different approaches. On the one hand, Aerie is telling me to choose dignity over achievement and walk out on the band if it's not willing to change. On the other, Griff is telling me to choose achievement over dignity and be happy to be a small part of a big-name band, as opportunities like this don't come often. But my question is, why do I have to choose between the two? Why can't I have both?

What makes it even more unfair is knowing that Bodhi doesn't have to choose either of those things. That he's accepted not because of his talent or work ethic but because of his whiteness. Something I don't have and can never have, even if I tried. (Not that I would.)

Anyway, what's the point? I don't have an alternative, and with the year almost over, I have no choice but to agree to go with the Blake's marketing plan.

As soon as class gets started, Blake mentions the song needs to be rearranged to fit Bodhi's range. There's an awkward silence, which I then realize is because Blake's expecting me to work on it again. Is he for real?

"I'll make sure it gets done." Bodhi cuts in before I say something I might regret. "I got you." Bodhi nods his head up at me like he's doing me a favor. It's a wonder he can find a beanie big enough to fit his head. I only did all the work with coming up with the song, the lyrics, the arrangement, all of it. And now he's going to do the very simple task of changing the key to it and receive all the glory? I'm about to tell him as much, but the words get caught in my throat. Seriously, confrontation is my kryptonite.

"Great. Sounds like you guys know what to do. I'll leave you to it." Blake signs off, and now it's just the three of us. Griff fiddles with his drum kit, loosening and then tightening the screw on top of the hi-hat. A nervous tic of his I've noticed during our countless hours together. It's his tell. Guess that means he's not fully on board with this plan either, which motivates me to say something.

"Actually, I have an idea," I say, surprising Bodhi. I can't change who I am, but it's still my song. And that's something I can change. "Now that the song is becoming a solo, the song will be imbalanced. If you don't want it to sound flat, you're going to need a harmony." It's not much; I'll only be the backup singer. Still, it's better than having no voice in the song at all.

"You really think that's necessary?" Bodhi raises an eyebrow at the suggestion.

"Think about it. The chorus had two people singing alternate lines. Now we have one person doing it?" I give him a pointed look. "If we want to change it to a solo and keep it interesting, we have to add layers."

After a long, drawn-out pause that honestly seems unnecessary, he eventually nods. "Yeah, okay. I see your point."

"Why don't we try it again with the harmony? That way we can be sure," Griff suggests.

Bodhi agrees, and we go through what we have of the new version, ending with my harmony in the chorus. When we finish, Griff nods approvingly. "I think Riley's right. The harmony adds a richness to it. I like it."

"Fine," Bodhi says. Despite his reluctance, he asks me to repeat the harmony so he can jot down notes on the sheet music. So much for him doing the work. Whatever. At least I'm back in the song. Even if it's not a lot of words. At least it's something.

I leave the music room to find Xander leaning on the side of the building.

"Hey," he says, getting up and following me.

"Were you waiting for me?" I ask, looking around my shoulder. "Bodhi's probably coming anytime now if you want to make a run for it."

"What?" His face distorts in confusion.

"I mean, I won't be offended if you want to keep your distance because of what Bodhi insinuated the other day." I'd be more insecure of how pathetic I sound if it wasn't for the fact that Xander's had a front-row view of my pitiful downfall. "Xander's opinion of me is the least of my worries. The upside of hitting rock bottom.

His eyes grow wide. "Wow, so that's how little you think of me?"

I stop myself from correcting him by saying that's how little I think of *myself*. Turns out I do care about my last shred of dignity.

"Just saying, no one would judge you if you didn't want people to get the wrong idea." I keep walking, eyes forward.

"No one takes Bodhi seriously," he chuffs. It doesn't escape my attention that he neither confirmed nor denied his feelings about being romantically associated with me.

"Really? 'Cause according to the marketing polls, an 'overwhelming amount' of people would disagree."

He sighs heavily. "That was shitty; I won't disagree with you there. Just do me a favor and don't take it personally," Xander says.

This makes me stop. "*What?*" My eyes harden. It's so easy for him to tell me not to take it personally. He'd never be called out for not being American enough.

"Blake's got a history of . . . Well, let's just say he did this to Jake and Jeremy last year."

My position softens. "What happened with them?" Ever since Griff mentioned they left on principle, I've been meaning to ask.

Xander looks around as if to make sure no one's listening, which only adds to my already piqued interest.

"It's not really my place to say," he says cautiously. "Let's just say Blake told them what part they should play, and they didn't like it. So they left."

What does that mean? Did he tell them to play backup too? Or did he make them do all the work and get none of the glory? I have a million questions running through my mind.

"And seriously, don't worry about Bodhi. He's a douche."

My mouth betrays me, tugging up at the corners.

"Is that a smile?" he teases.

I can't help it. His argument is solid. Bodhi *is* a douche. "I thought you were friends with Bodhi," I say, remembering their connection.

"I am. Doesn't mean I don't call it like it is. Besides, he kind of had a rough start."

My brow arches way up. "Bodhi? What, like, did he have to

ride coach on planes or buy off the rack like the rest of us plebs?"

Xander doesn't crack a smile. "Bodhi's mom and dad were never together." He corrects himself. "I mean, they were *together*. Obviously. Just not a couple or anything. When Bodhi was born, she didn't even tell Blake. He found out when Bodhi was almost ten."

"What?" I'm not sure I heard him correctly.

"Yeah, the whole thing got really messy, and Bodhi lived with us for a little while. Anyway, he doesn't talk about it, so don't say anything to him." He puts a finger to his lips.

"I won't."

I always thought something was off with Bodhi and his dad. First of all, he calls his dad Blake, which I guess isn't that unusual in some circles. There's also the fact that I didn't see any evidence at Blake's house of a warm and fuzzy father-son vibe. Then again, that's not everyone's story. But now that Xander's told me the real story, it all makes sense.

"Anyway, I have to go to the editing room. I just wanted to check with you and make sure we're good. So are we cool?"

Hold up. I didn't realize that's what he was doing.

New revelation: Xander *cares* about what I think of him.

"We're cool," I say, even though I'm nothing of the sort.

As I watch him walk away, I try to figure him out. This doesn't involve the documentary and doesn't involve him. He didn't have to care, and yet he does. Why, though? Serious question.

Long after Xander is out of sight, I'm walking slowly in the direction of the dorms, still overanalyzing what this means, when I run into Aerie and Jason coming down toward me.

"Did you forget about ASA?" Aerie asks. "Doesn't matter, you can come with us." She links arms with me, and I follow her back down the hill I just walked up.

"I've been so distracted, I forgot that's happening now."

"Oh, what's with the look?" Jason sing-songs. "Is someone in love?"

"Is it Brandon?" Aerie clutches her chest, all hope.

"What? NO." I shut it down. "I had a good day with the band, that's all."

Aerie gasps. "You reported Blake? OMG, is Blake fired?"

"No, it's not that." I stop Aerie from getting ahead of herself. I'm about to tell her how I came up with a harmony that made me part of my song, then realize it makes me sound pathetic. And then I'd have to explain Griff's argument, which sounded convincing to me but won't be to her. Anyway, Aerie's been acting weird, which I suspect has something to do with my lack of contributions to the club, so I may as well just address it.

"Sorry I didn't have a chance to come up with a suggestion for the ASA project."

"It's okay. I'm sure you can contribute in other ways," she says, surprising me. Maybe I've been reading into it too much.

"Sure, I'd love to help." It's then I realize I haven't seen Nari in a while. "Is Nari coming?"

I swear Aerie and Jason tense up at the mention of Nari. What's that about?

"She's going to meet us there" is all Aerie gives me. We get to the classroom, and I don't have a chance to ask a follow-up question. As soon as the classroom is settled, Aerie and Jason start with the agenda.

"Thank you to everyone who submitted suggestions for this year's legacy project," Jason says. "We valued each and every one of your ideas. They were super creative—from skits, to songs, to a documentary short. We wish we could do them all."

"What struck us most was the different perspectives each suggestion had," Aerie says. "Some wanted to dismantle white normativity while others wanted to highlight Asian cultures. These ideas are no doubt a great way to reach a broad audience. Then it occurred to me . . . how can we focus on trying to get people to think we belong in this country when there are people here at Carlmont who don't think we belong?"

Heat begins creeping up my neck. Where is she going with this?

"It got me thinking that we should be more open about sharing our experiences with each other. My own roommate, Riley, was a victim of racial injustice right here at Carlmont. By her own advisor."

Oh my God, oh my God, oh my God. Make. It. Stop.

"There's real power in sharing our stories, and it's surprising how much support you can find right around you." Aerie leans over and asks me, "Do you want to come up and share with everyone what you've experienced?"

I'm good in front of an audience. But not like this.

I try reminding myself that Aerie is, and has always been, a good friend. I know she's trying to be helpful. Except I'm having a hard time seeing how Aerie thinks this is helpful. Feeling solidarity for being victimized, to me, feels like reliving the prejudice over and over. I just want to forget about it. Move on.

I shake my head. "Sorry" is all I can say.

A fleeting look of disappointment appears on her face before it's replaced with understanding. "I totally get it. Sorry for putting you on the spot."

"It's okay," I say. Her heart might be in the right place, but this is one serious leap.

"Th-the point is, even our faculty advisors are acting in ways that are downright racist," Aerie says, faltering. "If we want people to stop treating us like we're invisible, we have to make ourselves visible. We have to share our stories and make our voices heard." I swear she looks at me an extra beat when she says this. She goes on to explain the project. How they'll be collecting essays of people's journey in their Asian American identity, including their experiences with different degrees of racism, and turn them into an anthology to be kept in the library. That way we can leave our stories for future students of Carlmont. A noble if not meaningful cause. Still, that doesn't give Aerie the right to put me on the spot like that without a warning. I mean, we walked in together. We *live* together. She had every opportunity to bring it up with me, and she didn't.

Then, as soon as our meeting ends, she heads back to the dorms without waiting for me. Great, now she's acting as if I've let her down when she was the one who betrayed my trust. Which is so unfair.

Aerie wants me to be a poster child for this initiative, which is a spotlight I've never wanted. And even if I did, she should have asked me first before ambushing me in front of everyone. I've never liked being put in a position where I'm forced to be something I'm not. It's the same feeling I got when people expected me to be friends with Pring or to play K-pop. I'm even more offended knowing Aerie of all people is pigeonholing me the same way. What's more unfair is that she's expecting me to stand up there and speak openly about my experience when she's been insinuating that I'm not Asian American enough. She can't have it both ways.

The thing about boarding school is, is that there's no escape from it. Every hour of every day, you're at school. So I kinda feel the looks of judgment from kids in ASA not just at lunch but at all the meals. And not just during the day—at night too.

After study hours are over, I spend an extra long time in the shower, finding relief in the solitary confinement of the stall. When I start feeling guilty about the water waste, I turn it off. I'm putting my robe on and wrapping my hair in a towel when I hear some juniors come into the stalls next to mine. They're talking about me.

"Isn't that messed up?" the first girl says. "I get why she didn't want to be put on the spot at the moment, but she doesn't even want to share her written story with everyone else."

Holding my shower caddy in the damp stall is uncomfortable, and I'm dreading the direction this conversation is headed. But I can't seem to get myself to leave.

"It's because she's from Arkansas," the second girl says.

I am so sick of that being an excuse. Part of me is annoyed with Aerie since she's the one who's probably telling people that. Then again, I know that Aerie isn't responsible for everyone readily accepting my Arkansan origins as a viable excuse for not wanting to be at the center of this cause.

"Who even is from Arkansas?" the first girl asks.

"That family from *Duck Dynasty*?"

They both erupt in laughter.

Oh God. A familiar dread fills me. It's like I'm back in Bentonville.

"Girl, get your facts straight. The Robertsons are from Louisiana, not Arkansas," the first girl says.

"Louisiana, Arkansas, same diff."

They howl, like this is the funniest shit they've ever come up with.

I take it back. This is worse than Bentonville. It was easier when I knew the people making the comments were so different from me. Well-meaning white people who were just as starved of a diverse community as I was. Excusable at best, if not defensible. Rage bubbles in my chest. I've never felt at home in Arkansas, but who are they to judge? I'm guessing after their comment that *they've* never even been there. And thinking about it as some Podunk, uncultured town is as ignorant as the white supremacists who hurl racist slurs at random Asian people.

In Bentonville, my defense mechanism would flare up, and I'd be working overtime to show people their assumptions about me were wrong. But lately, it feels like it's more than just Bentonville. It's everyone. My band, Aerie, even my parents don't seem to understand who I am.

VISUAL	AUDIO
Wide shot of Blake Collins on Zoom.	The song's coming along, and it sounds real tight. I have to hand it to the technical crew at Carlmont. They really elevate the performance. But ... [Taps finger to his lips.] It feels like it's still lacking something. "Stardust" has the potential to be a hit. It's just missing that great hook. It doesn't have to be complicated; it can be, like, a one-liner that's catchy or a phrase that rolls off your tongue. It has to be that thing that ties the whole song together.
Wide shot of Bodhi Collins in the music room.	Everyone knows Marc is coming to the Spring Concert. It's all over the school's website, our socials. There's too much at stake for stupid mistakes like this. With the concert right around the corner, we have to fix it ASAP. We're lucky Blake caught it in time.
Wide shot of Riley Jo in the music room.	I told them that when you change a song from a duet to a solo, there's an entire element of the song that's being taken out. It's more than key changes; it's going to leave a hole. It's like if you're on a Ferris wheel and two people are sitting on opposite sides of the car. What happens when one person gets out? Yeah, it's like that.
Wide shot of Griff Torres in the music room.	Does it matter who said it first? The important thing is, we're addressing it now before the performance. There's a lot riding on this personally and professionally. My parents put everything they have into me. I mean everything. They're amazing people, but they don't have any connections in the music industry. If this doesn't work out, I'm not sure I'll have another chance like this again.

TWENTY-THREE

Xander's camera battery died, so he went back to change it out while we brainstorm how to fix the hole in our song.

"If we're going to add a bridge, it should be concise," I say.

"Agreed. Since it's a love song, we should add something sweet and sentimental," Bodhi adds.

"I mean, even though there are a lot of elements to the lyrics that suggest it's a love song, it's never explicitly mentioned," Griff says diplomatically.

"It's so obvious. *I always wanted to be your light*? It's got first-love vibes written all over it."

Despite not writing a single line in the song, it's impressive how Bodhi can speak with this level of authority.

"Well?" Griff isn't convinced.

"It's whatever you want it to be." I shrug.

"Ha!" Bodhi points at me. "I knew it. You just don't want to admit it."

"Um, not true. I prefer to leave it open-ended for people to interpret it however they want." That's probably as much as I'll admit. I may not be singing my song, but at least this way I can keep a tiny piece for myself.

"So you're saying it doesn't mean anything specific to you?" Griff narrows his eyes at me like he's not buying it.

"No, that's not what I'm saying. 'Stardust' has a deep and personal meaning to me. If I put it out there, then the song's about me. I want it to be for everyone."

"Can't you see how that doesn't help us when we're trying to create a bridge that encompasses the meaning of the song?" Griff usually doesn't get frustrated about anything. Seeing him get worked up about this one detail is startling. "Just tell us what it means, Riley."

I could easily tell him what "Stardust" means, but I don't want to. I shouldn't have to. I've given enough of myself to them, and I draw the line here.

I level my gaze with Griff's. "It's what you think it is." I enunciate each word so there's little room for misinterpretation.

"Hey-ho. Looks like we need to cool off." Surprisingly, it's Bodhi who's playing referee. "Why don't we sleep on it and come back tomorrow with some fresh ideas?"

Neither of us disagrees that we could use some time to think about the change, so we end practice early.

As if butting heads with my bandmates wasn't bad enough, my other classes are suffering from collateral damage. I haven't been able to finish the assignment in music composition about voice. After school, I go to find Ms. Morales to help me. The truth is, I'm not in the right headspace to be creative. I can't just turn it on when I need to. I'm not a machine.

Honestly, the way people are treating me, though, is like I'm supposed to be a machine. I'm supposed to turn it on for Aerie when she wants me to be the face of advocating for Asian voices.

I'm supposed to turn it on for my parents and be happy about coming back to Bentonville. I'm supposed to turn it on for the band and do all the work but remain invisible. In Bentonville, at least I had one thing I was trying not to be. Here there are so many. It's too much.

"Riley, is that you?" Ms. Morales says when she notices me standing in front of her room, a snotty mess.

I nod. With everything cycling through my head, I hadn't even realized I was crying.

"Hey, it's okay," she says, standing up and putting her arms out to hug me, then retracting her arms. "Sorry, I'm not supposed to hug students. You know, in case of misunderstandings. It's a preventative measure. I hate that a small percentage of sexual predators ruin it for the rest of us." She puts a hand to her mouth. "What I mean is, I wish I could give you a hug right now. You really look like you could use one." She hands me a tissue instead.

"Thanks." I take the tissue from her and wipe my nose.

"Do you want to tell me what's going on? I might not be able to give you a hug, but I can listen." She motions for me to sit in the chair across from hers, so I do.

"I haven't been able to complete the composition on voice. Everything I've tried just doesn't feel like me. Probably because I've been feeling like people are expecting me to be this or that, and I don't know what to think anymore." It all comes spilling out of me.

"Does this have to do with the song? Bodhi was here yesterday asking me to help change the key. I suspected this might happen."

"That's part of it. It's not all, though. I mean, I get that I have to be able to make some compromises if I want to be white-famous—sorry." I stop myself and wonder if I've offended Ms. Morales. "I mean famous."

She smiles kindly at me. "Riley, look at me. I'm a fair-skinned Latina from Mexico; people assume stuff about me all the time. And because I'm white-passing, I've heard a lot worse than that."

"So do you know what it means?"

"Of course! You want to be Britney, or Miley, or Taylor. And the industry says you can't, and you can never be like them."

Finally. Someone who understands. I'm relieved I don't have to explain myself. Or at least try to. And I always knew Ms. Morales was cool. So I tell her about everything. How every step of the way I can't do something without feeling like I'm letting someone down—my parents, Aerie, Griff, even Bodhi.

"I understand your frustrations, I really do," she says in that too-real way. And for a second, she looks like she herself might cry. Like this is a feeling she might have felt at one point in her life. "After listening to you, I'm hearing that most of it is rooted in other people's happiness. I haven't heard from you yet. What is it that you want?"

Her question takes me by surprise. No one's ever asked me what I want. It takes me a while to peel back all the layers to get to what started this chain of events.

"I just want to play music." It sounds so simple when I say it. But the reality of it is much more complex. "Is it impossible to think I can be like Taylor or Miley?"

"Do you think you're like Taylor or Miley?"

"Aside from their looks, I do think my sound is like them, like a blend of both of them."

"I'm not just talking about looks or your sound. There's a lot you need to do to get yourself recognized in the industry. Taylor

Swift's dad bought a record label just for her, and Miley Cyrus's dad is a country singer-songwriter and actor."

I stare, open-mouthed. I feel so stupid. I know a lot about musicians and bands; how come I didn't make this connection earlier?

Then again, my fascination was with the musicians. It's never been about the industry.

"That's not to say those women aren't talented in their own right. But they had a monumental leg up." She tilts her head at me. "All I'm saying is, it's a lot of pressure to put on yourself. Breaking into the music industry is hard enough. Don't think about being white-famous or even famous. Just think about being you. Remind yourself who you're playing for. Is it for others, or is it for yourself?"

After Ms. Morales's advice, I had a good night's sleep—well, more like an okay night's sleep. She's the first person to give me actual advice that doesn't leave me feeling resigned or frustrated. I still haven't been able to come up with any ideas on how to fix the song, though. I hope Griff and Bodhi had more luck because I'm counting on them.

During class later, Blake asks me, "Have you fixed the song yet, Riley?" His weathered face projected on the screen is staring at something off camera.

"Me?" I startle.

"Bodhi mentioned some disagreement with the song choice, and I think it's easier, considering the short notice of time, if you figured it out. You know what they say, too many cooks." He starts shuffling papers around, more focused on rearranging the clutter on his desk than actually giving me the time of day. "Anyway, since you wrote the song, you'll know how best to fix it."

All I can hear is the blood rushing to my head. "So let me understand this. I wrote the song but can't sing it, and every time there's a problem with it, I'm supposed to fix it? How can we call ourselves a band of inclusivity if this is how we're operating?"

It gets super quiet in the room. Blake stops what he's doing, making it look like his screen is frozen. Griff and Bodhi are distancing themselves from me, which is not reassuring whatsoever.

"If you're unhappy, Riley, no one's forcing you to stay," Blake says, breaking the silence.

I think about what Xander told me, how Jake and Jeremy felt like they had no choice but to leave. And as Griff pointed out, it didn't really work to their advantage. So I hesitate. Quitting is only going to make things worse for me. It's not even about being famous, white or otherwise. Ms. Morales asked me if I want to play for others or for myself. And the sad truth is, I won't be able to play for anyone, let alone myself, if I walk away from here. So my only choice is to stay.

"Attagirl," Blake says, which doesn't make me feel good like his compliments used to. I feel stupid for thinking he saw something special in me that day when I performed my song at his house. Because it wasn't me he saw at all.

In the dorms, I spill everything to Aerie. I pace back and forth in the room, telling her about how even though the song's been taken away from me, I'm the one doing all the work. It's just so unfair. By the time I'm finished, I'm so amped up, I'm out of breath.

"I'm confused," she says, which kinda catches me off guard. In the past, she's gotten up in arms about issues I thought weren't that big of a deal. Now I'm telling her a huge deal, and she's just . . . confused? I thought she'd be pissed. I thought she'd be outraged by my outrage. I thought she'd *care*.

"Didn't you see this coming?" Her brows furrow.

"What do you mean?" Part of me wonders if I heard her correctly.

"I mean, you didn't speak up the first, second, or even third time you were discriminated against. What they did to you is wrong, but you had every chance to do something, and you didn't. You basically gave Blake permission to keep taking advantage of you," she says matter-of-factly.

"So you're saying that because I didn't report him, I asked for this to happen to me?" I can't believe those words are even coming out of my mouth—out of *Aerie's* mouth.

Sitting at her desk, Aerie twists her body to face me. "Of course I don't think you asked for it, but you set yourself up for disappointment. How many times did we ask you to submit a complaint to the administration office about Blake? Or to share your story at ASA?"

"That's so unfair!" My hands flail at my sides. "You put me on the spot before I was ready to share my story."

"Fine. I should have asked you if it was okay to call you up, and I'm sorry. I only did it because I thought that's what you wanted."

"Why would you think that?" My brows clench so hard trying to make sense of what she's saying.

"Because it was easier for me to believe that you needed help than to think you'd intentionally not speak out about your advisor." Her eyes soften just a notch. "Riley, I tried to be a good friend to you. I saw you hurting, and I hurt for you. And when you turned away your chance at sharing your story, I was hurt. It made me realize I can't help you if you don't want to help yourself."

"What's that supposed to mean?"

"Being able to talk to each other is great, and I'm glad we have a community here to do that. But at some point, you're going to have to take action. And I just wonder, what's it going to take for you to *go there*?" She sighs as if I'm too much for her. Seriously, though, she's not the only one who was hurt.

"Because I didn't want to talk about my experience in a public setting, you think I don't want to help myself? You make it sound like there's only one way of being Asian American, and I'm tired of feeling like I'm not acting like one. I mean, we can't all be like you."

"*What?*" It's Aerie's turn to be offended.

"You and Nari keep saying I'm from Arkansas like it's an excuse for not being Asian American enough, or that I've got white fever. How's that supposed to make me feel?"

"We didn't mean it like that."

"How else is it supposed to be meant? When people look at you, you are what people think you're supposed to be—you speak Korean, understand the culture, play classical music, and have Korean American idols like Sarah Chang. When people look at me, I'm nothing like what they expect—I don't speak Korean, I don't play K-pop, and none of my idols look like me. I didn't grow up with an Asian American community, and it might take some time for me to be comfortable enough to *go there*. And because I can't make that leap overnight, you're going to hold that against me?"

"If you think I've got it any easier than you, you're wrong." Aerie points an angry finger at me. "You think it's easy growing up with parents like mine? I have to work harder than most to keep up with a culture that isn't around me. And if you think it's any easier in orchestra, then you're sorely mistaken. Nari and I might be cochairs this year, but then what? I just found out that the graduating class at Juilliard is almost fifty percent Asian, and yet all the major symphonies and orchestras are a fraction of that. Asians are the most non-underrepresented minority in the classical music industry. You think you're the only one who deals with this type of injustice? Racism exists *everywhere*. Why do you think I'm so active in ASA? Because I'm frustrated too!"

Someone knocks on our door. It snaps us out of our argument.

"Quiet down in there, ladies." It's our dorm head, Ms. Nelson. We stand in silence, staring at the ground. Neither of us moves for what feels like an eternity. Our whole conversation is a blur. Like after waking up from a dream, it's distorted and disjointed when I try to remember it.

Did I—

Did she—

Did *we* really say those things to each other?

Later, when we're in bed and the lights are off, Aerie says, "We all have a responsibility, Riley. Whether you're in orchestra or pop rock. Whether you're from LA or Arkansas."

I don't say anything back. Maybe she'll think I'm sleeping.

TWENTY-FOUR

I hardly slept last night. Aerie's words kept gnawing at me. I was mad when we argued. Now, I'm not sure what to think.

On my way to lunch, I'm lost in my thoughts when footfalls close in on me.

"It's spaghetti time, Jo." Xander appears next to me with a huge grin on his face.

"What?"

"I've been thinking about it since you told me about the questionable pairing. I think I'm brave enough to try it," Xander says, rubbing his hands together.

I don't say anything at first. No one's forcing him to try it. Not sure if he wants me to throw him a parade or something. Then again, it's not Xander I'm mad at. He just caught me in a salty mood.

"Okay," I say with a forced smile.

Just then, Bodhi flies past us. "What's up, you two?" His brows bounce up and down suggestively. "Have you hit that yet, Xan?" Of course he waits 'til he's far out of reach to say that, coward that he is. And bonus, because he's far, he yelled it, and a few other students start catcalling.

"Up yours, Bodhi," Xander says without faltering. Then he turns his attention back to me. "As far as pickles go, does it matter what type? Like, can they be dill, sweet, or even the fancy cornichons?"

I eye him suspiciously. Is he seriously unfazed by Bodhi and the other catcallers?

"What?" He peers over at me, confused. We're standing right outside the dining hall doors, and I realize what's bothering me.

"Why do you let Bodhi talk to you, talk to *me*, like that? If he's your friend, why don't you say something to him?" I can't help but think about the incident on Halloween when my mom told me that the best we can do is hope that someone like Professor Wilkins, or in this case Xander, speaks up for us. Because when people like them speak up, others take it more seriously.

He swats a hand. "It's just Bodhi. When it comes to him, you just have to learn to shake it off. He's gone through some stuff, and I think that some of his antics are because he knows I know about the past he's trying to forget about. With Bodhi, you just have to understand that it's not personal."

Xander might be able to excuse Bodhi, but I can't. Not while we're sharing the same space in the band.

"Hey, are we going to get lunch or . . . ?" He looks around, utterly confused at why I've stopped.

"I'm not hungry," I say. As let down as I am with Xander, I'm more upset with myself for expecting him to stand up for me.

I go to the library for the rest of lunch since there's way too much idle time left before class starts. And honestly, if I'm not going to walk out of the band, I might as well get to work. The lyrics aren't going to write themselves.

Seriously, I could give myself a brain aneurysm from the eye rolls. How is it that no matter what I do, it's always one step forward and two steps back? I'm beginning to think that maybe Aerie is right. Maybe I don't want to help myself.

In fact, the more I think about it, the more her words ring true. Every step of the way, I've been given a choice. I could've walked away at any time, and I didn't because I thought this was the only way. My self-pity turns to rage. Rage swells in me like a hive of angry bees. The familiar sensation of too many feelings rising. There's only one thing I can do when I'm filled with this kind of restless energy.

Instead of fixing the lyrics to "Stardust," I pick up my pen, grab a notebook, and start scribbling. I think about how Griff doesn't say the things he feels. And how my mom felt pressure not to speak up in her workplace. And the countless times I'd been too scared to bring up the fact that people were putting their racial biases on me because I didn't want to make things harder for me than they already were. It's not that we're being silent. It's that we're being *silenced*. There's a big difference. We want to say the things that matter, but we don't feel like we can.

I left Bentonville to get away from being misunderstood. I came to LA thinking it would be about the music. And now the sad truth is, I've felt more discrimination and blatant racism in this industry than in all my years in Bentonville. Aerie's right: At some point, something's going to force me to go there. So I let myself go there.

Go There

Am-C-Em-Am

Shut up and shut down
Turn that frown right round
How many ways can you say
I'm not enough?

Each step that I'm taking
Every choice that I'm making
Is tearing me down while it's tearing me up

I might be shooting for the stars
Even though I know I won't be getting very far
Because this world wants, yes, this world wants me to go
nowhere
So instead, I'm going to go there
Yeah, instead, I'm going to go there

At under an hour, it's the fastest I've ever written a song before. With only a few minutes left during lunch period, I march over to the sound booths, clutching my scribbled notebook and guitar. Surprisingly, there's an open spot, and I race over before anyone else can claim it. I press record on my phone facing me, and I put the lyrics to music. It sounds exactly the way I hoped it would. It's hurt and disappointed. It's hopeless and bleak. It's not a song that evokes joy whatsoever. A stark contrast to "Stardust." Probably the most revealing song I've ever written. I think about what to do after the adrenaline subsides. If Blake's marketing team or whoever has an issue with me singing "Stardust," I'm pretty sure "Go There" isn't going to win them over. But it's too important to just keep to myself. So after thinking about my options, I decide to post it on my TikTok account, which I've been neglecting. And at the very least, I feel better about releasing some of the anger. Which is what I need to get through the Spring Concert.

Days go by, and before I know it, it's showtime.

The Spring Concert is a weeklong event. Monday it's musical theater since it takes the longest to get the stage set up. The orchestra is playing the background, so Aerie's been preoccupied with that. Tuesday, the film department showcases their projects, ranging from short films to docs. Xander got special permission to show his after our performance since he wants to include that in the final cut. Orchestra is a two-day event because it's such a large portion of the program at Carlmont. Wednesday, the whole symphony performs, and Thursday is for soloists. Aerie is chosen as one of the violin soloists, and her performance moves me to tears. Not because she's an exceptional violinist (which, for the record, she is). But because I know that talent alone isn't enough to secure her spot as a musician at Juilliard, or any other orchestra out there. My heart breaks for her, and I feel so self-involved for thinking I'm the only one struggling to fit in in my surroundings.

Later that night, after she comes back from dinner with her parents, I muster up enough courage to approach her. With her performance over, we can't keep pretending we're too busy to talk. One of us has to take the initiative. Might as well be me (for once).

"Aerie, I know things are weird between us. And I miss you."

At this, she exhales, and I can tell relief fills her. "OMG, me too. I've been so worried that you hated me." She steps closer to me.

"What? How could I? You were the one that was always there for me, and you gave me a hundred every time. And you weren't wrong. We all have responsibilities, and I need to own that." I shift, fidgeting with a loose thread in my sleeve. "But if I'm being real with you, I was hurt that you chose to share something I told you in confidence to make a point."

"Riley, I am so sorry for putting that added pressure on you. I shouldn't have pushed you to share something you weren't ready to. The truth is, I was envious of you."

"What?" Her words are a complete surprise.

"Sometimes I think I could do more for the Asian American community if I were in your position. Like I could do more if I weren't in orchestra. Because it's something people expect of someone like me, so I can't even challenge the stereotype. If I were like you, though, people would have to listen. They'd have to hear what I had to say. And believe me, I'd have a lot to say. I just wish I had the platform to be in that spotlight. Guess I was trying to live my secret dreams through you, and it was wrong of me."

Hearing Aerie say she's envious of me throws me for a loop. I never considered myself to be in a position anyone would want to be in. It helps me understand why Aerie would push me to do something so unlike me.

"I appreciate it." I say. "While we're apologizing for stuff, I shouldn't have made the assumption that things were easier for you just because you had more community support or because you played orchestra. I'm really sorry for stereotyping you the way I hate being stereotyped."

We both share a smile, and the tension instantly evaporates.

"Friends again?" I ask.

"There is no 'again.' We've always been friends." Aerie hugs me, and I hug her back. When we release from the hug, Aerie's face turns pensive.

"Can I ask you a question?"

"Of course," I say.

"Riley—and don't take this the wrong way—but do you . . . only like white guys?"

I try to give Aerie the benefit of the doubt. It's hard to, though, with a question like this. "What do you mean?" I say in the nicest way possible.

"Well, Nari . . . she's kind of upset."

"I thought she might be. Is it over the ASA stuff too?"

"Not exactly. You know that crush she has? The one she's being tight-lipped about?" When I nod, Aerie continues. "Well, it's Brandon."

"Brandon? You mean—"

"The one who has a crush on you."

As revealing as the news is to me, I'm having a hard time following where this is going.

"I told you and Nari, though. I don't like Brandon."

"Right. Because you like . . ."

I blink.

"Come on, Riley. Are you going to make me say it?"

"Say what?"

"Okay, fine. I'll just get to my point. Nari thinks you don't like Brandon because he's Asian and that you only like white boys."

I try not to take my frustrations out on Aerie, especially since we just made up, but I can't help it. This is super frustrating.

"First of all, I don't know how that's relevant. If I don't like Brandon, I don't like him. Shouldn't matter why. I mean, do you like every Asian boy who has had a crush on you?"

"What?" Aerie is taken aback.

"Because that's how ridiculous it sounds to me. You're talking in absolutes when this is my first crush ever. I hardly have a track record for you to call me out on anything, so it just feels like unfair judgment. And if I only like white boys, why does that bother Nari when the bottom line is none of my decisions have anything to do with the fact that Brandon doesn't like her?"

"I understand what you're saying. And I can't speak for Nari. I can only try to explain why it could be perceived as problematic." She pauses, gathering her thoughts. "It's like . . . some people don't like when an Asian woman only date white men, because they think it's a relationship based on hierarchy. That Asian women see white men as superior, physically or socially or both, or that it perpetuates the stereotype that white men see Asian women as submissive."

I blow out a sharp breath, motioning a hand going over my head. "That's way deeper than it actually is. If I understand what you're saying, then you've got it all wrong. This thing with Xander . . . it's based on a feeling. A spark. Chemistry. The feels—all the other romantic clichés."

"Look, I believe you, and you don't have to prove yourself to anyone. If you like him, you like him. You should be with someone who gives you butterflies, someone who treats you right. But, like, you can see how others might think that about you. Especially seeing how you are with your band, the way you seem to be prioritizing their needs before yours—it seems like a pattern. That you see yourself as inferior to white people."

Her words sit like a brick in my stomach. That's what it seems like?

TWENTY-FIVE

It's the day of our concert, and I'm on pins and needles. I put on my outfit for the performance—distressed jeans and a loose-fitting top, aptly chosen to provide max ventilation for the perspiration that's already an issue. Which reminds me to double up on the antiperspirant.

Just before I get to the theater, my phone rings. A FaceTime call from Elise. I'm not really in the headspace for an Elise conversation. If I don't take this call, though, she'll send a thousand emojis I definitely won't have enough in me to decipher. So I pick up.

"Hi!" Mom, Dad, and Elise say in unison. They're all scrunched together in a car.

"We just wanted to wish you good luck today," my dad says.

"Sorry we couldn't be there," my mom says, even though she doesn't look that sorry. In fact, it looks like she's hiding a smile.

"It's okay, and thanks for calling." Then I notice the car looks different. "Did you get a new car?"

The three of them look around at one another.

"My car's in the shop. It's not a big deal." My dad tries to brush it off.

"What happened?" I ask. Something tells me there's more to the story.

"Are you nervous?" Elise asks, changing the subject.

"Yeah, is it that obvious?"

"We know you're going to be great. We wish we could be there to see it." Even my dad is acting weird.

"What's going on? What happened to your car, and where are you?"

"We took Elise somewhere," my mom says, and I sort of get it. Knowing them, they probably are on some big trip for Elise's sake and aren't mentioning it to me because they don't want to hurt my feelings. If they didn't want to hurt my feelings, then they should have prioritized my interest in music for a change. I guess that's too much to ask, though. Whatever. I don't want to get into it. Especially now.

"Well, good luck, Riley. We're rooting for you," Dad says.

"We're with you in spirit!" Mom says before we hang up.

Backstage, I spot Bodhi and Griff right away. Bodhi's pacing while muttering lyrics to himself, and Griff is practicing his part on an imaginary drum kit.

"Whoa, is that a tie?" I point to the slim black tie hanging off of Griff's neck. His hair is freshly dyed platinum blonde.

"Don't ask." He rolls his eyes at himself. "My parents put me up to it." He snorts.

"Looking smart there, Riley," Bodhi says when he sees me.

"Looking pretty much the same there, Bodhi." I eye him up and down. He's got the same beanie on his head, with a T-shirt hanging over his skinny jeans.

"Haters gonna hate," he says, probably at my clearly unimpressed tone.

"Slackers gonna slack," I let slip out. I don't know where that came from. Actually, I do. After Aerie pointed out how my choices seem like I'm prioritizing Bodhi's needs over mine, it's been gnawing at me. I've been going along with Blake's marketing plan, a plan that benefits Bodhi, so I don't make Bodhi uncomfortable. In return, for the sake of his comfort, I end up bearing the brunt.

"What was that?" Bodhi asks. I can tell he didn't fully catch what I said.

I want to tell him it's unfair that he didn't do the work but is getting all the credit. That it's unfair that because he's a white male, he doesn't have to prove himself; he can just be. The words are at the tip of my tongue, and for once, I don't feel anything holding me back.

"RGB, we're ready for you!" Of course it's that moment that the stage manager calls us over for a sound check. The irony is, I'm finally finding my voice, but it's too late.

We do a run-through of the song. The whole time, I'm eyeing Bodhi. The entire performance feels wrong even though it sounds okay. But by this point, with people trickling into the auditorium, the moment to say something has definitely passed.

While we wait for the auditorium to fill up, we hang back in the green room. Nervous energy overflows the room like bad cologne. I pace the small rectangular space blocked off by PVC pipes with curtains hanging from them. Bodhi and Griff go check to see if their families have arrived. I don't join them since I know mine isn't out there.

This day is supposed to be the culmination of the year. To showcase the thing we've been working all year for. And for me, it meant something else. My ticket out of Bentonville. All

I've ever really wanted was to be understood, and music has been the only way I can express myself. But if I go out under these pretenses, not having a voice in my own song, then I'll be no better off than I would have been staying in Bentonville. It eats at me to know that after a year at Carlmont, I've made no real progress.

"Just confirmed Marc is with Blake." Bodhi comes over from peeking behind the curtain. "So get your game faces on."

Griff comes back looking sheet white. "Oh my God, my cousins are here too."

"What's wrong with that?" I ask.

"My dad is the oldest of five, and my mom is the middle of six. Each one of them have at least three kids in their family. You do the math."

"Oh wow." When he said large family, I thought two or three siblings. Four, max. He's talking *big* big.

When we hear the announcer over the sound system welcoming Blake to the stand, we snap to attention. Next thing I know, I'm being herded onto the stage.

We find our marks in the center of the unlit stage while the spotlight is shining on a podium off to the side. Blake gets up on the podium, and the crowd erupts for him, a celebrity in his own right. He pretends he doesn't love it, trying to settle them down. When the crowd starts to lull, he does his lame signature move, angling his face and cocking one eyebrow up at the audience, like he's saying, *Hey, girl*, and the audience goes nuts again.

When it finally gets quiets, he says, "Today is a big day. And not just because it's Carlmont's annual Spring Concert. We also have Marc Rubinstein in the audience with us." Another huge burst of applause while he gets Marc to stand up. Even if he didn't stand up, I could spot him easily in his low-cut T-shirt, dripping in gaudy jewelry.

Once everyone settles down again, Blake continues. "I'm proud to represent RGB, a brand that encompasses our band not just by name but by what it represents. RGB stands for red, green, and blue—the primary colors of light. Not only that, but red, green, and blue can be combined to get any color on the visible spectrum. And like the colors, we want people to know that this isn't just a band for everyone. It also represents everyone."

Not one mention of me coming up with the idea, which is not surprising. What is surprising, though, is how he motions to us first collectively, then pauses an extra-long time on me and Griff as if he's presenting us as props for his diversity project.

"We don't see color. We see love." He does the stupid prayer hands. "And with that, I present to you RGB," he says, then disappears offstage.

That's it. The final straw that breaks me. I can't hold it in anymore. When the spotlight turns its attention to us, something clicks in me.

The next thing I know, without having control over what I'm doing, I'm walking up to the mic positioned in front of Bodhi. He glares at me, but in his shock, doesn't move. The applause tapers off, and I'm not sure what I'm going to say, yet I hear my tinny voice through the speaker.

"Blake's right. We don't see color here. In fact, you don't see me at all; isn't that right?" I don't even know who I'm asking. Blake, Bodhi, Griff? The audience shifts around. Dr. Buckley, our headmaster, looks over at Blake for his reaction.

I realize I've started something I can't stop, so I might as well stop resisting it and "Go There."

"If you're like me and you're tired of being overlooked, under-valued, and misinterpreted—" I snort. "I mean, how many of you think I'm going to sing K-pop when you see me?" The question hits with a thud. My ears are ringing from the silence. People look embarrassed *for* me.

I should probably be embarrassed. Surprisingly, I'm not. I think I'm too numb or something because I can't feel anything at all.

Griff and Bodhi slowly move away from me, offstage. Apparently I'm too much for them too.

"I see. You're happy to have me in the band if I'm quiet and do all the work. The minute I start wanting to be valued, I'm too much—invisible when it counts, visible when it doesn't." I adjust my guitar. "Well, here's what I have to say to that."

Without thinking, I launch right into "Go There." I haven't even had time to play it since I recorded it, which I did in one shot. So technically, I've only played this song once all the way through. Doesn't matter, though. All I know is that this is the only way I can fully express myself, and I'm going for it. At Blake's house, when I first performed "Stardust," Marc said he liked the raw confessional style of my music. Wonder what he's going to think of my performance today.

My voice comes out angry and at times rage-y. Some of my high notes even sound guttural. More than anything, it's honest. It's an honest look at what it feels like to be misunderstood by the people around me. How it feels to be overlooked and under-valued by my bandmates. And what it feels like being taken advantage of by an industry I've had my heart set on. By the end, I'm panting, staring up at the lights, with my arms stretched out to the sides like a goddamn hero.

Only when my eyes adjust back to the audience, I come down from my high.

Because this performance was completely unplanned, the sound engineers weren't prepared, and the feedback from the mic screeches through the speakers when I finish. The entire audience flinches. Marc and Blake are gone. Dr. Buckley is glaring at me, his arms folded across his chest. And I can only imagine how pissed Bodhi and Griff are at me.

Suddenly, like a light switch has turned on, I feel like I've been caught naked onstage. A good portion of the audience left mid-performance. The righteous indignation I felt earlier turns to embarrassment in an instant. Regret hits me at once. My whole life I wanted to be like everyone else so that the average person could relate to me. How can anyone relate to me after *that*?

I'm about to do the walk of shame off the stage when the remaining audience starts doing something I don't expect. They clap. There are a few people who stand, and it signals others to stand. Soon everyone is on their feet. They're all cheering for me. At least the audience that chose to stay for the entire performance gets my song—they get me. I see Aerie in the audience, jumping up and down, screaming for me. Even Jason and Brandon are whistling loudly. And I can't help but feel proud of myself. I finally said the things I wanted to say.

Then I see them. Mom, Dad, and Elise, sitting in the front row.

TWENTY-SIX

I have to fight the crowd to get out of the theater. People all around make way for me, staring with polarizing looks. Half of them stare in admiration, the other half like I'm a circus attraction. Whatever. If it doesn't blow over by next week, I'll be out of here next month. Besides, if it wasn't apparent by my performance, I no longer care what people here think of me. The only people I care about now are my family.

After I spot them in the crowd, I take them to the back lot of the campus. Now that the theater department's performance is over, it's quiet in these parts.

"What are you guys doing here?" I say to my parents.

"We thought we'd surprise you. But wow, we were the ones who were surprised." Mom forces a smile that I can tell she's doing for Elise's benefit, not mine.

"That was . . . something." Dad pats me on the shoulder with an equally forced smile.

"You killed it, Ry! That was fire!" Elise says, handing me a bouquet of grocery-store flowers.

"Thanks." I take them from her. I can tell she's genuinely impressed, unlike my parents, who are clearly pretending.

"If I'd known you were coming, I wouldn't have—"

"Let's talk about that later," Mom says, cutting me off. "We have big plans for this weekend."

Yes, that's right. Let's pretend something ugly didn't happen for Elise's sake. And it's okay because they're making a bad decision to avoid a worse one. *Right?*

Then again, I don't say anything while they proceed to tell me our weekend plans because I don't want to cause A Scene. So maybe I'm being a hypocrite.

My parents fill me in on the rest of their surprise, which is a trip to Disneyland and a day at the Santa Monica Pier. I'd be stoked if I hadn't just thrown away my one chance at a record deal. *FML* doesn't even begin to cover it. I go back to my dorm and pack a weekend bag. On my way back to my parents' rental car, I spot Xander walking toward me.

"Is everything okay?" he asks, face full of concern.

I sigh, shaking my head. Now that some time has passed since the performance, I'm second-guessing everything.

"Your performance? What . . . was that?"

My mood shifts when I see from his expression that he's not concerned for me. He's *embarrassed* for me. My cheeks flare.

"Do you think I made a mistake?" I ask, unsure of what to make of his reaction.

"I don't know what to think. Honestly, you kind of lost it in there."

"*I* lost it?" I let out a sound like a balloon deflating. "Blake humiliates me in front of the whole school, and you think *I* lost it?"

"No one thought you were humiliated. If you had gone on with the performance—"

"Then what? We would've gotten a record deal, and all my

problems would be solved?" I let out a humorless laugh. "That's not the way it goes for people like me. You of all people should know how effed up it is."

"Me?" His head jerks back. "I'm the one checking in with you to see if you're okay."

"You think checking up on me is going to make everything better?" It was naive of me to think that Xander and I could have a friendship without talking about race. Not only is it a big part of who I am, but there's a bigger picture we're both part of that shouldn't be ignored. The system that puts people like him on the top and me on the bottom.

"I'm trying," he says in a strained voice. "What do you want from me?" There's a look of regret on his face like it was a huge mistake coming here.

"I want you to take responsibility for the part you played in it." I started this tirade; I can't stop now. Now that he's here, I'm going to tell him what's bothering me. "The world of entertainment and music is overwhelmingly white. The odds are already stacked against people like me, and then here you are, son of so-and-so, and you'll get the job not just because you worked hard to get there but because you have the right parents and the right look. The system is built for people like you to succeed. So whether or not you don't think you have anything to do with what's happening to me, you're wrong. You're part of the problem."

"Wow." He slow blinks, letting out an incredulous laugh. "This is the thanks I get for trying to be a friend? You're taking out your aggression for an *entire industry* on me, and I'm the one being effed up?"

"Let me ask you something. Are you going to put any of this in the doc?"

He raises an eyebrow.

"I mean, a documentary *by definition* is a film based on factual events. I assume you're going to include Blake's bad behavior with how he treated Jake and Jeremy and me."

Xander avoids my eye.

"Or Bodhi and his insecurities about his past. Is that going to make it into the doc?"

I didn't want to believe that Xander could be this superficial, but his face tells it all.

"Unbelievable," I say like a sigh.

"It's not what it looks like. I just don't want to cause trouble," he says. That's when I lose it.

"You think I do?" I seethe. "All I've ever wanted to do since I got here is not cause trouble because I have too much at stake. But you? You don't have to worry about your future; you're all set. And yet you *still* can't be bothered," I say. "Maybe Blake's not the only one who's colorblind. Maybe you are too."

"What is it you want from me?" he says, avoiding my eyes.

"All I want for you is to recognize that this isn't fair."

He's silent, which disappoints me.

"And you can't even give me that."

I leave to find my parents. They've been waiting for me for a while now; I was beginning to worry they were going to come look for me and accidentally overhear my argument with Xander. As I approach the car, it's clear by their expressions that they've witnessed everything. They might have heard everything. And yet when we make eye contact, they plaster on their smiles.

Elise doesn't even notice me getting into the car because she's on her iPad, which I know is being used as some shield. They probably just handed it to her as soon as they saw me talking to

Xander. It's like she's in a soundproof room when she's on that thing.

"Everything okay?" My parents crane their necks to face me in the back seat. I figure if they're going to ask me a ridiculous question, I'll answer them in an equally ridiculous way.

"Peachy."

The next morning, we wake up at the ass crack of dawn. Even though Disneyland doesn't open until eight, Elise wants us to be the first ones at the gates when they open. And what Elise wants, Elise gets.

I'm not really mad at her; I'm just mad. I did the thing I thought I was supposed to do: stand up for myself. Why does it feel worse than before?

Most of the morning, I'm quiet. I can easily pass that off as being tired and cranky. Something I don't have to try hard to convince anyone of since I've never been a morning person. As soon as the gates finally open, though, I plaster a smile on my face because I'm officially at Disneyland. Literally the happiest place in the world.

The rides are a good distraction, and after the first one, I don't have to fake my smile anymore. Plus it's nice to hang out with Elise again. The phone calls only show snippets of our lives, and I'd forgotten how infectious her free-spirited personality is. Being with Elise is easy; she fills the silence with her endless knowledge of random facts about the theme park. How Mr. Disney's office was once in the pink castle, how the land used to be an orange grove, etc., etc. And seeing her happy makes me happy. Truly.

The next day, however, we're not at Disneyland, and there's less chatter to fill the void. If Disneyland is the state of California, Santa Monica Pier is Catalina Island. That is to say, small by comparison. There's a Ferris wheel that Elise wants to go on. I don't like them much because being suspended in the sky in a tin can–like contraption is seriously not my idea of fun. My dad, God bless him, is a saint and obliges her even though I know he's just as scared of heights as I am.

As if on cue, the second Elise is out of sight, my mom opens up to me.

"I talked to the assistant dean at Bentonville U about you," she starts, hesitantly.

"You did?" Guess I should show more interest since that's all I have left.

"I told him you wanted to continue pursuing your music education in addition to your undergraduate degree. Since there isn't a music department there, he agreed to let you do an independent study."

"Wait, what?" I'm not sure I heard her right.

"There would be assignments of course. You'd have to write papers on how you're furthering your music knowledge. That is, if your deal with Marc is still happening." She treads carefully, then nudges me with a smile. "Who says your mom doesn't have connections?"

If this were a month ago, I'd be over the moon. Mom's finally come around to supporting me, or at least her version of it. She's even made it possible for me to go to college like we agreed.

"Thanks, Mom." My enthusiasm is muted.

"I thought you'd be more excited." She cocks her head to the side, her brows furrowed.

"I am . . . but . . . I don't know if I'll be working with Marc."

Mom stares at me curiously, and I know I have to tell her everything. So I tell her everything, starting with the first day of school, when Blake assumed I played K-pop, right up to my performance.

When I'm done, she sighs, pulling me in for a hug. "Oh, Ry," she says, and I start to cry into her shoulder. "I knew this might happen."

I pull back, staring at her. "You *knew* this might happen?" The tears in my eyes dry up almost instantly.

"And now you have not one but two college acceptances to choose from." She smiles as if to say, *You're welcome*.

I'm not glad I'll be going back to Arkansas; in fact, my mom's reaction is bringing up all the reasons why I don't want to go.

"Can you hear yourself? Because it sounds like you're saying you've been waiting for me to fail."

"Oh my gosh, Ry. No. It's not that I'm waiting for you to fail. I just remember how crushed you were when you didn't get the part of Cosette. I can't watch you go through a lifetime of that. No parent would. I did what I thought was best for you."

"That's where you're wrong. I was upset with the *Les Mis* audition because I thought I didn't get the part because I didn't look like Cosette." I motion around my face, and my mom's own face falls, understanding my meaning. "Then when I got to Carlmont, my advisor did it to me again. But this time, he openly used my Asianness against me."

Mom sniffs. "Can't you see why I wouldn't want this for you? No parent wants to see their child struggle."

"Even if it was hard, it would have been less hard if you supported me." I try to keep my frustration in check. "For so long I didn't think you believed in me, and it made me lack the confidence or the conviction in myself. I'm not saying it's your fault. I just wish we could have been more honest with each other." This time I'm not only talking about her support in my music. It's everything.

"Riley." Her voice quivers. "I'm so sorry—"

At that moment, Elise comes skipping toward us. "Did you see us? We were waving to you from way up there." She points to the top of the Ferris wheel. "I was yelling at the top of my lungs. Did you know that sound travels faster in warmer air than colder air? I'm not sure it worked because you didn't look up when I was trying to get your attention. Isn't that right, Dad?"

Dad picks up on our tense mood, unlike Elise, whose only flaw—aside from being spacey—is not being able to read the room. He tries to steer Elise away from us and onto the Third Street Promenade, where there are rows of stores and restaurants. Elise, as usual, is in her own world.

"What were you guys talking about? It seemed serious." She twirls as she's talking to us.

"We were talking about how much fun yesterday was," Mom says without skipping a beat.

My heart sinks at the realization that the breakthrough I was about to have with my mom isn't actually a breakthrough. She goes right back into her old habit. I'm not sure why I'm surprised. Her *let's-not-talk-about-the-fact-that-we-don't-talk-about-it* act is very on-brand for Mom.

Elise buys it and chatters on about her favorite parts of the day yesterday. The Matterhorn, the teacups, etc., etc., while I seethe the whole way to Third Street. When we get to the intersection, Elise stops.

"I kind of want to go to the LEGO Store, but I also want to go to the bath-bomb store, and they're on opposite ends of the promenade, and we're in the middle." She taps a finger to her lips as if she has the weight of the world on her shoulders. I want to shake her until her ponytail comes loose and tell her those aren't real problems. That there are bigger issues out there to deal with and this is not worth her time or energy.

"I wish I could be in two places at once," Elise continues to ramble. "You know, if we go to the nearest border, which I think is Nevada, we can technically be in two places at once. Just put one foot on one side of the border and the other foot on the other side." She holds up two fingers like a peace sign. "Did you know that in Korean culture, the peace sign doesn't mean peace? It means victory. See?" She holds up her two fingers in my face and traces them with her other finger "It's a *V*!"

I finally snap.

"When are you going to grow up, Elise?!" My mom, my dad, and Elise all flinch in unison. I had my limit of family-fun time, and this is tipping me over the edge. "Who cares about these things? These stupid facts that mean nothing. One day you're going to have to face real problems, and none of these random facts are going to help you."

Elise shrivels, and for a second, I think she's going to cry. Mom swoops in and says, "I think there's an ice cream shop farther down. Let's go check it out."

I almost roll my eyes at how childish my mom is treating Elise, except when ice cream does the trick and works to distract Elise, it hits me like a ton of bricks. Elise *is* a child. And my mom is treating her in an age-appropriate way. Unlike me.

God, I'm such a dick. I screwed up. Again.

I seriously need to get a grip on my emotions. I feel awful. Worse than before, which I didn't know was possible. I'm angry at a lot of things, but Elise isn't one of them. She didn't deserve to be at the receiving end of my outburst. Knowing Elise, how sweet and forgiving, if not forgetful, she is, she won't hold it against me. I envy her and her innocence. I hope she never changes, and at the same time, I hope she does.

On her way past us, my mom gives my dad a tag-you're-it look. Elise goes happily traipsing off with Mom. I know I've been left with my dad to be dealt with like I'm some kind of untamable creature.

"What's on your mind?" he asks me when it's just us.

"I don't even know where to start. . . ." I blow out hot air and run a hand across my face. There's too much on my mind to make sense of anything. "Sometimes I think if I grew up in a place with more Koreans or if I wanted to do something Koreans are stereotypically good at, then I wouldn't feel so out of place all the time," I say, thinking out loud.

"I'm sure it's not as bad as it seems," Dad says without hesitation.

Something about his optimistic tone sets me off. I always thought his outlook on life was half-full. Smiling when he's had to give up so much—his comfort food, his language, his passion. Now it seems defeatist.

"Dad, can I ask you something?" I continue without waiting for an answer. "Why didn't you teach us more about Korean culture?" I ask, not able to keep it in any longer. By this point, there's nothing holding me back from saying what I've wanted to say all these years.

Startled, his eyes grow wide.

"I mean, if we're going to keep getting accused of being

foreigners here, I wish I at least had more ties to the homeland I'm accused of coming from. The truth is, we don't keep up with any of the Korean traditions you grew up with, so now I feel like I don't belong anywhere. I'm not Korean; I'm not American. I'm not even Korean American."

He opens his mouth to say something, but nothing comes out. A minute later, he tries again and says, "Riley, I'm so sorry."

"That's it?" The words come out harsher than intended, but I feel he at least owes me an explanation.

It seems like he's continuing to walk unfazed. Then I catch a glance of his face cracking. A thin film of moisture appears on his eyes from his side profile.

"I just want to understand why," I say in a gentler tone.

He eventually moves to the edge of the sidewalk, taking a seat on the curb. He motions for me to join him, so I do.

"When I came to Arkansas, I didn't know anyone," he says after a while, a faraway look in his eyes. "It was lonely at times. And then I met your mother. She had a familiar face and was Korean, so we had that in common." A faint smile comes to his lips, even though his tone isn't cheerful. "I was instantly drawn to her because of our similarities, but it was our differences that interested me more. She spoke fluent English, ate eggs and bacon for breakfast. She taught me about cultural differences and etiquette, like how slurping is considered rude here. I was shocked. How are people supposed to know the food tastes good if we don't make a lot of noise eating it?"

We both let out a light laugh.

"I came to the US when I was just about your age." He peers over at me. "At the time, I wasn't only accused of being a for-eigner; I was one. Every day was a struggle at first. I had a lot to learn, and with your mom's help, over time I learned how to be more American—talk like them, eat like them, even dress like them. And things got easier. I didn't want you to go through what I went through, so your mom and I decided to raise you and Elise as American."

"Oh, I didn't know that." Like anesthesia wearing off, my sensations are returning. Searing guilt stabs at me.

"To hear you still struggle makes me realize I failed you. I only wanted to make you feel more American. I can see now that in doing so, I made you feel less Korean."

Tears are streaming down my cheeks. The pain is now unbearable.

I've been so focused on not being seen in the band. But this whole time, I wasn't seeing my own dad.

TWENTY-SEVEN

That evening, my family drops me off at the dorms. It's silent the whole drive, and the air is stale. Leave it to Elise to break the silence.

"What's going to happen next after you graduate from Carlmont, Ry?"

My head whips over to her. "Elise, you said Carlmont." It's the first time she hasn't botched the name.

"I could always say it. I just didn't want to."

"Why?"

"Because I thought you liked it more than living at home with me."

"That could never be true, Lise." I pull her in for a side hug. "And I'm sorry I yelled at you earlier. I didn't mean it. I was frustrated with myself, not you."

"I know," Elise says, releasing from our hug. We never fight, not like that. It's been awkward for us both. "So does that mean you'll be moving back in with us?"

I feel Mom's and Dad's eyes shifting to glance at each other even though going back to Arkansas was always the plan. Guess that means there's a part of them that actually believed I might have gotten that record deal and found a way to stay out in LA. Anyway, now that I've ensured I won't be getting a record deal—not after that performance—going back to Bentonville isn't just part of the deal, it's my only option.

"Yep. Maybe we can be roommates." I nuzzle her under my arm again.

"Good. Because I'm your biggest fan." She holds up two fingers, making a *V*.

I can almost hear the collective sigh from the front of the car.

"I'm going to teach you guys how to make kimchi," my dad announces.

"What? Euge, you don't even know how to make kimchi." My mom cranes her neck to face him.

"We'll learn together," he says, grinning wide. His optimism never ceases to amaze me.

"I'd like that," I say. I don't know why I made such a fuss about going back home to Bentonville. It doesn't seem so bad now. The only thing I'm sad to leave behind is the dream of becoming a music artist. Like Dorothy, I made it all the way to Oz only to discover that the thing I'd been searching for my whole life never existed. The music industry is a reality for some, not for everyone.

Mom walks me to my building. Before I go into the dorms, she pulls me aside.

"I'm not trying to shield Elise from anything; I just wanted to have a private conversation with you." She holds up her hands in surrender.

"Mom, I might have come across too harsh earlier."

"Maybe," she says. "But that doesn't mean it wasn't true." She sighs. "The truth is, my parents were immigrants, and it was hard for them because they didn't speak English or have college degrees, so they worked manual labor jobs. They worked so hard for me to go to college, the thing they thought would free us from economic burden and give us better lives. Now here I am, not only a college grad or a graduate student but a college professor! I'm the one helping people get college degrees, and I'm living my dream thanks to my parents." She sighs again. "And as much as I wanted to give you the freedom to be yourself, I'm still your mother. I want to see you succeed. So I did the only thing I knew would ensure your success. I kept pushing you to go to college."

"I'm sorry, Mom. For being such a bad daughter. For not listening and for being selfish and only thinking about my dreams." The tears spring out at once.

My mom shushes me, pulling me in for a hug. "Don't apologize for expressing who you are. It's very brave of you, and I'm sure it was painful to think I didn't support you. I want for you to follow your dreams, but it's hard for me when I see your dreams are causing you pain."

"Does it help to know that it causes more joy than pain?"

She laughs through her tears, which makes me crack a smile. "A little. And maybe you're stronger than me. I don't know if I could survive that type of cutthroat industry."

I sniff, thinking about my mom in my shoes. "Mom, I'm not trying to be judgmental. I just wish you could have felt more confident to speak out more. Maybe it wouldn't have been so hard for you."

She cocks her head to the side. "Ry, I grew up in a different time. When people asked me where I was from, I told them Korea because I knew what they meant. Then they would accuse me of making up a fake country because to them, Asians were either from China or Japan."

"Mom, that's super messed up."

"It was messed up," she says. "Now, with K-pop and K-dramas, we're ... well, we're probably more fetishized. Or is it tokenism?" We both laugh. "My point is, there wasn't any awareness when I was growing up. We didn't talk about these issues because we didn't have the language or the community support to combat these issues back then. So I'm sorry if I didn't talk about them with you. I'm not always sure if I can since I'm still learning myself."

"I understand. And, Mom, for what it's worth? Your story, as hard as it may be for you to share, is something I needed to hear."

She blinks back tears, and we hug goodbye.

Making my way to my room, I'm thinking about how much it helps hearing my parents share their stories. I didn't want to share mine with ASA or even talk about what happened. I kept feeling ashamed that it was happening to me. But holding on to my shame served no one. And if you really want to get down to it, it's probably—definitely—responsible for the public meltdown (make that meltdowns) I've had. Bottling things up isn't healthy. I get that now. You could say I was sweeping it under the rug, the very thing I accused my mom of doing. What a hypocritical idiot I've been.

There are clusters of girls in the common areas and in the hallways, whispering about me. Guess it's going to take a few more weeks to get over the drama. Worst-case scenario, it'll last until the end of the school year, in which case, it's a *really* good thing I'll be out of here for good.

When I get to the dorm room, I'm glad to see Nari's there with Aerie because I've been wanting to talk to her ever since Aerie told me how she felt.

"Nari, I'm glad you're here because I've been thinking about something, and I needed to get it off my chest."

"Riley, you don't—"

"I know I don't owe you an explanation, but I care about you and our friendship, so I want to clear the air." I put a hand up to her, and she lets me finish. "You might think I didn't give Brandon a chance and that I'm rejecting him for superficial reasons. The truth is, I have feelings for someone else. And that's why I don't like Brandon. It has nothing to do with the fact that he's Asian."

Nari waits a beat before she says, "I'm sorry for doubting you. You're right. You don't owe me an explanation. When Brandon didn't . . . It stings, you know?"

I nod because I know what she means.

"Anyway, that's not an excuse. I'm sorry for accusing you of anything. And especially now, after the doc, I feel even worse. How could I have ever doubted you?" Nari's face falls.

My brows furrow. "Why would that make a difference?"

Aerie and Nari exchange a curious look.

"What?" I ask. Something's definitely up.

"You haven't seen the doc?" Aerie asks.

"Xander's doc?"

Aerie and Nari nod.

"I didn't know he was finished with it. Did he post it somewhere?" I'm not sure how I'm the last one to know this, considering the documentary was based on a band I'm part of. Or used to be part of.

Nari pulls up her phone and hands it to me. "Here. Look at this."

VISUAL	AUDIO
Wide shot of Ms. Susan Morales sitting at her desk in her classroom.	We have three disciplines of music at Carlmont: voice, orchestra, and band. A few years ago, uh, [shifts in her seat] a certain parent thought there wasn't a fair opportunity for contemporary music artists. He—or, I mean, this person—took it upon themself to create a subset genre. [Subtle eye roll.] I mean, look, I teach the fundamentals. At this level, all the students here have talent and knowledge, not to mention, the majority of the kids here have industry connections. Whatever they make of their careers is up to them. We're not supposed to be a packaging school that assembles bands. That's not what Carlmont is about. Well, it's not what it's supposed to be about.
Wide shot of Dr. Warren Buckley sitting behind his desk in his office.	Losing Jake Harris and Jeremy Williamson almost ended the contemporary band program here. But I told Blake we had an exceptional candidate apply at the last minute, one who could fill the hole left by Jeremy and Jake. Riley Jo could not only play the guitar, she could also write songs. Something Blake had mentioned was *essential* to the candidate selection process.
Wide shot of Nari Hitomi sitting on a bench in front of the girls' dormitory. Text on lower third: Nari Hitomi, Student at Carlmont	Um, I'm Nari. [Tucks her hair behind her ear.] I'm a student here at Carlmont, and I play the violin. Over the summer, I worked in the admissions office. Two students dropped out in the summer, and the school was scrambling to fill the spots. I didn't understand what the big rush

	was, and then I overheard a call from Dr. Buckley's office. He had it on speaker, so I could hear everything. It was Blake Collins for sure. I knew because the office assistant announced who it was before Dr. Buckley picked up the phone. Anyway, Blake was upset that Dr. Buckley had agreed to accept someone without his approval. I believe he said, "Riley *Jo*? How am I supposed to work with that?" [Shakes her head incredulously.] I mean, he couldn't even have the decency to refer to her as a human being.
Wide shot of Ms. Susan Morales.	It was bad enough I overheard that call, but for a student to hear it? It was a major violation from my point of view. Guess that shouldn't surprise anyone. I mean, inviting students over to your house as a faculty advisor in the presence of alcohol? A huge violation of— I'm not even going to go there. I know that's not what this is about. As usual, no one listens to me, not when money's involved.
Wide shot of Dr. Warren Buckley.	We pride ourselves on being a diverse community, so when we accepted Riley Jo before Blake had a chance to listen to listen to her audition, he was upset at first. Then I reminded him that this isn't his record label or Boyz Club. The school's admission process falls under my jurisdiction, not his. Anyway, since then, I haven't heard a peep out of him or the band, so I assume everything sorted itself out. And by the looks of it, with the attention the new song is getting, it sounds like it more than sorted itself out.

Wide shot of Blake Collins leaning back in a chair in a classroom.	It wasn't easy at the beginning of the year. I had my work cut out for me. Jeremy and Jake weren't perfect, but we had a lot of reconfiguring to do with Riley part of the group.
Wide shot of Jake Harris and Jeremy Williamson sitting on a couch in their apartment. Text on lower third: Jake Harris and Jeremy Williamson, former Carlmont students	I'm Jake, and this is Jeremy. We both were at Carlmont up until last year. I play bass guitar. Jeremy writes songs and plays rhythm guitar.
Wide shot of Jeremy Williamson.	I wrote a couple of songs for Blake, and he zeroed in on "Real Love." He said it had all the makings of a hit—it was pop, a love song, and, with our commercial looks, it would be a smash hit. Then I told him the inspiration of the song. That it was about my first time being in love and that Jake and I were in a relationship together.
Wide shot of Jake Harris.	Blake said it was fine, that we could do whatever we wanted—in private. But for the sake of our public image, we had to keep that part of us hidden. It wasn't a hard choice. If we continued with Blake and made a name for ourselves under his label, we'd have to give that part of us away. Like signing a deal with the devil.

Wide shot of Jeremy Williamson.	So we walked out. Easiest decision we ever made. Once we passed our high school equivalency test, we enrolled at Berkeley City College. On the weekends, we play at a local bar down on Telegraph. It's not a record deal, and we're far from famous, but at least here no one's telling us to hide who we are. [Holds hands with Jake.]
Footage of Riley Jo singing her original song at Blake's house. Cut to footage of Blake Collins with Marc Rubinstein shaking hands with Riley Jo.	Blake Collins voice-over: How do I spot a star? I look for their range, skill. I look for the spark of potential.
Footage of Bodhi Collins singing lead to "Stardust" during practice.	Blake Collins voice-over: And then it's my job to take it and make it into a product that people want to buy.
Wide shot Blake Collins sitting on a lounge chair by the pool.	Sometimes it seems like tough love. That's the way the industry goes. You gotta be professional and check your emotions at the door.
Wide shot of Carly Rae Blake at her kitchen table.	When Blake acknowledged Bodhi as his son, I made sure the agreement included everything down to the amount of hours he would contribute to helping Bodhi with school. I had to. The way Blake fought me tooth and nail to prove he wasn't Bodhi's dad? [Shakes her head and laughs.] I'm sure Blake wouldn't have done it otherwise. I mean, why do you think he's Bodhi's advisor? Because it takes care of two birds with one stone. If Blake can make money off of Bodhi, he will. That sort of backfired on me, didn't it? Bodhi's almost eighteen, and then Blake will be free of his "paternal duties." [Scoffs.] As if real life works that way. Have you realized he hasn't made a

single song after his one-hit wonder from the nineties? Blake Collins's only talent is leeching off of others. Just watch, now that Bodhi's close to getting a record deal, I bet Blake won't let him out of his sight. The irony! After all that time Blake spent trying to get away from his son, now that he sees dollar signs, he won't let Bodhi out of his sight.

TWENTY-EIGHT

So *that* happened.

"I can't believe what Blake did to Jake and Jeremy. I can't believe Xander posted the documentary on YouTube. I can't believe how many views it has." I go on like this for a few more minutes.

"I know," Aerie says. Then after a beat, she asks, "What happened between you and Xander?"

I make a face. "What do you mean?"

"Why would Xander post this if . . ."

I wait for her to finish the sentence. She never does. So I fill in the blanks for her. "What are you saying? He has feelings for me?"

"I mean, maybe? Didn't you say you had feelings for him?"

I blush hard. "Guess I did. You know what's messed up? I didn't think he would feel the same way about me." I shrivel. What does that say about my self-esteem? "What's wrong with me?"

"Nothing!" Aerie says right away. "There's nothing wrong with you. A crush can be terrifying, especially if you don't know if it'll be reciprocated."

I peer over to Nari, feeling self-conscious.

"I wasn't sure at first," Nari says. "That is, until Xander interviewed me. Then I could tell how much it meant to him. And I'm no relationship expert, but *giiiirrrrl.*" Nari squeezes my shoulder. "I don't know if anyone would have followed through with something like this unless they cared about you. Like really cared. As in more than a friend. As in—"

"Okay, got it." I cover my face with my hands, embarrassed by how big my smile is. "Do you really think he likes me?"

"Only one way to find out."

Aerie says I should talk to Xander, so naturally I . . . go to the snack shack and get a packet of Skittles.

Before I leave the student union, I rip into the packet and pop a few Skittles in my mouth. I suck on the candy until the outer shells melt away, then chew on the white gummy remains. Ever since Elise told me about the insides being the same, I can't eat them any other way. I laugh thinking about how I didn't take her seriously when she compared Skittles to people. *On the inside, we're all the same—gummy and tasteless. Without the outer shell, we're missing some of the best parts.* As I sit there eating deconstructed candy after deconstructed candy, it's starting to make sense to me. Yes, we're all human, and to a certain degree, very similar to each other. But we're also complex creatures with layers of unique individuality, like the crunchy and colorful— not to mention flavorful— outer shell of the candy. We should embrace the differences as much as we appreciate our similarities. I've always thought that since I'm the number-one daughter by birth order, I should be setting an example for Elise. Maybe I've had it wrong the whole time. Maybe Elise is the one who should be giving me advice on life, not the other way around.

Halfway through the bag of Skittles, my blood-sugar levels are probably off the charts. I fold the packet of remaining candy and pocket it. I still don't know what to do about Xander when all of a sudden there he is, in the passenger seat of a car, getting dropped off in the main parking lot. I don't even know what model or make the car is, just that it's fancy as hell. He wasn't kidding when he said his dad had a thing for cars. After he gets out carrying an overnight bag with him, he leans down and says something through the window, then waves bye to presumably his dad.

For a split second, I think about bolting. Confrontation is my kryptonite, remember? Then again, avoiding things is what got me in so many pickles in the past. So maybe it's time I tried something different.

"Hey," I say, approaching him. My voice is quieter than usual.

Xander looks around himself, his bag slung over his shoulder. "Are you talking to me?"

It occurs to me that he doesn't know I've seen the documentary. So I tell him.

"You watched it?" he says, his eyes shying away. He fidgets with his shoulder strap and stares at the ground. Aerie was convinced he released the doc online because he likes me. Now that I'm with him, I'm not so sure.

"I devoured it in one sitting. Like a plate of spaghetti and pickles."

He cracks a smile.

"Sorry, I mean French fries with a packet of ketchup squirted right in my mouth."

His smile grows wider, reaching his eyes. "Gross ... also funny." My stomach flutters.

"I thought you might be mad," he says, peering over at me.

"No way. It took you months to collect enough material for

the documentary. Then you somehow manage to get all those interviews and edit it together in a weekend? I'm impressed."

"Thanks," he says, rubbing his chin. A few people walk by, and I might be paranoid, but I think they're staring at us. I can't tell if it's because of my "performance" at the Spring Concert or if it's the documentary.

"Why'd you do it?" I ask.

"Because . . . it's wrong." He answers like he thinks it's a trick question.

"I know it's wrong. And I know you know it's wrong. But it doesn't always mean it's easy." I stare at him questioningly.

He shrugs. "After our last conversation, I was pissed. I didn't realize you could think of me like that. I kept thinking, 'I'm a good person; why can't you just see that?'"

"No one's saying you're not, Xan—"

"Please, just let me finish," he says. I nod, closing my mouth. "I was editing the documentary, going through footage in the editing room. And watching it all together, I started to see it." He pauses, and I hold myself back from saying something. "You know those optical illusions where they could either be an outline of two faces staring at each other or a vase?"

I nod.

"Well, it's like going through life only seeing the vase, and then one day, someone points out the profiles of the two faces. Now all I see are the faces. You know?"

Again, I nod.

"Through the footage I'd captured, I got to know you—all of you—through the interviews. And then everything you said began to sink in. It's just so unfair, and I felt bad for you."

"Hold on." I put a hand up. Everything was sounding okay

until that last part. "Are you saying you completed the documentary the way you did, out of *pity?*"

"What? No! Of course not." He lets out a frustrated groan, raking a hand through his hair. "What I'm trying to say—not very well apparently—is that I got to know you through the interviews, and you were different from the others. With you, there weren't any pretenses. Like, you were going through it for the first time, and you didn't hide it. Then we started talking, and it was like that in person too. You were real with me, and I liked that I could be real with you."

I'm stunned into silence. Is he . . . Which means Aerie is . . . Does Xander have . . . *feelings* for me?

"Xander," I finally say. "Do you . . . ?" I struggle to find the words because I'm afraid I'm going to sound like I'm reading off a script right out of *Relationships for Dummies.*

His phone pings before I can finish my question. He ignores it. "Do I what?"

"Do you like—"

His phone pings a few more times in rapid fire. He and I both look questioningly at each other.

"You should get that," I say at the same time he says, "I should probably check that."

When he unlocks his phone, his eyes get tense. Real tense. The way he's not moving is giving me a bad feeling.

"Everything okay?" I ask.

Without looking up, he shakes his head and says no. Then he hands me his phone so I can read what's on it.

HERE'S A NEW SONG FOR YOU: DOCUMENTARY REVELATIONS PLUS INAPPROPRIATE RELATIONS EQUALS MUSIC DEAL EXPLOITATIONS

In the wake of a shocking documentary that was leaked revealing the music industry's blatant use of racial bias and its direct correlation to the lack of Asian American musicians in the American pop music genre, another bombshell has been revealed. It has been suggested that the documentarian, Xander McNeil, and one of the subjects of the documentary, Riley Jo, have been in a close relationship this whole time. It's ex-plosive, ex-ploitive, and according to an anonymous source close to the band members, maybe an ex-band?

As the film's director and creator, Xander McNeil, has all the balance of power in his control. Getting too close to the subject matter is not only unprofessional, it's an exploitation of his position of power. (#MeToo Movement much?) However, our source has a different perspective to offer. This person is wondering if the influence didn't go the other way around, and Riley Jo didn't somehow influence the outcome of the documentary. "All I'm saying is that everything was fine until it was decided by Ruby Records that Riley wouldn't sing the lead. Now suddenly, this documentary is leaked. So you start to wonder . . . Who's the puppet and who's the puppet master?"

Still, the documentary served as a big platform for Xander McNeil, leading to talks with film schools and major motion-picture companies. It's hard to say who the documentary benefitted more. But one thing is for sure: The inappropriate conduct between the film's director and subject while filming is one that should be looked at more closely.

TWENTY-NINE

The bell rings, signaling the start of first period, and I'm not in class. I'm making my way to Dr. Buckley's office, where I've been summoned to. As soon as I open the door to go in, I see that I'm not the only one. Xander's already there.

"Good of you to join us," Dr. Buckley says, as if I had a choice in the matter. "Please sit down." He motions to the seat next to Xander.

I lower myself into the chair, glancing at Xander. My eyes search his to see if he knows what this is about. He does a subtle headshake to say he's in the dark as well. We don't get to finish our silent conversation, but his expression tells me we're in this together. Whatever this is. Judging by the stone-faced expression on Dr. Buckley's face, I'm pretty sure it's not to award us for our behavior.

"It's come to my attention that there might have been questionable methods used on a school project that involves both of you." Dr. Buckley's eyes flick back and forth between us behind his tortoiseshell glasses.

Xander and I both start talking at the same time. Dr. Buckley puts a hand up to shush us.

"I'm not asking anyone for answers. *Yet.*" He raises an eyebrow at us. "It's my job at this time to inform you that there is going to be an investigation on this matter starting today.

Here at Carlmont, we not only value your talents—we value the whole student. So while we applaud the success of your documentary"—he nods to Xander—"and your . . . performance"—he looks to me, shifting in his seat—"the question of ethics is just as much emphasized as the quality of your final projects, and as a result, your final grades might be affected."

I knew there would be retribution for upstaging my bandmates, but I didn't foresee how I could feel responsible for the outcome of Xander's fate. I shoot him an apologetic look. He shakes his head, telling me not to worry.

"Unfortunately, given that a formal complaint has been made, we have no choice but to speak to your classmates as well as your advisors to determine what the consequences of your actions will be. Bear in mind that the outcome might affect your acceptances to colleges, as they would need to be notified of an investigation of the ethical nature."

Hold on. Xander and I stood up to Blake over his discriminatory treatment of his advisees, and it's *our* ethics that are under investigation? Even though Xander's future is secure thanks to his family connections and mine isn't, it isn't fair for either of us.

"Is Blake going to be under investigation?" I blurt out. "Or Bodhi for that matter?" For once I don't feel the words trying to claw their way out of my throat. They come out easily this time.

"Excuse me?" Dr. Buckley is taken aback. Even Xander cranes his neck to face me.

"If you're invested in the ethics of the methods we use when it comes to our school projects, then you should be looking into Bodhi and Blake as well. Because leaking a false story for the sake of personal advantage and discriminating against a student based on racial bias would, I think, fall under that category." I don't know what's come over me, except that I've been pushed enough to "Go There."

"Riley, however upset you are, deflecting is not the answer." Dr. Buckley's eyes harden, calling my bluff. But I'm far from bluffing.

I draw in a measured breath. "I would appreciate it if you didn't put words in my mouth. I'm not upset; I'm merely pointing out the facts," I say firmly but calmly. "If what you're saying is true about Carlmont's policy on ethics, then I want your assurance that a fair investigation will be carried out."

Dr. Buckley's face turns mad-hot red. "Y-yes, of c-course," he stammers, adjusting the collar of his tweed jacket. "I have no doubt we'll be doing thorough investigations. Thank you for coming." He stands up abruptly before I can add anything else that might make him more uncomfortable.

As soon as we step outside the administration building, Xander busts up laughing. "Oh my God, did you see the look on his face? I swear, for a second, I thought he was going to shit himself. Where did that come from?"

"I don't know," I say, shaking my head. "The more he spoke, the more he seemed like he was using the right words on the wrong people, and I just had to say something." I feel light-headed and tingly all over.

"I'm glad you did. I was feeling the same way. Just didn't know what to say."

"Look who it is." Bodhi's voice cuts into our conversation like permafrost. "What're you two scheming up this time?"

"If anyone's scheming, it's you. Did you leak the story to the reporter or did your dad?" Xander gets right in Bodhi's face, jaw clenched.

"I have no idea what you're talking about." Bodhi holds his hands out to his sides. "If anyone is mad, it should be me. How could you put that stuff in the doc about me and my dad? I trusted you!" He points an accusing finger at Xander.

"You trusted me? Since when?" Xander's head jerks back. "Don't pretend that there's anything between us but a one-sided competition. You want to forget about your past, fine. But by constantly putting me down, you're the one who's holding on to your unresolved issues, not me." Looks like I'm not the only one who's found their voice. It's about time Xander finally tells Bodhi what a shitty friend he is.

"Save it for someone who cares, Dr. Phil. I don't need your touchy-feely psychobabble you learned on WebMD. You know what you did was wrong, airing my personal business like it's some cheap gossip column."

"What part of this isn't personal?" I cut in. "I put myself out there as much as you did. And because it makes you look bad, you think we did something wrong? Did you for once think that maybe you're part of the problem?"

"You're one to talk, hijacking the performance like that. After everything I did, after all the hard work I put into the performance, you stole the spotlight just like that." He snaps a finger.

"Well, now you know what it feels like to be me. Because that song was mine. From the beginning. I did everything to make you part of it, and instead, you had to take it all for yourself, piece by piece. Where do you get off telling me I stole anything from you?" I chuff out an incredulous laugh.

"Yeah, well," he says, flustered. His face is puckered and red, like he's about to implode. "You wouldn't have had a chance if it wasn't for me."

I want to fight back, but there's truth in what he's saying, and it stings. I don't know if we would've gotten a chance with Marc—or with anyone for that matter—if I remained the lead singer of the song. It's a sad but true fact that I had to learn in the process.

A few students trickle over to see what's going on, distracting us. There are usually no students in this part of campus near the administration buildings, but our voices must've carried. And in the intersection of so many buildings, I hear their conversations echo.

"That's the couple from the article."

"He's the one who posted the documentary about the band."

"I heard they're dating, and they ruined their chances at getting a record deal."

"All because she ruined their performance."

"All because he leaked the documentary."

I try to shut their voices out, but they're everywhere and in stereo sound. Bodhi backs away, distancing himself from me and Xander. More people start crowding around us, pointing and whispering. It's too much. They'll get the wrong impression and make it worse for Xander, especially with an investigation going on. I don't have time to explain it to Xander, not with an audience. So I run.

It isn't until I'm almost at the dorms that the weight of what Dr. Buckley told us hits me. I lost everything—the record deal, my band, and maybe even my acceptance to college. All because

I let myself "Go There." I start to second-guess myself. Was it worth it? Should I have just dealt with it like Griff suggested? If I did, we might be signing a contract at this very moment and not wondering if I'm going to graduate high school. Aerie sometimes makes it seem so easy to stand up for injustice, but it comes at a price.

My walking has slowed to a crawl, and I barely make it through the doors when I see Ms. Morales in the common area of our dorms.

"Riley. I just heard the news that you were at Dr. Buckley's office. I came straight here to check up on you. Is everything okay?" She can already tell I'm not okay, and she has a concerned expression on her face.

"I'm so sorry," I say to Ms. Morales. Hot tears spring out at once. "I tried to do what you said and remind myself who I play for. I just didn't think about how it would affect others." I blubber on about what Dr. Buckley said, how he's launching an investigation, how both Xander's and my futures hang in the balance of the outcome of it. "I messed everything up," I finish. The tears have slowed down even though the snot hasn't. I wipe my nose with my sleeve, which is gross. But I've got bigger problems than that.

"No, no, no. Don't say that." She approaches me, then hesitates. "Actually, you look like you could use a hug."

I nod, head hung low. When she hugs me, I start to cry again.

"You should be so proud of yourself," she says. "You finally found your voice. In fact, I gave your song an A for the assignment."

"You did?" I smile through the tears. I'm glad Ms. Morales understands. Even if she's the only one.

"Hey, that's meant to be good news. Why are you crying again?"

"I messed everything up with that performance."

"What you did was brave. And yeah, it created some problems. That's a good thing, though. Maybe people will listen now."

"How? I ruined my chance at becoming someone in the music industry." I sniff.

She tilts her head at me. "Over this?" She shakes her head. "Music is a long game. You've got your whole life ahead of you to figure it out. There are no timelines or mile markers you need to make."

"What if time isn't the only issue? What if I'm too much for the music industry? If Carlmont isn't ready for me, then why would the music world be ready for me?"

Ms. Morales smiles, but there's sadness behind her eyes. "Oh, Riley. Don't put that kind of pressure on yourself. No one's asking you to declare who you are right out the gate. You think John Legend could have debuted with 'Preach'? Or that Sam Smith could have come out as nonbinary in 2012 when they released their first breakthrough single? Don't compare yourself now to what these artists have spent ten plus years making." She follows it up by saying, "No matter what, don't give up on yourself. The music landscape has changed a lot in my lifetime. Think of how much more change can happen in yours. And you can take an active part in that if you choose to. So don't get discouraged. If people aren't ready for you or your type of music, that's their problem, not yours."

"You really think I could find another record label that would want me? After the way things went down with Blake and Ruby Records?"

"I wish I could answer that for you." She shrugs. "It's true that Ruby Records is under one of the major record labels, but that doesn't mean they speak for the entire industry. If this is what you really want to do, I hope you can find a label that treats you fairly."

I don't know what kind of answer I was expecting from Ms. Morales. It's not like she can tell me my future; no one can. And after the meeting with Dr. Buckley and knowing that not only is my future in music uncertain but also my future in here and even in Bentonville U, I'm not sure about anything anymore.

THIRTY

As a formality, we still have to go to band practice, which is ridiculous. Not only do we have nothing to practice now that the Spring Concert is over, but I'm an outcast in the band. Under normal circumstances, I'd find humor in the irony that in trying to be more accepted, I've made myself a reject. But it's not actually funny.

Bodhi and Griff are already in the music room when I get there. It's clear I've interrupted a pleasant conversation, but as soon as they see me, their smiles evaporate, and it's all business.

The projector is turned off, which means Blake isn't going to make an appearance during practice today. I hope that means he's under investigation, though I don't have much faith that he'll actually be held accountable.

Although I don't completely agree with Griff's methods when it comes to Surviving Microaggressions 101, I know he was collateral damage, and I feel bad about that. I try to give him a look to convey everything I'm feeling, which is impossible. When we get onstage, I stare at Griff, willing him to look at me. He doesn't glance up once. In fact, he seems to be actively avoiding me. Guess I kind of deserved that. Just as we're about to start practicing, though, Bodhi cracks a joke, and Griff *laughs*. What's that all about?

By the end of practice, I follow behind Bodhi and Griff until they part ways. And as soon as there's enough distance between them, I fast-walk to catch up to Griff.

"Hey, do you have a sec?" I ask from behind him.

He stops under the shade of a giant oak tree, his eyes on Bodhi, who's walking up the hill. Probably making sure he's far from earshot.

"What is it, Riley?" His voice is clipped.

"I was going to say sorry for the record deal getting squashed. I know how much it means to you, to your family. Now that I'm here, though, I'm not sure I'm actually sorry."

"Okay." He lets out an annoyed sigh. "Is that it?"

"No, that's not it." I steady my breath. "I thought we were friends. Not just bandmates. We shared similar stories of struggles about not fitting in. And not just in life. In music too. I understand why you're mad; I just don't understand why you're mad at me. The way I see it, in circumstances like this when Asian people are being discriminated against, we should be leaning more on one another, not distancing ourselves from each other. How will people support us if we can't support ourselves?"

"Riley." He folds his arms across his chest. "We do know each other well. Which is why I thought you of all people should know what it is we need to do to get ahead in life. Put your head down, do the work, and then we'll get to where we need to be."

"I've seen my parents and even yours do that, and on a surface level, it seems to have worked for them. They may be financially stable and give us the opportunities to follow our dreams, but at what price? The anti-Asian hate crimes are rising, and we can't ignore the fact that some of it is in part due to prior generations of Asian Americans who didn't fight back."

Griff's fists are balled up. This time I can see he's not mad at me. There's no denying that bigotry is the real enemy here.

After chewing on his bottom lip for a minute, staring at the ground, he finally speaks. "I guess I understand why you went off-script at the Spring Concert. And despite what you think, I don't think what Bodhi and his dad did to you is okay. But the fact remains, we—and I don't mean just me and you, I mean *everybody*—need people like Blake and Marc to help us make it in the music industry. They are the gateway to becoming a legit band. So if you see me making nice with Bodhi, it's because I'm trying to play the game."

Before the Spring Concert I would have agreed with Griff. Now? I'm not so sure. Things have changed. *I've* changed.

"I've been thinking about that lately," I say, remembering my talk with Ms. Morales. I take a step toward him, my eyes softened. "Griff, you're talented. You really are. I don't want you to think your talent is only worth someone else's opinion. I want you to be your own success." I say these words to Griff even though I mean them for the both of us. I used to feel like my success could only be made possible through others, but when it finally happened, it didn't feel right.

"How?"

I shrug. "That's as far as I've got." I let out a faint laugh. "Hey, I can't do all the work for you." The mood lightens.

A small smile tugs at Griff's lips, and I'm glad this conversation has at least released some tension.

"Well, let me know when you figure it out. 'Cause it looks like I'm out of options." He runs a hand through his hair and blows out a breath.

"Do you know what 'Stardust' is about?" I peer over at him shyly.

Griff's head pops up with eyes two sizes bigger than they were before. "Are you finally going to tell me?"

I nod, smiling back at him. "When I first got to Carlmont,

we had this burst of energy—well, maybe not at first." He and I laugh, knowing I had a pretty rocky start. "Eventually when RGB came together and Blake seemed hopeful, I really believed we could be something big. Then reality crept in. I knew my time at Carlmont was a onetime thing with an expiration date looming over me. I didn't want to think that I finally started taking off with my music career only to have to go back to my old life. I started writing my hopes down about how I wish that my music journey, like a shooting star, will be more than a burst of light that disappears as soon as it appears. That the special part of the shooting star will actually be the dust that sprinkles on the ground. And even though we can't see it, it doesn't mean it's not there. That's 'Stardust.'"

Griff stays silent a moment, kicking around a pebble. Then a beat later, he lets out a light chuckle, rubbing his chin. "Bodhi thinks it's a love song."

"I know." I laugh.

"I kinda thought it was too. Except for the line: *But when you set yourself free / You can find out who you're meant to be*. I kept thinking, '*Free* from what?' Now that you explained it, it all makes sense."

"Right?" A smile takes over my face. "Anyway, Bodhi can have 'Stardust.' Because it doesn't hold the same meaning for me now. Having hope in something like a music career seems backward. I should have faith in the things that count, like people and relationships and, most of all, myself. And after everything the song went through, it makes it easier for me to walk away from it."

As I'm having this epiphany out loud, Griff seems to be having his own. He seems thoughtful, almost childlike.

"Thanks for sharing the meaning behind 'Stardust' with me

and for, you know, calling me out on my bullshit." He shifts his stance and looks up to the sky. "I'm mad about the way things are too, and I took it out on you. If I'm being honest, it was easier to be mad at you since there was less at stake."

"Um, ouch?" I say.

He rolls his eyes playfully at me. "You know what I mean. I mean this professionally speaking."

"I know what you meant." I lightly tap him on the shoulder. It feels good to be able to laugh with Griff again. "I'm just giving you shit. Again."

"Anyway, I prioritized getting what I want versus doing what's right, and I'm sorry for that."

"Thanks, Griff. That means a lot."

We stand awkwardly for a minute, kicking around pebbles with our toes.

"So what now?" he asks.

"I'm going to focus on the music. For once." I laugh at myself. Aside from "Go There," I can't remember the last time I played music. "Not gonna lie, it might be just me playing sad songs in my room for the next couple of months." I laugh again. This time, Griff does too. "At least I'll still get to play music."

"That's not a bad idea," he says. "I should probably do the same. I felt so much pressure to get the record deal for my family, I lost sight of what I'm doing."

"I can see that." I nod sympathetically. "You know what it reminds me of, though? Those airplane safety demonstrations when the flight attendant says to put your oxygen mask on before you help others with theirs. Maybe you should try that."

He peers over at me with uncertainty. "You mean save myself before I try to save my family?"

I roll my eyes, laughing. "It's a metaphor, smart-ass. Take care of yourself first. You'll be better off to help your family."

He nods, seeming to understand. "Thanks, Riley. I hope the best for you."

"Right back at you."

We part ways, and I go back to my dorm with a mix of emotions. I feel lighter having cleared the misunderstanding between us, but it feels like I'm saying goodbye to Griff even though we have another month of school left before we graduate. We won't be collaborating on any new songs together, and with the investigation ongoing, we're expected to keep a professional distance between us. After graduation, I'll be back in Arkansas, and he'll be in California. I still have hope, though, that one day our paths will cross again.

THIRTY-ONE

The next day, Xander and I get interviewed by Dr. Buckley and Ms. Nelson.

"Explain your relationship with Xander," Ms. Nelson asks.

"We're friends," I say. Or *were*? I'm not sure what we are anymore. We haven't talked since we were first called into Dr. Buckley's office.

"Did you talk about the documentary with Xander at all before the Spring Concert?" Dr. Buckley asks, not even trying to hide skepticism.

"Um, we did. But about the process of storytelling and not about the actual content."

"So you're telling me you never talked about the content of the interviews to a further degree than what was filmed?"

"Not never . . ." Panic sets in, and I can't seem to finish answering Dr. Buckley's question.

I feel like the floor is being ripped out from right under me.

"Aside from the interviews, did you discuss the song with Xander?" Ms. Nelson asks.

At once, the memory of us walking down Fake Hollywood flashes through my mind like still frames being shown on a projector. I didn't tell Xander about "Stardust," only that it had a special meaning to me. It causes me to hesitate. Dr. Buckley and Ms. Nelson begin scribbling notes furiously on their notepads.

Shit, shit, shit. This is bad.

There are a few more questions that Dr. Buckley and Ms. Nelson ask before I'm excused. I know Xander and I didn't do anything unethical, but their line of questioning is confusing me. Did our friendship blur the lines of ethics? Is it possible we let our personal feelings muddle our professional judgment? What's worse is that I can't talk to Xander about it, not with the investigation still going on.

On my way up to the dorms, I keep my eyes focused on the ground. I have to actively concentrate on avoiding Xander, which is easier to do now that the documentary is over. But it takes some effort not to run into him around campus.

Once I'm in my room, I find it empty. I'm sure Aerie's in the main part of campus hanging out with Jason and the others. I think about joining them to distract me from the investigation. The longer I'm in the room, though, the more I appreciate the quiet. Being talked at is exhausting. So I lie down in bed and stare up at the ceiling, glad for the alone time. Ironic if you think about it. This time last year, I was looking up at my ceiling in Bentonville, wishing for something better than what I had. A lot has changed, that's for sure. But are things better?

Guess that depends on how you define *better*. I thought a life where I didn't have to explain myself, where people just got me, would be the solution to my loneliness. That as long as people understood my music, they'd understand me. Now, without any prospects for a real career in music, I'm expressing myself in ways I never thought were possible. This year has taught me how to address my frustrations by trying to understand what is bothering me so that I can speak up when it matters. Most importantly, it taught me how to find my voice.

As difficult as it was to butt heads with my parents, Aerie, and even Griff, hearing their sides of the story, their struggles, helped me understand so many things about them as well as myself. It's painful, but there's also power in that pain. We can combat misunderstanding by just listening to one another more.

Suddenly, I get the familiar too-much-feeling sensation, and I jolt out of bed to pick up my notebook and pen. This time, instead of writing lyrics, I decide to share my story for the ASA anthology. For my essay, I write about my experience growing up as an Asian American in a community with few Asians. I could have written about my experience here with the band, but I feel like that story has been told through Xander's documentary. And it's time I shared some of the ways I felt isolated, not just in my majority-white community but also in an Asian American community. I talk about how Carlmont is and isn't everything I expected it to be. How being here at times made me feel like I'm not this or that or even a hybrid of the two. There's a sort of catharsis in writing it. Because even though I don't offer any solutions, I feel much lighter telling my truth. It's maybe not the most inspiring story. Then again, real life doesn't always have a storybook ending. At the very least, I hope someone out there reads it and is comforted knowing they're not alone.

The last month of school crawls by while I wait for the committee to make its decision. Nari and Aerie help support me when I need to vent. Seeing the way the investigation could potentially upend Xander's, Griff's, and my futures yet not affect Bodhi's or his dad's is frustrating to say the least. With my permission, Aerie and Jason form a petition to have Bodhi and Blake included in the investigation. My signature is the first name on it. It eventually does the trick, and Blake and Bodhi are called in for questioning just as Xander and I were.

The decision doesn't come until the last week of school. The school board eventually came to their senses and accepted Xander's doc on terms of completion. For his final grade, he got an A-, which I think he deserved. Xander didn't get the apprenticeship with J. J. Abrams, who incidentally saw the documentary as well. But this is where things took an interesting turn. Instead of hiring him, J. J. Abrams saw his potential and thought his talents would be better served elsewhere. He promptly recommended him to his friend, famed documentarian and filmmaker Davis Guggenheim. Now Xander'll be shadowing Davis for the summer. I'm happy for Xander, and I bet his dad is proud of him.

I, on the other hand, got a C- for my performance at the Spring Concert. Actually, Ms. Morales told me that the song itself got an A+, but my advisor felt that I should lose a crap-ton of behavior points for not demonstrating teamwork. Laughable, coming from my "advisor." By that point, I couldn't care less.

There were no consequences to Bodhi's grade, as the board couldn't find evidence that he tipped off the news reporter about my and Xander's unethical behaviors. Blake, however, didn't get off as easily since Xander's documentary showed damning evidence of his discriminatory behavior, which was unbecoming of Carlmont's ethical code of conduct. Dr. Buckley didn't ask him to be a returning advisor next year. Didn't matter, though, since Blake didn't have any plans to return next year anyway. After all, Bodhi is graduating. What would be the point?

My grade dropped my GPA, which made me sweat about my acceptances to Bentonville and Hartfordshire U. My mom talked to the dean about my situation. The dean not only assured me that my acceptances to both universities still stood, she also congratulated me on my upstanding behavior. Thinking that moving to a diverse, big city was going to make me more understood was a wrong assumption. Bias and discrimination can happen anywhere, even in the biggest cities. Now I can't wait to start school in the fall.

By the time I graduate from Carlmont, I'm able to take back control of my voice. But I couldn't celebrate, not fully. I may have changed my views of the way the industry works, but the industry wouldn't change its views on me that quickly. The fact of the matter is that pop culture has a huge influence on defining social norms. If TV/movies/music are showing Asian people as foreigners only glorified in their native country's work or as side characters in films only there to support white superheroes or main characters, and if industry executives are hesitant to take risks on people who don't traditionally have success in their desired market, then what hope is there for Asian Americans to stop feeling like perpetual foreigners? If I think too long on it, I get overwhelmed. So I remember what Ms. Morales told me: Don't give up, and focus on the music.

If people in the music industry aren't ready to accept me yet, maybe I can be part of music and inspire change from within, like how Ms. Morales helped me. Which is why I decide I want to go to Hartfordshire U to pursue a career in music. I still have a month to make my decision. I just have to think of a way to bring it up to my mom.

We're back in Bentonville, and it's my first dinner at home. Mom's in her Bentonville U sweatshirt at the stove, and Dad's helping her. Elise and I set the table and sit while Mom brings the plates of spaghetti. Time away has made me see things differently. Sure, this is Elise's favorite meal, but I don't always need to take center stage at home to know my parents love me.

Just as my mom sets down the last plate, the timer on the oven dings. She goes over to the oven and pulls out a tray of ...

"Mac-and-cheese grilled cheese?" I stare, open-mouthed.

"Your favorite," Mom says, setting the tray down.

My nose stings at once, and I feel the tears rising. Just to be clear, I don't need the mac-and-cheese grilled cheese to know my parents love me. Doesn't mean I don't appreciate it, though.

Dad joins us with a bowl in each hand. When he sets them down on the table, we see that one is filled with pickles and the other has kimchi in it.

"So this is new," I say, wondering which Asian market it came from.

"I helped make kimchi!" Elise shout-talks, reading my mind.

"Well, in that case, I can't wait to try." I start loading my plate with food. The rest follow suit, and manners go out the door. I smile through my slurping. While I'm glad things have changed, I'm equally as glad to know that some things haven't.

Dad takes his first bite with his eyes closed, and he honestly kind of sells it. But when Elise and I try it, we both decide the kimchi is too spicy for our tastes, and we prefer the pickle-spaghetti combo, the Jo family delicacy that we're used to.

"We have everyone's favorite for dinner," Elise says. "Except for yours, Mom."

I look around at the mishmash of a spread. "That's true, Lise. Mom, what's your favorite?"

"This," she says, looking around at all of us. "This is my favorite."

What is happening? Why does my vision keep blurring? I blink rapidly to dry up the moisture.

Since we're having a moment, I figure this is the best time to bring up my decision to go to Hartfordshire U. I ramble, telling my parents all the reasons why I want to go—the music program, the smaller class sizes, the fact that it's close enough but also far enough from home.

My mom says yes almost instantly.

"Are you serious?" I look to my mom, and she's nodding with a smile stretched as wide as it can go.

"In fact, I was going to suggest it, but your dad thought it should be your decision, not mine." Mom looks over to Dad.

"Riley," Dad says. "I'm sorry I haven't been a better role model for you. I gave up on my art and my culture; I can see that now."

"Dad, no—you're the best role model a kid could ask for. Elise and I are so lucky to have you as a dad. You're so—"

He gently shushes me. "I'm not, what do they say . . . fishing for compliments? Even though I appreciate hearing it." He lets out a chuckle. "Going to Carlmont, performing at the Spring Concert—they're all things you were hoping music could do to change your life. This is the first time I'm hearing what you can do to change the future of music. And if you want to go to Hartfordshire U, we'll support you one hundred percent."

"Thanks, Dad." I'm having a hard time holding back my sniffles.

"I gave up my art too easily. Not like you. Write all the songs, Ry. For you, for me," he says. "I'm really proud of you."

Now I'm crying—the ugly kind with snot and noises only animals make. I finally feel like my parents are starting to understand me.

THIRTY-TWO

Four months later I'm at Hartfordshire U, an hour away from Bentonville. My parents come often, and Elise's texts are even more frequent. I don't mind, though. I like having them close by. Lately, Elise has been texting me the victory emoji, formerly known as the peace-sign emoji. After explaining to her what I experienced in the band, we decided to celebrate the victory in our lives more than the peace. Because keeping the peace—I learned the hard way—doesn't always mean it's a good thing. I don't want me and Elise to have to only make the bad choices in order to avoid the worse ones. I want us to be able to make good choices too.

I was afraid of staying in Arkansas because I didn't want to end up like my parents. When I came to Carlmont, I thought things would be better. They were better in some ways but worse in others. Anyway, leaving Bentonville wasn't the answer. And I can't blame my parents for the choices they made to assimilate. They had their own struggles growing up, and they did what they thought was best to fit into their surroundings. I understand that now.

After music comp class ends, I'm packing up my bag when my professor stops me.

"Nice job today, Riley. I like your version of the Skylar Twist song. Most people take a song that's uniquely different to their sound for covers, then make it their own. You and Skylar sound so similar, and yet you've still managed to make it yours. I think it's really smart." She nods approvingly.

"Thanks." I can't help the childish smile from taking over my face. It's proving to me what I suspected—that being in LA or Hollywood or any other big city isn't the only way to pursue my dream.

Before I get to my car, my phone pings, and I reach to pull it out.

Aerie: We're boarding
our plane.
Nari: See you soon!

I smile at my phone and type back.

I'll be waiting for you at the airport!

Aerie and Nari are coming to visit me this weekend. They're excited to see what my hometown is like. I'm glad we finally cleared things up, and now we can enjoy spending time together outside of Carlmont.

I haven't spoken with Griff or Xander, and I definitely haven't kept in touch with Bodhi or his dad. Last I heard, Blake is going to take a chance on Bodhi as a solo artist, which doesn't surprise me. I'm sure he'll get a record deal; he might even have a hit. But that has nothing to do with me, so it doesn't bother me like it used to. I've been keeping up with Griff's social media posts, and from the looks of it, he's going for auditions and trying out for bands. He even got to fill in for the drummer of Pearl Jam when they were touring LA and their drummer got sick. They did an open-call audition, and Griff was picked out of hundreds who showed up. I'm not surprised; he's seriously talented. I like that he never gave up, and I hope to one day watch him perform.

My phone pings again in my hand. A TikTok notification. Despite not seeing the relevance of it, I kept up with TikTok. I post my new songs, snippets of me editing and riffing, that sort of thing. And plot twist, it's become a fun outlet for me.

I click on the notification and read it: XanTheMan likes your post.

The profile pic is blurry, so I click on it. Is it Xander? Hard to tell when the icon is an image of the text SARCASM: One of the many services I offer. Though, knowing him, this sort of humor does seem right up his alley. Could it be?

Inexplicably, my pulse quickens even though this could be nothing. This could be some rando for all I know. The truth is, I felt like Xander and I had unfinished business. With the investigation going on until the end of school and me moving back to Arkansas, we didn't have a chance to resolve things. We were the start and stop of a song that kept skipping, never able to be played all the way through. I hope our paths cross again, but with me being here and him being in LA, I doubt it'll happen. Still, I can always hope. Songs get second chances; maybe crushes do too.

THIRTY-THREE

New Development.

I just got off a call with a music producer at 88rising. It's a record label primarily for Asian American artists who release music in the US. I thought it might have been the documentary that got their attention. Surprisingly, the producer found me on TikTok and the meeting is going to be about "Go There," which I really wasn't expecting. After everything that went down at Carlmont, I honestly wasn't sure if I had a place in the music industry. "Go There" is about who I am, and if they're interested in talking to me after hearing that song, then it's already good news. I'm in my dorm room and there's still an hour before I go to the airport to pick up Aerie and Nari, so as soon as I get off the phone with the producer, I know who I have to call next.

My mom picks up after the second ring.

"Mom, you'll never guess what happened." I tell her about the call with 88rising: how they like "Go There" and how they're interested in hearing about other songs I'm working on.

"Ry, that's amazing!" She sounds as pumped as I feel. I was already riding high when I called her, but her enthusiasm takes me to another level. "I hate to bring it up, but do you think this is going to be anything like it was last time with Blake?"

"Not this time," I say. "Things are different."

"Really? What's changed?"

"Me," I say, smiling. And my mom doesn't ask what I mean. She knows.

When Ms. Morales asked me who I play music for, I couldn't answer her because I was ashamed. Music is such a personal expression, a part of me the way my limbs are a part of my body. It's an extension of who I am. But when I kept making changes to my song based on what Blake said would make it a hit, I wasn't playing music for me anymore. I was playing for him. Which doesn't make sense now that I think about it. Why would I want to try and imitate something that's already proven itself to be a success when the thing that made it a success in the first place is that it was something different and original? Anyway, Blake might have represented a big part of what is wrong in the music industry, but he doesn't represent it all. And I didn't know any better then, so I felt like I had to settle for what was being presented to me. I know now that there are other people in the industry who want to make a real change, like 88rising, and I'm excited to work with people who don't want me to compromise who I am to fit anyone else's idea of what a music artist should look like.

Past Riley would have shunned the thought of working at a label for Asian Americans. The truth is, I was scared to be different. I wanted to blend in, not stick out, be average. It's no wonder I was confused last year when I was trying to fight for my place in RGB. How could I take center stage in a band when I couldn't even take center stage in my own life? I have spent most of my life avoiding the things that define me. Who I should be friends with, what type of music I should play, who I should aspire to be like ... but my experience at Carlmont taught me that in trying to show people who I'm not, I don't get a chance to show people who I am.

As soon as I hang up the phone with my mom, my dad texts me. Riley, I'm so proud of you. You're really doing it!

And then, a second later, a bunch of celebratory emojis come in from Elise. Confetti emoji, music notes emoji, fire emoji—repeat ad nauseam. I smile at my phone.

This moment feels familiar and at the same time different. This time, I'm going into a meeting with a music producer and I'm not afraid to be different anymore. I'm not worried about trying to be like everyone else. I no longer care about people putting their cultural expectations on me. I'm just focused on trying to be the best me I can be. That's the difference between playing music and making music. Playing music is playing the notes on the page. Making music is putting yourself into the piece. My whole life, I was playing music—now I'm getting the chance to make it.

ACKNOWLEDGMENTS

I started writing this book as a challenge to the status quo in the American media industry. But as I began working on it, I discovered that it was impossible to separate Riley's struggles with being unplaceable in her life from my own. Most days, I didn't feel Korean enough, American enough, or even Korean American enough. Like Riley, I too left my small hometown and went to boarding school in LA hoping to find a sense of belonging. What I ended up with was so much more. As I'm writing the acknowledgments for a book literally inspired by my experiences at boarding school, I realize that in a full-circle moment, I have finally found my voice.

To my agent, Andrea. Thank you for your unwavering support in me and my work. You are my rock.

Eternal gratitude to my editor, Zareen, who handled all the iterations of this book with kindness and sensitivity. Working with you has been the best part of the process. Truly.

To the team at Kokila—Namrata, Jasmin, Joanna, Sydnee, Gnesis, Asiya, and Eunice. Thank you for the care with which you handled this book. Every piece of feedback was incredibly impactful, and I thank you for making Jo the best version it could be.

Thank you to the production team, Tabitha Dulla, Nicole Kiser, Ariela Rudy Zaltzman, and Hansini Weedagama, as well as copyeditor Kaitlyn San Miguel and proofreader Jacqueline Hornberger.

A HUGE thank-you to Kristin Boyle and Doejin Lee for really nailing the cover and capturing Riley's personality so perfectly. She truly shines.

This book in particular needed some extra conversations with music people to whom I am so grateful. Melanie Maras, Alice Dabell, Alex Lin, Allen Lau, and Nadya Geta.

To my family who love and support me regardless of my successes or failures. Mom, Dad, Sue, and David—I don't say it enough, but I love you all. Especially to my kids, Tyler, Troy, and Kate. You are the reasons I do this. And to Jin, of course. Thank you for supporting me in this journey. Not everyone has the luxury of pursuing their passions, and I do not take that for granted.

People ask me all the time what boarding school was like, and I tell them it's kind of like one long season of *The Real World*—communal living with random people with whom you experience some of the highest highs and lowest lows. By the end of it, you're bonded for life with the people who went through the same unique experience as you. Thank you to Esther, Sara(h), Jim, Ken, Mike, and countless other Webbie's who have stayed in my life after high school and beyond. I cherish our friendships.

Publishing, in a way, is also kind of like boarding school in that it's a unique experience filled with its own set of ups and downs. To my Kimchingoos who I started my publishing journey with—Jessica, Susan, Sarah, and Graci. I am bonded with you all for life and look forward to many more years to come.

In 2018, I was plucked from obscurity by Jesse Q. Sutanto in Pitch Wars to be her mentee and work on an early version of Jo. Jesse, your support of Riley's story from the early stages is what kept me going. Now, five years later, it has finally come become a real book. Thank you for always believing in me and in Riley's story. <3

Thank you to Kate Dylan, Julie Abe, Nicole Lesperence, Marley Teter, Margot Harrison, and of course, Stephan Lee. With you, writing never feels lonely.

There are countless others who I can't thank enough for keeping me sane. The MMMs—Shannon, Kristi, Ragen, Jeni, Andi, and Lisa Rose. I can always count on you for a good time (every night is girl's night, amiright?). To Sassy 6 (+1,-1), Karen, Cindy, Esther, Esther, Helen, and Eunice—if wealth was measured by the quality of one's friendships, I'd be set for life. To the BBNG East Bay Crew—Tammy, June, Christine, Helen, and Kristy. Thank you for the years of friendship and support. Special thanks to Jennifer Chang, who probably knows more about the publishing industry than a person outside of the industry should know. Love you dearly.

And finally, to you, reader. Thank you for picking up this book. If it's inspired you in some way, just know that this book was written especially for you.